# TRAGIC TOPPINGS

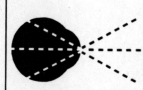 This Large Print Book carries the
Seal of Approval of N.A.V.H.

A DONUT SHOP MYSTERY

# TRAGIC TOPPINGS

## JESSICA BECK

**WHEELER PUBLISHING**
*A part of Gale, Cengage Learning*

GALE
CENGAGE Learning·

Detroit • New York • San Francisco • New Haven, Conn • Waterville, Maine • London

GALE
CENGAGE Learning·

**LIBRARY OF CONGRESS CATALOGING-IN-PUBLICATION DATA**

Beck, Jessica.
    Tragic toppings : a donut shop mystery / by Jessica Beck. — Large print ed.
      p. cm. — (Wheeler Publishing large print cozy mystery)
    ISBN-13: 978-1-4104-4532-2 (pbk.)
    ISBN-10: 1-4104-4532-1 (pbk.)
    1. Coffee shops—Fiction. 2. Private investigators—Fiction. 3. Doughnuts—Fiction. 4. Large type books. I. Title.
PS3602.E2693T73 2012
813'.6—dc23
                                          2011047213

Published in 2012 by arrangement with St. Martin's Press, LLC.

*To the faithful NC morning donut crew!*

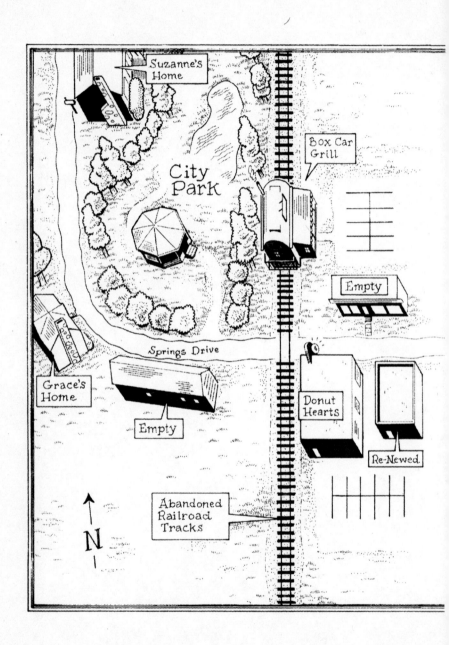

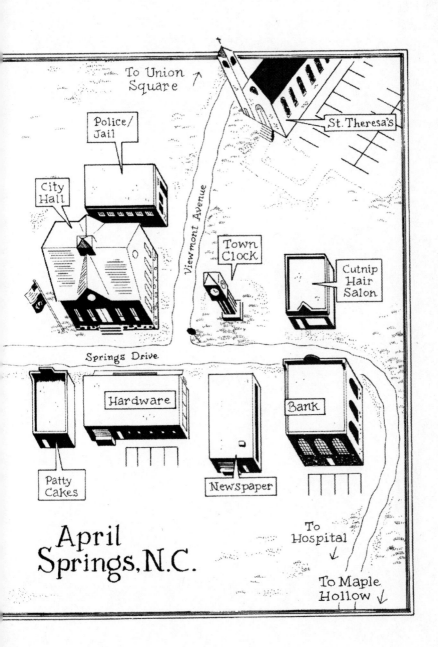

"Don't miss the donut
by looking through the hole."

— Author unknown

# CHAPTER 1

The day Emily Hargraves disappeared after visiting my donut shop, I had no idea that it would be the beginning of a series of seemingly unrelated events that would ultimately lead to the death of one of my dearest friends.

To be honest, I didn't think much about my encounter with Emily at the time. As the owner of the only donut shop in my small North Carolina town, I speak with a great many people in the course of running my business during the day, and Emily really didn't make much of an impression on me at the time. I did remember that she said she was on her way to Two Cows and a Moose — her newsstand just down the block from Donut Hearts — and while she wasn't exactly a regular at my shop, it wasn't unusual for her to visit when she wanted a sweet iced pastry treat. Emily didn't indulge that often, but when she did, it was all the way. No topping was too outlandish, no combination of tasty additions too much for her. In other words, she was my kind of gal, and we'd been friends ever since she'd come back to town after graduating from college.

I wish I had taken the time to chat with her a little more before I served her a blueberry donut with chocolate icing, sprinkles, stars, and a chewy sour gummy worm coiled on top — all per her request — along with a pint of the chocolate milk we sold in cute little boxes, but she came in when things were crazy, and I barely had time to do more than share a smile, serve her, and then take her money.

As it turned out, it appeared that I was the last one to see her. At least that's what Chief Martin tried to tell me a few hours after Emily had visited my shop. He wasn't all that pleased with me, but that honestly wasn't unusual. I wasn't sure if his frustrated relationship with my mother had anything to do with his attitude toward me, and I wasn't about to ask. It was a sore subject between the three of us, one that I was very careful to avoid whenever possible. Chief Martin and my mother had been trying for months to arrange their first official date, but every time it approached, Momma had found a new and sometimes ingenious way to postpone it. She finally promised the police chief that she wouldn't drag her feet anymore, and they were slated to finally go out on their first real date later that night.

Until then, things would continue to be tense, and I'd been doing my best to avoid the police chief for the past few weeks, but now with Emily's disappearance, that wasn't going to work anymore.

When it came down to it, there weren't many folks in town who wanted Emily found more than I did. April Springs was very much like a small family, and when one of us was in trouble, it felt as though all of us were.

"We've been over this already," I said to the police chief as we stood in my donut shop covering the same ground again. Chief Martin purposely avoided looking at any of my donuts as we spoke, since he'd been on a diet ever since his divorce had become final. His weight was dropping, even if it was ever so slowly, but I'd never seen a man go to such lengths to avoid a donut so thoroughly in my life. I explained yet again, "She came by for a donut and a pint of chocolate milk, and that's the last time I saw her."

"What kind of donut did she buy?" he

asked as he jotted something down in a small notebook.

"Does that really matter?" I asked.

"It might," he answered. "You never know with these things."

"It was blueberry."

"Just blueberry?" he asked, his pencil still poised over the paper.

"No, it had chocolate icing, sprinkles, stars, and a chewy sour gummy worm on top."

He scowled at me. "Suzanne, this is no time to trot out that odd sense of humor of yours. This could be serious."

Why was I not surprised he didn't believe me? "I'm telling you, that's exactly what she ordered, but I can assure you, there wasn't anything wrong with what I sold her." I was probably a little too defensive about it, but my donuts had shown up in police investigations a few times in the past, and I didn't want to even consider the possibility that the donut Emily had bought from me could be connected to her disappearance.

"Take it easy," he said as he jotted the donut's complete description down. "I have to ask. Who knows? It might turn out to be important." He closed the notebook, and then added a little apologetically, "Suzanne, I'm just doing my best to collect information right now."

I lowered my voice as I asked, "Why the fuss, Chief? She hasn't been missing that long. It's not like there's any reason to suspect foul play, is there?"

He shook his head. "No, at least not from what I've been able to uncover so far."

"Then what gives?"

The police chief almost whispered the next thing he said to me, and I had a difficult time hearing him. "Truth be told, she had an appointment in her shop with the mayor about a zoning waiver she's been trying to get for parking, and when she turned up missing, the boss was afraid it reflected badly on him somehow."

I wasn't all that fond of our mayor, and I knew that he wasn't afraid of throwing his weight around, especially when he was soon going to be up for reelection.

"I'm sure it's nothing. Is that all you need from me?" I asked, completely finished with this conversation if I could manage it.

"We're good for now," he said as he put away his notebook. "If you happen to think of anything else, give me a call."

I nodded my agreement. "You know, you really should speak with Gabby Williams. She spends half her day looking out her front window, so she might have seen something everyone else missed." Gabby was my nearest business neighbor. She owned ReNEWed, a secondhand shop that specialized in nice clothing gently used. If something was going on in town, chances were good that Gabby knew something about it. I'd used her as a source for information in the past myself, and though the facts and rumors she gave me were often valuable, they never came without some kind of price, even if it was just sharing a cup of her favorite tea and listening to her latest spin on the world of April Springs.

"We've already spoken," the chief said abruptly, and for a second, I actually felt sorry for the man. He was usually able to hold his own with folks around April Springs, but I knew that going up against Gabby, he'd have a battle on his hands. Most folks did, and I always tried my best to keep dancing that fine line that kept me off her expansive list of enemies.

"Did she have anything helpful to add?" I asked.

"Only that Emily walked into your shop, and that's the last time she saw her."

I shook my head. "Do you honestly believe that she still might be here? Feel free to search the place if you'd like. Emma's in back doing dishes, but I guarantee you that

Emily's nowhere to be found on site."

The two young women had been friends for years, sharing the root of a common name, and my assistant was upset by Emily's disappearance. Conversations could get confusing if both of them were in the room at the same time, something the young women always had fun with.

"How's she holding up?" the chief asked softly.

"I didn't realize you knew how close they were."

He nodded and smiled briefly. "Believe it or not, I know quite a bit about our little town. Why don't you wait on your customers out here, and I'll go have a word with Emma in back."

I would have loved to listen in on that interview, but I still had a shop to run, and I needed our customers to know that I was on the job. Besides, there was no doubt in my mind that Emma would tell me everything they talked about once Chief Martin was gone.

"Suzanne, what's happened?" my mother asked six minutes later when she came bursting through the front door of Donut Hearts. She was a petite little thing, but anyone who judged her by her size was in for a rude awakening. My mother could take a stand against a grizzly bear and a mountain lion teaming up together and send them both scampering for the hills.

"Emily Hargraves is gone," I said.

My mother looked shocked by the news. "What do you mean, she's gone? You're not saying that she's dead, are you?"

I fervently hoped not. "No, she apparently missed an appointment with the mayor in her shop, and now everyone thinks she's vanished completely."

Momma wasn't buying that, though. "Nonsense, no one just disappears."

"Apparently that's exactly what happened. The mayor arrived at her newsstand ten minutes after she left here. He found the door open, and no sign of Emily anywhere."

"Couldn't she have just stepped away for a while?" Momma asked.

"I was wondering the same thing myself, but I can't imagine her not locking the front door on her way out. After all, the guys were all in there." The "guys" I was referring to were the store's namesakes: Cow, Spots, and Moose, three much beloved stuffed animals from Emily's childhood that she'd named her newsstand after. They now occupied a place of honor in her store on a shelf by the register. Emily took it one step further, dressing her three mascots in whatever seasonal outfits struck her fancy. In years past, they'd made appearances as Santas, superheroes, leprechauns, Uncle Sams, and a host of other characters.

Momma looked hard at me for a moment. "And how do you figure into all of this?"

"What makes you think I'm involved?" I asked, trying to muster as much indignation as I could manage. "I'm not a part of every odd thing that happens in April Springs."

"No," Momma said, "but you're usually in the middle of most of them, so don't bother denying it."

"Why do you think I am this time? It's pure coincidence that Emily came by the shop this morning."

My mother pointed outside to the police chief's cruiser. "Perhaps, but I know Phillip wouldn't ordinarily be visiting you here unless it was related to business, given his strict diet."

I wasn't above using our police chief's presence to motivate my mother to change the topic of conversation. "You shouldn't even be here then, should you?"

"Why ever not?"

"Isn't it bad luck to see him before your first date?"

"We both know that's when you get married. Suzanne, enough nonsense. I won't discuss my love life with you."

"Fair enough, as long as mine is off limits, too," I said.

Momma chose to let that slide. "Where *is* Jake this week?" she asked.

"He's in Dillsboro," I answered. My boyfriend was a state police investigator. As a matter of fact, that was how we'd first met. Our dating life had been turbulent for a while, but these days, the only problem we had was too much time apart as he traveled the state solving crime.

Momma nodded. "That's right, I read about it in the newspaper this morning. Who could imagine that someone might rob a train in this day and age?"

A pair of daring bandits had robbed a recreational train that traveled private tracks in the North Carolina mountains, sticking up its passengers car by car, and then vanishing into the woods on waiting four-wheelers before anyone could stop them. It wasn't exactly the Great Train Robbery, but it was enough to spur Jake's boss into action. It didn't hurt that the governor's daughter had been on the train on her honeymoon. I'd ridden that train more times than I could count, but fortunately, I'd missed that particular trip.

"Jake said they made off with a lot of loot," I said. "He's working the backcountry with dogs searching for them right now."

"The things that man does in the course of a day's work," my mother said.

"Don't kid yourself. He loves every second of it," I said.

Chief Martin chose that moment to come out of the kitchen. He had a stern look on his face that quickly melted when he saw my mother.

"Hello, Dorothy. You look lovely today."

So help me, I almost caught my mother blushing. "You should save some of that praise for later," she said.

"Oh, trust me. I've got plenty more where that came from." It was odd seeing that boyish grin on the police chief. I nearly told them to get a room, but I kept my mouth shut just for a change of pace. He smiled broadly at her and said, "I'll see you at six."

A troubled look crossed my mother's face. "Should you be going out on a date with me when you're just beginning a new case? If you'd rather postpone and keep searching for Emily, I'd understand completely."

"Not on your life," he said. "I'm not willing to wait another minute for our first date. Believe me, I've waited long enough." That much was true; the man had been pining over my mother since they'd been in grade school together. In a softer voice, he added, "Besides, I'm not even certain this is a real case. Emily's a grown woman, and until we hear differently, I'm not jumping to any conclusions about where she might be."

I was happy my mother was going out again, but I didn't need to hear any more from them at the moment. "Chief, did you need me for anything else?" I asked.

He looked surprised to see me still standing there. "What? No, we're finished, at least for now."

"Good. If you'll excuse me, I've got work to do." That was a big whopping lie, since we didn't have a single customer waiting to be served, and Emma clearly had things in back under control, but I wasn't all that crazy about having the police cruiser parked in front of my shop, no matter what folks thought about the fond relationship that existed between cops and donuts.

"Yes, I'd better be moving on myself." I couldn't believe it when he tipped the brim of an imaginary hat to my mother, and I was about to say something when Momma said, "I'll see you this evening, Phillip."

"I can't wait," he said as he left the shop.

After he was gone, Momma said, "I'm afraid you'll be on your own for dinner tonight, Suzanne."

"That's fine," I said. "I've already got plans myself."

"Jake's not going to have time to come back to April Springs just to take you out to eat, is he?"

I shook my head. "No, but it's the next best thing. Grace and I are going out on the town." Grace Gauge was my best friend, and frequent coconspirator. She liked nothing more than digging into an investigation with me, but things had been quiet lately.

At least they had been until Emily stepped away from her shop without telling anyone where she was going.

I was just getting ready to close the donut shop for the day at the crack of noon when something caught my eye outside. A man was approaching Donut Hearts with a halting, limping gait, and for a moment, I didn't recognize him. But as he got closer, I saw that it was George Morris, a retired cop and good friend who had been injured, not in the line of duty, but following a lead for me. I'd been overwhelmed with guilt since his accident. No, "accident" wasn't the right word. His injury had resulted from a purposeful event, and my part in causing it was something I still had a hard time coming to grips with.

I rushed to open the door for him, and did my best to hide the sadness I felt when I saw him. With my bravest smile, I said, "George, you're looking good."

He grinned at me. "Suzanne, you're lying through your teeth, but I appreciate the sentiment. How are you?"

"That's what I should be asking you," I said as I stepped aside and let him in.

"I'm fine." He paused, and then grimaced slightly as he came into the shop. "Well, at least I'm getting better all the time. What more can anybody ask for than that, right?" He tried to smile, though I could see that it was a little forced.

"You're getting around pretty good."

He tapped his cane on the floor. "I do my best. Now enough about me. What's this I hear about Emily Hargraves?"

"How did you hear about that? News travels fast around April Springs, doesn't it?"

"Faster than you can imagine. How did you get involved in Emily's disappearance?"

I frowned at him. "What makes everyone think that I'm involved?"

"Come on, Suzanne, I'm not a cop any-more, but when I retired, I didn't give up my skills *or* my contacts. I hear things. The

24

whole town's buzzing about her last being seen here at the shop." He tapped his cane again. "This thing has slowed my pace down some, but in a way, it's been a blessing. You'd be amazed how folks open up to an old man with a cane." He paused, and then added, "If you're not involved in the case, you might consider looking into what happened to her yourself."

"Why do you say that?" George certainly knew how to get my attention.

"I've heard talk that some folks around town suspect that you're the reason she's gone." He said it flatly, as though he were announcing baseball scores for Little League.

"Just because she was last seen here doesn't mean I had anything to do with her disappearance. Besides, we don't have any reason to suspect that anything is even wrong." My voice must have gotten a little louder as I spoke, and a few folks in the shop glanced over at us. "Hang on a second," I said to George. I wasn't about to get into that conversation with customers still in the donut shop. I put on my brightest smile and said, "Folks, it's closing time. Thanks for coming to Donut Hearts, and we hope to see you all again tomorrow."

After everyone was gone, I locked the door

and turned back to George. "I'm sorry," I said once I'd managed to calm down a little. "I shouldn't have raised my voice like that."

"Don't apologize to me. I'm just telling you what I've heard. We need to do something, to help."

I grabbed a broom and started sweeping. "Slow down. Whether I look into this or not, you're not going to be involved in it this time. You're recuperating, remember?"

"This?" he asked, waving the cane in the air. "It's no hardship; more of an inconvenience, really. I might not be able to chase anyone down in a footrace, but that doesn't mean I'm completely useless."

From the tone in his voice, I could tell that I'd angered George, the last thing I wanted to do. "Don't you understand? Look at it from my point of view. I can't risk letting you get hurt again," I said, the honesty in my answer surprising me as much as it clearly did him.

He just shook his head. "Suzanne, a meteor could fall from the sky in the next ten seconds and I'd be just as dead as if something else happened to me. Just being alive is a constant risk, but it's not something I'm ready to give up on." He rubbed his chin for a moment, and then added, "You don't have to include me in your investigation, but that doesn't mean you can stop me from digging around into what happened to Emily on my own. She's a friend of mine, too, and I aim to find out what happened to her, with or without your blessing. Do we understand each other?"

I knew I was fighting a losing battle, so the only hope I had of reining him in was stepping in myself, whether I believed there was cause for alarm or not. "I get it, but I'm still not sure there's any reason to panic, at least not yet. Want a donut?" I asked.

"No, thanks, I've already had my breakfast, and I'm headed out to lunch now."

"You can put it in a bag and take it home for later," I said as I grabbed a plain cake donut and slid it into a bag. As I handed it to him, I said, "After all, it's still all I'm able to pay you for your professional investigative services."

He took the bag with a smile, and then asked, "What, no coffee anymore? I used to get both when I worked for you. Times are tough, I suppose."

I laughed, despite my reservations. "One coffee to go, it is. You drive a hard bargain."

George smiled at me. "I don't know; you're no pushover yourself."

I filled a to-go cup, and then gave it to him.

"Now we're in business," I said with a grin.

"When do we start?" George asked.

I'd agreed to enlist his help more to keep him from going off on his own than for a real need to dig into Emily's life. After all, I wasn't so sure I'd want anyone overreacting if I stepped away from Donut Hearts without taking out a full-page ad in the newspaper. "As soon as I finish closing up the shop I'll call Grace. Why don't you disappear for half an hour or so, and then come back?" Hopefully Emily would show up on her own before that.

"You're not going to do anything without me, are you?" The look of concern on his face was clear.

"I have a lot of work to do before I can leave Donut Hearts," I said. "Emma and I have to finish cleaning the place up, and I've still got to cash out the register and run my reports. Those things take time." I touched his shoulder lightly as I added, "Come on, George, don't be so paranoid. It doesn't suit you."

"Point taken," he said with a shrug. "I'll go grab a bite to eat. See you later."

After he left the shop, I watched him walk away. I wasn't sure if it was just my imagination, but I could have sworn that George's limp had suddenly gotten better. I suspected that having a purpose again was helping take his mind off his injury. As I replayed our conversation in my head, I realized that he had been completely right. I had no business trying to tell him how to run his life. If George wanted to take a few risks in order to feel alive, I wasn't about to stop him. All I could do was try to make the dangers more manageable, and I couldn't do that if he was off investigating on his own.

I kept working in the front, and a little later, Emma came out drying her hands on a dishtowel. "The dishes are done and the trays are clean." She glanced at the case. "I see you boxed up the last couple of dozen donuts. Anything else I can do to help out here?"

"No, we're good. You can go on. I'll balance the register, and then I'm taking off myself."

She grabbed a broom. "That's okay. I can sweep up if you'd like."

"I took care of that already," I said. I looked carefully at her and then asked, "Emma, are you stalling for some reason?"

"Honestly? I don't want to go home," she said, and I saw her fighting tears.

"Why not?" I asked softly. I knew she and her father had difficulties sometimes, but

I'd never heard her hesitate about going home after a long shift at the donut shop.

"Dad means well, but he's going to ask me a thousand questions about Emily, and I don't know how to answer a single one of them. I'm a little concerned about where she might be, and he's not going to make it any easier for me. Emily's not just another story for his newspaper to me; she's my friend."

"Mine, too," I said, touching her shoulder softly. "I'm sure she's fine, and that she has no idea how worried we all are about her."

"I hope you're right."

"Don't worry. I'm calling Grace, George has already promised to help, and we'll all do our best to track her down. In the meantime, you can't keep avoiding your dad. Tell him what you just told me, and ask him to give you a break. He's not a bad guy if you give him half a chance."

"I know," she said, and suddenly tried to smile. "I'm okay."

"Good girl," I said, and let her out. The cash register balanced out on the first try, to my unending joy, and I prepared the bank deposit. When I was ready to lock up, I grabbed my phone and called Grace at home. I knew she was there doing paperwork, part of her responsibilities as a super-

30

visor for her company.

"Hey there," I said when she picked up.

"I was just getting ready to call you," she answered.

"What's going on?"

"Believe it or not, I've got a problem. Someone I know just disappeared."

It didn't even surprise me that she'd already heard about Emily. "Trust me, I know. I'm not entirely certain that it's worthy of all this fuss, but she was last seen at the donut shop this morning."

There was a long pause on the other end of the line, and then Grace asked, "What on earth are you talking about, Suzanne?"

I was baffled by her response. "Emily Hargraves is missing," I said. "Isn't that who you're worried about?"

"No, someone else in town has disappeared. It seems as though we've got an epidemic on our hands."

# CHAPTER 2

"Who are you missing?" I asked Grace as I clutched the telephone.

"Tim Leander was supposed to be here two hours ago to do some work for me, but he never showed up."

I knew the town handyman well, and one of the things Tim prided himself on was his punctuality. If he couldn't make it, he'd always call. Tim was a man we'd all grown to count on. Two years before, our furnace had died in the dead of winter, and Tim had dropped everything and rushed over in the middle of the night to fix it for us without question or complaint. There were dozens of reasons for all of us in town to love him for his willingness to always lend a hand when we needed him. "Maybe he got held up at his last job," I said, hoping that was true.

"That's not like him, and you know it. He would have called me," Grace said. I knew the two of them had a special relationship, though I could never get more specific details for the reasons behind it out of Grace. All I was certain of was that whenever Grace called him, no matter what the circumstances, Tim came running.

"I know it sounds out of character for him not to show up," I said, "but it doesn't seem likely that *two* people from April Springs could disappear at the same time." A sudden thought struck me. "They couldn't be together, could they?"

Even as I said it, I doubted that there was any set of circumstances that could explain Emily and Tim vanishing at the same time.

"Sure, maybe they eloped," Grace said with a laugh. "And to think they'll miss my coronation as Queen of Bogatavia later today."

She had a point. On the face of it, the two of them had nothing in common. "I know, it doesn't make much sense, but how do you explain it otherwise?"

"I can't," Grace said, "unless it's just a coincidence, and I don't believe in them any more than you do. That's why I think we should investigate."

"Funny, that's exactly why I was calling you. So, who should we look for first?"

"I don't think we have the luxury of putting either one on the back burner now that we know that both of them are missing," Grace replied. "This could be serious."

"Or they could just be in Union Square having lunch together," I said.

"What if they're not, though?" she asked. "I can look for Tim, and you can hunt down Emily."

"You know I don't like splitting up," I said hesitantly. There was real safety in numbers, at least for the two of us. George could and did go off on his own at times, but he was a trained investigator, while Grace and I were just amateur sleuths.

"If we're going to work together, then we'd better get busy."

There was a tapping at the door of the donut shop, and I looked up, startled. I'd been so engrossed in my conversation with Grace that I hadn't even noticed someone approach.

George was standing outside, grinning and looking certain that even with his cane, he'd still managed to sneak up on me.

"George is here," I said to Grace as I opened the door and told him to shush. "He's going to help us look into this."

He did as I commanded, but nothing would wipe the smile off his face.

Grace said, "I'll meet you there. Don't go

anywhere without me."

"I'm not making any promises," I said.

"Suzanne Hart," she said, and before she could get wound up, I butted in.

"Grace, I'm kidding, but don't take too long. There are two dozen donuts here, and I don't want to eat every one of them by myself."

"You don't have to worry about that. I'll be glad to help," George said.

"Save some for me," Grace said, and then hung up.

I flipped open a box and said, "Go ahead. Help yourself."

"I was just kidding. I told you I was having lunch when I left here. I'm stuffed."

"So, my donuts aren't good enough for you as dessert?"

He started hedging his bets instantly. "I give up. I'll take one. Have any lemon filled, by any chance?"

I peered into the boxes. "Sorry, there's no lemon left. I've got a German chocolate I can offer you instead." That was just plain mean. I knew George hated that particular flavor of donut from a test I'd done years ago.

His smile faded as he answered, "Sure, I guess that will be okay."

He started to reach for one, but I couldn't

take it any longer. I snapped the box top shut and said, "You aren't getting any, so stop pretending that you like them, or that you even have enough room to eat one."

The look of relief on his face was comical. "Honest, I'm too full to eat another bite, but I'll take some coffee, if there's any left."

The pot was empty, but that was an easy thing to fix. "I'll make more. It should be ready by the time Grace gets here."

"Don't go to any trouble on my account," he said.

"I won't," I said with a grin. "I want some, too."

George nodded, and then asked, "Do you mind me asking if it's your blend, or one of Emma's?"

"You don't care for our more exotic offerings?"

It was clear that George wasn't sure if I was teasing him or not, but he said, "You know me; I'm usually up for something different, but Emma's taste in coffee and mine aren't even close to being the same."

"Trust me, I'm not always a fan of what she brews myself. It was all I could do to get her to agree to one exotic flavor one day a week."

As I started to prepare the coffee, I asked, "What do you think happened to them,

George? Are they somewhere together, or did they just vanish? Are we worrying over nothing?"

"They?" he asked, clearly perplexed by my question. "Suzanne, what are you talking about?"

"That's right. You haven't heard." As I filled him in on our discovery that Tim was missing as well, I could see George take it all in.

When I was finished, he said, "They aren't together. I'm sure of that."

"How can you possibly know that?"

He frowned as he pondered it all, and then said somberly, "Call it a hunch, or a cop's intuition, but I've got the feeling that one of them is in trouble, and the other's just fine."

His statement sent a chill through me, and for some reason, I believed what he said with all my heart, though he didn't have a single fact to back up his statement. "Why would you say that?"

"Suzanne, I honestly don't know. It's just a feeling." But let's keep our minds open and hope for the best until we learn differently."

That effectively killed our conversation, and we were both left to our own dark thoughts.

The coffee was ready just as Grace tapped

at the front door. I'd made it a point to watch for her so that I wasn't startled twice in fifteen minutes.

I opened the door for her, and Grace took a deep breath as she stepped inside the shop. "My idea of civilization is anywhere there's coffee to be found," she said.

I smiled gently at my friend, always happy to be in her presence again. "I'd disagree with you, but I know it would be a lost cause."

After I locked the door behind her, I poured us all cups, and we sat at the bar side by side. I hadn't meant to snack on one of the leftover donuts, but it was so natural to have one with the coffee that I instinctively grabbed one and passed the boxes down to the other two. It was no wonder I never managed to lose weight. I should be thankful I rarely put much on, either. Somehow I'd found an equilibrium I could live with, even though it was quite a few pounds over what I considered my ideal weight should be.

I was about to tell Grace George's theory about the fates of our subjects, but I couldn't make my lips form the words. There was just something too depressing about it for me to voice the thought aloud.

It was Grace who finally broke the silence.

"That was great, but we're burning daylight here. Where should we get started?"

I was about to answer when George said, "You two should look for one of them together, and I'll tackle the other."

"How should we decide how to split our subjects up?" I asked. I knew George would never let us take the one he believed was in serious trouble, and I was curious about his answer.

Grace kept me from ever finding out. "I think we'll have more luck with Emily's mom than George will." She swiveled in her chair and faced George. "You two don't exactly get along, do you?"

George put his mug down and pivoted so he could make eye contact with Grace. "How did you know that?"

"My dad used to tell me how you two would tease Christine in school, and she always held it against both of you."

George smiled. "Hey, we were a couple of rambunctious boys. In our defense, we teased everyone pretty mercilessly, including each other." He took another sip of coffee, and then added, "I really miss your father."

"I do, too," Grace said softly.

"I'm sorry, Grace," George stammered.

"Relax. I know you two were best friends

growing up." She patted his hand, and then added, "I'm sure you miss him nearly as much as I do."

George nodded. "Yes, that sounds just about right." He drained his mug, and then asked, "Are you two ready to get started?"

"It sounds as though we have a good game plan," I said.

"Then we divide and conquer," Grace replied as she took a last sip of her coffee, finished the bite of donut in front of her, and added, "We need to meet again this evening to compare notes on what we've found."

George stood as he said, "I'll see you both later, then. If anything major comes up before that, call me."

"You do the same," I made him promise. I might not be able to dog his steps, but I still wanted to know what he was up to.

After I let George out of the shop, I turned to Grace. "As soon as I rinse out these mugs, I'll be ready to go."

"That sounds great," she said as she threw the napkins we'd been using into the trash while I walked in back with the three mugs.

When I rejoined her at the front, I found Grace looking into the boxes of donuts I'd left behind.

"You're welcome to take some of those

home with you if you're interested," I said.

Grace shook her head. "The offer's tempting, but I don't think so. Thanks for the gesture, though. I hate it, but you're just going to have to throw them away."

I smiled. "Don't worry; it won't be anything that drastic. I have an idea." I combined the boxes into one, and though it was crowded, it looked quite festive with my little offerings wedged in close together. In particular, the iced éclairs and the sprinkled donuts were really very pretty side by side.

"Don't hold out on me," Grace said. "What are we going to do with them?"

"We're going to use these to get in Christine Hargraves's front door."

"Suzanne, is there any news?" Christine asked as we came to her door fifteen minutes later. She was a heavyset woman with carefully styled hair and nice clothes. I knew that Christine was barely in her fifties, but at the moment, it was difficult to tell how old she was, given the harried look on her face. That wasn't the worst of it, though. It was as if someone had turned the light off behind her eyes, and it was just about all I could take looking at her. She was known around town for her heightened sense of melodrama, but I wasn't entirely sure that I

41

blamed her this time.

"You shouldn't let your imagination run away with you. It might be nothing."

"I keep telling myself that exact same thing," she said. "But I'm having trouble believing it. Regardless of what some people around town might think, my daughter has a good head on her shoulders. I know she can seem flighty at times, but this just isn't like her."

I shrugged, not knowing what to say. "We brought you these," I said as I offered her the donuts. "We thought they might help a little."

"That's so sweet of you," she said, almost automatically, as she took the box of donuts from me. "Where could that girl of mine be? I've tried calling her dozens of times, but her phone is turned off."

"We wish we knew," Grace said. "Do you have a second to chat, Christine?"

"Of course I do." She shook her head gently, as though clearing the fog from her mind. "Where are my manners? Would you two like to come in?"

"We'd love to," I said, "if it's not too much trouble."

"Honestly, it's no problem at all," she said. "I'd be delighted."

"We're not disturbing your husband, are

we?" Grace asked as we all walked into the living room. The furniture was more than a little dated, and the carpet over the hardwood floors had seen better days, with frays and a few spots testifying that there wasn't a great deal of money in the Hargraves household, at least not available for home improvements.

"No, he's gone," Christine said simply.

"Is he out looking for your daughter?" Grace asked.

She shook her head. "Actually, he left for Tampa this morning, and I haven't been able to get in touch with him. As soon as he lands, they say they'll have him call me here. Honestly, I'm losing my mind," she admitted as she pushed the donut box around on the table, though it was still unopened. I doubted that she even realized she was doing it. "We weren't sure we'd be able to have children, and Emily has been a blessing from the beginning."

"Maybe it would help to talk with us about where she might be," I said. "Do you have *any* ideas? Does Emily have a new boyfriend, by any chance?"

Christine nodded slightly. "It's complicated. I hate to admit it, but she hasn't confided in me much lately. We were really close before Emily left for college, but since she's moved back in here with us, it's like she's a stranger sometimes."

We were on familiar ground now. "I know it can be tough getting used to having her live with you again. It's got to be hard on all of you. It surely was for Momma and me after I moved back in after my divorce."

Christine looked surprised by the news. "You two had trouble getting along? I find that hard to believe. I thought you always seemed more like sisters than mother and daughter."

Grace and I both laughed, and Christine asked, "Did I say something funny?"

"No, ma'am," I answered quickly. "It's just that it's felt a lot different from the inside of the relationship. Trust me; we've had our share of rough patches along the way."

"More than their share, if you ask me," Grace added.

Oddly enough, the news made Christine smile.

"Now I'm the one who's wondering what's so amusing," I said.

She laughed gently as she said, "I just thought you two were the perfect example for the rest of us to try to live up to. It's a little reassuring hearing that you've had some problems along the way as well. It gives me hope for Emily, if you want to know the truth."

"It's not easy coming back home. I know sometimes I feel smothered," I said, trying to soften the blow of what I was about to say. "Is there any chance she just had to get away?"

"And leave the shop unlocked and unmanned? I can't imagine it, especially with the three amigos there. She might leave everything behind in the world that she holds dear, but she would never leave Cow, Spots, and Moose unprotected and unguarded. Especially Spots."

"Why Spots in particular?" I asked, my curiosity getting the best of me. "I didn't realize that she had a favorite."

"Spots was always *her* cow. Cow was mine, and her father reluctantly adopted Moose, though in the end he embraced the fantasy as much as we did. When she was younger, Emily insisted that each of us have our very own pal, and that's the way it worked out in the end." She lowered her voice, as though someone besides us could hear her. "I know it's silly, but I couldn't just leave the three of them in the shop. I've brought them home and tucked them into her bed, just like they used to be in the old days."

"Where should we start looking for her?" I asked.

The question seemed to surprise her. "You're getting involved? I didn't realize you and my daughter were that close."

"We were closer than you might think," I explained, "but that's not the only reason. The last time anyone admitted seeing her was at Donut Hearts. Whether I like it or not, in a way I'm tied to her disappearance until we find her."

"I can understand that," Christine said. She was clearly about to add something when her cell phone rang. "Emily?" she asked breathlessly.

After a pause, she said, "Hi, Chet. I'm afraid I've got some bad news. Our baby is gone."

She hesitated, and we could hear the wail on the other end of the phone. "Chester, snap out of it. She's not dead."

Another pause, and then she said, "She's missing. The shop was unlocked, and the guys were still inside. You have to come home. I need you here with me." Two heartbeats later, she said, "Let me know when you get a flight home. I love you, too."

After Christine hung up, she turned back to us. She looked startled by our presence, almost as though she'd forgotten we were there. "I'm sorry. I can't really talk right now. I need to be alone."

"We understand completely," I said as Grace and I stood. "If you think of anything that might help, don't hesitate to let us know."

She nodded, and as we walked to the front door, I asked, "I know you said her love life was complicated at the moment, but do you happen to know who she dated most recently, by any chance?"

"I do," Christine answered, though it was clear that she was reluctant to admit it.

"Would you mind sharing a name with us?" Grace asked.

Christine frowned, and then finally said, "I was hoping we'd be able to avoid this, but if anyone can get him to tell the truth, it's you."

"Me?" Grace asked.

"No, you," she said as she pointed to me.

"Why would I be able to help there?" And then, without any reason or evidence, I knew why she was reluctant to tell me anything. "She's been dating my ex-husband, Max, hasn't she?"

Christine nodded. "I've been phoning him all afternoon, but he's not picking up, and he won't return any of my calls. Would you speak with him, Suzanne?"

47

"Just try to stop me," I said with a smile.

I was out on the steps before Grace called out, "Hey, slow down a second and wait for me."

I stopped and turned to her. "Why doesn't it surprise me that Max is involved?"

"Maybe because you know him so well?" she asked.

"Yeah, that must be it." We got into my Jeep and headed to my ex-husband's apartment. Leave it to Max to get mixed up in this. What did Emily see in him, anyway? I suddenly realized that I knew the answer to that without voicing the question out loud. Max was many things, good and bad, but near the top of the list had to be how charming he was. He could talk a woman dying of thirst out of her last sip of water if he put his mind to it. I couldn't blame Emily for falling for his lines.

It was just amazing to me sometimes that *any* woman could resist him.

"Do you think they're together somewhere right now?" Grace asked as I drove to Max's place.

"It wouldn't surprise me one bit," I said, my gaze glued to the road.

Grace said carefully, "They're both single, consenting adults. You know that, right?"

"Of course I do," I said. "Believe me, I

48

don't have a problem if they're together. I just want to make sure that Emily's okay."

We got to his place, and I turned to Grace. "Let's go see if we can get any answers out of him."

I rang the doorbell twice, and then knocked on the door, but there was no answer.

"He's not here," Grace said.

"Let's give him another second," I said as I leaned on the doorbell, hearing it ring constantly inside.

Max finally came to the door, looking more than a little frustrated. "Suzanne. Grace. What are you two doing here?"

"We need to talk to you," I said.

He glanced back inside, and then said, "Sorry, but I'm a little busy."

"With Emily Hargraves, by any chance?" I asked.

"How did you know about that?" he asked.

"Max, you're a grown man. I'm not asking just to be nosy, but do you know where Emily could possibly be?"

He was about to answer when I saw Emily herself pop out from behind him.

"Suzanne, what's wrong? Why are you both looking for me?"

"Everyone in town thinks you've disappeared," I admitted. "You missed a meeting with the mayor, and you left your news-stand unlocked this morning."

She looked ashen. "Are the guys okay?"

"They're fine," I said, finding it touching that that was where her mind had gone first. "Your mom has them at home. She's going out of her mind with worry."

Emily shook her head, and then smacked Max's shoulder. "I told you I couldn't leave work like that without telling anyone. You convinced me that it would be impulsive and fun and daring, but all you've been for me since we met is trouble."

As she raced past us out of the apartment, Max looked sourly at me and said, "Thanks a lot."

I gave him my best smile as I said, "You're most welcome. Have a good day."

Back at the Jeep, Grace asked, "Should we track George down and bring him up to speed on what we've found out?"

I looked at my watch and saw that it was nearly five. Momma was going to be getting ready for her big date soon, and I'd promised to be there to hold her hand. If I didn't, I had a feeling that she'd find another way to back out yet again. "Why don't I drop you off at your place, and you can call everyone and tell them they can stop worrying about Emily, including the chief of police. I need to get home."

"Okay by me."

I had no problem letting Grace make those happy calls on her own.

I had something to do that was even more important, supporting my mother as she took the first small steps to a new life after my father.

She was counting on me, and I wasn't about to let her down.

## BUTTERMILK DONUT VARIATION

These are really good, especially with the combination of the buttermilk and the pumpkin spice mix. With spices like cinnamon, ginger, nutmeg, and allspice, what's not to like!

### Ingredients
- 1 egg, beaten
- 1/2 cup sugar
- 1/2 cup buttermilk
- 2 tablespoons butter, melted
- 2 cups all purpose flour
- 1 teaspoon baking soda
- 2 teaspoons pumpkin pie mix

### Directions
After beating the egg, add the sugar, buttermilk, and melted butter, mixing thoroughly. In a separate bowl, sift the flour, baking soda, and pumpkin pie mix, then add to the egg mixture. Roll the dough out to 1/4 inch, then cut out rounds and holes. Put in hot canola oil (375 degrees) for 4 minutes, flipping halfway through. Drain on paper towels or rack, then dust with powdered sugar or ice as preferred.

Makes approximately 6 donuts and holes

# CHAPTER 3

Grace understood when I told her that I had to go. "I nearly forgot about your mother's big date. Need any help getting the old gal ready to go?"

I grinned at her. "No, but I'd love to be in the room and hear her response when you ask her that way yourself."

She laughed, and I knew again why Grace was so dear to my heart. "Not on your life, and if you repeat it, I'll deny that I ever said it."

I smiled as I shook my head. "You would, wouldn't you?"

"You can bet on it," she replied. "Ordinarily I'd say that our investigation trumps everything else, but this is important; helping George find Tim can wait until tomorrow. Drop me at my car so you can get home."

"We're still having dinner together later, right?" I asked.

"You can count on it. Suzanne, I just love being your backup when your boyfriend is out of town," Grace said.

"Which is most of the time," I admitted. "Do you honestly mind?"

"Are you crazy? I love the company, especially since my love life is so stagnant these days. When is Jake coming back to town?"

"As soon as he finishes up in Dillsboro, I guess, and honestly, who knows when that will be?"

"No worries, then. In the meantime, you've got me as a happy and willing substitute," Grace said.

I dropped Grace off at the donut shop where she'd left her car, and as I drove my Jeep back to the cottage, I couldn't help wondering what was going through my mother's head at that moment. Was she nervous? Certainly, she had to be. After all, it had been a long time since she'd gone out on a date, and I wouldn't be surprised if it had been all the way back when my father had been courting her. Was she a little scared? Without a doubt. The real question, though, was whether she was the least bit excited about dating again. I had to hope that there was a spark left within her that was open to the possibility of love coming back into her life.

"I'm home," I said loudly as I came into the cottage we shared. The park was beautiful where we lived, filled with love and memories, but the house meant even more to me. Moving back in with my mother had been tough on both of us as we worked through a rocky adjustment period, but at the moment, I couldn't see myself being anywhere else.

"I'm back here," she called out.

I followed the sound of her voice and found her in the master bedroom, if you could call the cramped space that with a straight face. To be honest, there wasn't much masterly about it, though it did have a small half-bath off the bedroom that helped make it a suite.

I was surprised to find my mother sitting on her bed in her white slip, with six dresses laid out carefully on the comforter around her.

"Is everything okay?" I asked as I came in and leaned against the door frame.

"It's fine," she said, her voice barely showing any emotion at all. "It's too bad, but I'm afraid that I won't be able to go out tonight."

"Why not?"

"I have nothing suitable to wear," she said

as she looked around the room.

I wanted to laugh, but I realized that would be exactly the wrong thing to do.

"What about your red dress?" I asked as I pointed to it.

"I tried it on, but it's too festive for the occasion," she said.

I wasn't exactly sure what that was supposed to mean, but I wasn't going to pursue it any further. "Okay, then how about the black one?"

"Too somber," she replied. "It's no use."

We could have gone on like that all night if I didn't do something. "I've got an idea. Do you want to borrow something of mine?"

She looked at me as though I'd lost my mind. "Suzanne, you are six inches taller and thirty pounds heavier than I am. Anything you own would drape on me like a curtain, and I would swim in that much material."

"Wow, you could have stopped with the fact that we're not the same size," I said with a smile. "Mentioning my weight was just plain mean."

"I didn't mean anything by it," she said with a frown, finally breaking out of her level tone.

"I know that," I said, trying to laugh. "Do

you want my honest opinion?"

"Of course I do," she said as she looked at me. It was as though she were drowning, and I might have a rope to pull her out.

I studied the dresses again, and then made my choice. "You should wear the blue one."

She glanced at the dress to her left, looked away, and then studied it again. "Do you honestly think so?"

"Absolutely. It's perfect."

"Fine," she said. "Blue it is."

After she slipped into it, I applauded. "Wow, Momma, you look beautiful."

"Nonsense," she said, but I could see her trying to hide her smile. "I haven't been anywhere close to beautiful in years."

"I beg to differ. Look in the mirror."

She glanced at the full-length mirror, and I could see a glint of approval in her eyes as she brushed a few non ex is tent wrinkles away.

"I suppose that it will just have to do," Momma said.

"Don't sell yourself short; it's a lot better than that. Chief Martin will be ecstatic."

"Not too delighted, I hope," Momma said.

"Trust me, you could come out in a track suit and a floppy pink hat and he'd still be impressed. All of this is just a bonus."

"I don't know what I'm doing," she said.

"I'm too old for this foolishness."

I hugged her. "You're wrong there. I think you're exactly the right age for this foolishness."

"Is it too late to call it off?" she asked, a hint of worry in her voice.

There was no way I was going to let her back out now, but I was saved when the front door bell rang. I looked at her and smiled. "Yes, if I had to guess, I'd say that it's too late. It appears that your date has arrived."

I almost had to drag her to the door, but once I opened it, I made myself scarce by stepping into the kitchen. I wasn't going to get in her way, but I wasn't about to go anywhere out of hearing range, either.

Chief Martin whistled softly the second he saw her. "Dorothy, you look absolutely breathtaking."

"Thank you, Phillip. You look nice as well."

From the crack in the door, I could see him brush at his gray suit. It was so new, I was surprised that a tag wasn't still hanging somewhere off it.

He nodded. "Thanks. Should we go?"

"Of course," Momma said. As she headed toward the front door, she called out, "Have a nice evening, Suzanne."

"You crazy kids have a good night, too," I said as I popped out.

Momma kind of snorted a little, but the chief surprised me by laughing heartily. "Don't worry about us; we will."

I stepped out before they could go. "Did Grace get hold of you?"

"No, why?"

I smiled, happy to deliver a bit of good news myself. "You heard about Emily showing up, didn't you?"

He nodded. "Her mother called the moment she walked in the door," the chief said. "I'm glad that turned out okay."

"Me, too," I said. "I'm just hoping Tim turns up soon as well."

"Don't worry, he will." He turned to my mother and asked, "Are you ready?"

"I am."

I ran to the window and got there just in time to see the police chief escorting my mother to a nice blue sedan parked in front of the cottage. That was surprising. The man really had gone all out for their big date. He held the door for her, a point in his favor, and as they drove away, I saw the rental sticker on the back of the car. The only vehicle he normally needed was his police cruiser, but I was glad he hadn't tried to take her out in that.

Sixty seconds after they were gone, Grace drove up and parked in the space where he'd been.

"That was perfect timing," I said as I joined her outside. "They just left."

"I was waiting at my house on the front porch watching for them. I nearly missed them in that rental car. Wow, he really did it up right. He wasn't in uniform, was he?"

"No, it looked like a brand-new suit."

Grace looked at me and grinned. "Should we follow them?"

"Don't even think about it," I said. "We're going to stay as far away from the two of them as we can possibly get. Agreed?"

"Yes, ma'am. Where are we going to eat?"

There was only one place in town that I could think of where I wanted to eat. "Why don't we go by the Boxcar and see what Trish is serving."

"As long as it's cheeseburgers, it sounds good to me," Grace said.

A sudden thought struck me. "I've got an idea. Why don't we leave our cars here? We can walk through the park to the Grill easier than we can drive it, since it's a lot closer on foot."

Grace nodded. "Why not? It's a beautiful night."

We strolled through the park together,

past the Patriot's Tree, the swings, and the horseshoe pits. When we got to the tracks, we followed them a short way to the Boxcar Grill. The diner was lit up, and I fell in love with the restaurant all over again. Having a donut shop in an old train depot was wonderful, but I was glad there was another remnant of the days when folks traveled by train in town as well.

"Trish's place is hopping tonight," Grace said as we approached. "Do you think she'll have room for us? We could always just grab a pizza and watch an old movie."

I locked my arm in hers. "Come on, I've got a feeling she'll evict someone from their booth if she has to so she can seat us."

Grace nodded. "She's lucky she's so popular. Otherwise she'd have to be a little more careful about who she might offend."

I laughed at the thought. "Trish has a mind of her own."

"Like you don't," Grace said with a laugh.

"I'm not so sure about that. I don't have the luxury of turning anyone away from Donut Hearts." It was true. The difference between red and black ink on my books could be just a few dozen donuts in the course of a day, so I had to do my best to make sure that every customer was happy with their order, though there were times I had to bite my tongue to keep from expressing how I really felt.

I didn't want to think about that at the moment, though. Donut Hearts was in good shape financially, and the nest egg I kept for rainy days was as healthy as it had been in a while.

When we walked in, Trish was clearly glad to see us, even though the place was crowded. That was one of the things I loved about her. She always seemed to have a smile for me.

"It's Ladies' Night, I see," she said with a laugh. "Is there room for one more at your table? I haven't had a bite all afternoon, and I'm starving."

"Can you just leave your post like that?" I asked. "I thought you had to be the hostess all the time when Hilda isn't here."

She lowered her voice. "That's usually true, but I just hired Lilly Jackson's daughter, Allison, and she's been bugging me to run the front along with the register all day. If we're within twenty dollars either way at the end of the shift when she's been working the front, I'll consider it an unqualified success." She looked at me and smiled as she added, "To put it in a way you can appreciate, she's a few glazed donuts short of a dozen."

"Why don't you just fire her?" I asked.

Trish shrugged. "I wish I could, but I owe Lilly a huge favor, and this is going to just about cover it."

"But Allison could hurt your business," I said as I looked around.

"It hasn't so far," she added, and then explained, "Don't worry; I've heard that she gets bored before she's worked a week anywhere. I thought for sure she'd hit you up for a job by now, Suzanne."

"She's probably next on the list, especially if she's going about her job searches geographically," Grace said.

I wasn't in any hurry to tangle with Lilly myself, so it was a conversation I hoped I'd never have to have. "Who knows? But honestly, can you imagine anyone but Emma and me putting up with the hours we have to work every day? Then again, there's a good chance it may never come up. You never know; Allison might just work out here."

"Bite your tongue," Trish said.

I looked around for a table, but there was no luck finding an empty seat, let alone three that were together. "We'd love to have you join us, but where are we going to sit?"

"Don't you worry about that. I'll take care of it," Trish said.

Trish walked over to a table where three older fellows were lingering over nearly empty glasses of iced tea. "Any chance you gentlemen are about finished?"

One of them said with a smile, "Not quite just yet. We've solved half the world's problems, and now we're going to work on the other half."

Trish kept smiling as she asked, "Tell you what, why don't you save that for another day?" She looked at one of the men and added, "Travis, I'm willing to bet that Patty's out somewhere looking for you right now."

One of the other men laughed. "No doubt about it, she's got him on a short leash for sure."

Travis shrugged. "I've been married to the same woman for forty-one years. Bob, how many years does the time you had with all three of your ex-wives add up to?"

The third man said, "He's got a point, Bob. Come on, guys, let's clear out and give this lady a chance to eat."

The three old friends stood, and they were still teasing each other as they walked out of the diner. A party of two women directly behind them laughed as well, probably happy that they hadn't lost their spot, too.

After Trish cleared the table and wiped it

down, Grace and I took our seats.

"Let me guess. Cheeseburgers, fries, and Cokes?" Trish asked.

"Times three, if you're still joining us," Grace said.

Trish nodded. "You bet. That sounds good. Let me give Gladys our orders, and I'll be right back."

After Trish returned with three sodas, I asked, "What happened to Hilda? You didn't fire her to give Allison a job, did you?"

Trish looked at me as though I'd lost my mind. "Fire Hilda? No way. She's too valuable, but she's been meaning to visit her daughter in West Virginia, and we both figured Allison's stay would be just long enough for her to take a vacation."

I looked around and noticed several folks glancing our way as we chatted. At first it felt friendly, but then I caught someone's curious gaze, and I could have sworn that they looked away with an expression filled with equal parts fear and condemnation.

When I looked back at my friends, Grace said, "Sorry, Suzanne. I was hoping you wouldn't see that."

"What's going on?" I asked.

"It's got to be Emily's disappearance," Trish said. "I wish folks around here would just mind their own business sometimes."

"But she turned up safe and sound this afternoon," I said.

"What?" Trish asked, clearly surprised to hear the news. "I hadn't heard."

Grace explained simply, "She was with Max."

Trish shook her head. "Now, why am I not surprised? That man is smooth as silk when it comes to women."

"Tim Leander is still missing, though," I added.

"Tim's gone? I hadn't heard. What's happened to this town?" Trish asked.

"I wish I knew, but at least Emily's safe." I couldn't help myself from adding, "Trish, we're going to investigate Tim's whereabouts."

Trish nodded. "I understand that completely. Listen, if there's any way I can help, all you have to do is ask."

"We will, but it's good news that Emily isn't guilty of anything more than bad judgment."

"There are quite a few ladies in town who can echo that." A second later, Trish looked over my shoulder and said, "Good. There's our food. Finally."

On a tray, Allison brought us one cheeseburger, a salad, and a plate of fried chicken.

"Dibs on the cheeseburger," I said before

she could set the tray down.

"There's no need to arm wrestle for it," Trish said. She pointed to the tray, and then said, "Allison, check the order, and then look at your tray."

"I got it right this time. You're at Table Nine," Allison said proudly. She had shiny black hair, fair skin, and the brightest blue eyes I'd ever seen. All in all, she was a pretty girl. It was just too bad that she didn't have anywhere close to the intellect to match.

"The only problem with that is that we're at Table Six," Trish said. I noticed that she was keeping her temper and attitude in check, something that I wouldn't have sworn she'd be able to do. What did Lilly have on her, anyway?

"Does that mean the cheeseburger isn't mine?" I asked.

"Sorry," Trish said. She stood and gathered everything together and placed it back on the tray. "I'll be right back."

She turned to her newest employee and said softly, "You. Come with me."

Allison followed closely behind, and I could see a fleeting expression of worry on her face. I couldn't blame her for being concerned. I doubted Trish would keep her on after all of the mistakes she'd been making, regardless of the possibility that she'd have to incur Lilly's wrath.

Trish vanished into the kitchen after she delivered the food to the right table, and soon reappeared with our food on her tray.

"Sorry about that," she said as she served us.

"Where's Allison?" I asked as I took my plate from her.

"She's taking the rest of the night off," Trish said.

"You didn't fire her?" I couldn't believe it.

"I have to wait it out," Trish said with a shrug. "Do me a favor, okay? Can we just eat and forget about it?"

"That's a fine idea," I said, trying to lighten the tone of my voice. For the moment, it was important that I put my own situation on the back burner so I could enjoy this time with my friends. If being involved with police investigations in the past had taught me anything, it was that it was important not to take the people I cared about for granted.

We had a fine meal, and after we were finished, Grace and I helped Trish gather up our dirty dishes.

"Thanks for everything," I said as Trish walked us out.

I laid enough cash on the counter to cover our meals, and as Trish rang it up, she took the money and said, "Thank you. I feel a little guilty charging you."

"But just a little, right?" I asked.

"Just a little."

I smiled at her. "If it helps, I stiffed you on the tip."

Trish grinned back at me. "That helps exactly the right amount. Good night, you two. I had a lot of fun. See you both soon."

Grace and I walked out of the diner and I felt the light touch of the September air in the approaching dusk. It was just a little cool now, though the day had been warm, and I knew that colder weather wasn't far from coming to stay in our part of North Carolina.

As we left the abandoned train tracks and neared the park, Grace said, "I don't know how you didn't freak out all of the time at night living here as a kid." She hadn't been allowed out much after dark when we were growing up, while my parents had no problem with letting me roam the park practically anytime I liked. Grace added, "There are so many shadows around here that I still see bad guys behind every tree and bush."

"You hung out with me enough growing up," I said. "You never seemed to be scared of this place then."

"That's because we were almost always

together when we played here," Grace said, "and we can't forget the fact that I had to go in at the first hint of dusk."

"If you can believe it, I find the shadows comforting," I admitted. "Everything's familiar, and yet just a little different. Besides, it's not like it's completely dark yet. The moon's putting off enough light to let us see, and full dark is still half an hour away. You should try this walk when it's pitch-black. That would really give you the willies."

"Are you saying you've never been afraid here before?" Grace asked. "Not even when we were younger?"

"I wouldn't say that," I admitted. "You know my imagination, but if I jumped at every shadow, I'd never make it home."

I glanced around and tried to see the darkened park through Grace's eyes. It probably did look a little spooky if you didn't know the shapes behind the shadows. Besides, her folks had put so many fears about the night in her head, it was amazing she'd even walk home with me now that we were both grown.

"Look over there," I said as I pointed to a cluster of bushes. "What do you see?"

"I can just make out a maniac with a knife," she said. I honestly couldn't tell if

70

she was exaggerating, or being completely honest with me, but I assumed she was telling me the truth.

"You're looking at it the wrong way," I said as I pointed to the outline. "If you look carefully, you'll see that it's really just a fat old man with a butterfly net chasing a moth."

She frowned as she peered into the darkness. "I guess I can see that."

After a few more steps, Grace pointed to another shadow. "Surely that's scary. It's clearly a man with a machine gun."

I laughed. "Funny, that's not my take on it at all. I see a woman with a pool cue trying to make a tough shot, and from the way she's standing, she doesn't have a chance."

"You're too much," Grace said. She pointed again, and I saw that she was motioning in the direction of the Patriot Tree. "Tell me that doesn't look like someone's hanging from the branches."

I froze as I took in the tree and its surroundings. "Grace, call 911."

"Why? What's wrong?"

I looked at it carefully, but as we got closer, there was no mistaking it. "That's no shadow, Grace. There really is a body hanging there."

# CHAPTER 4

As Grace dialed the number on her telephone, I started walking with dread toward one of my favorite places in the park. The Patriot Tree was a living testament to the loyalty of our ancestors, and a stark reminder of the way they treated traitors in the Revolutionary and Civil Wars. It was a place of comfort for me, but there was nothing comfortable or reassuring about it tonight. As I approached, I couldn't tell the sex of the victim, let alone guess who it might be. The only time I'd ever seen anything hanging from its branches before had been when local high school kids had hung a stuffed effigy of the principal there as a prank, but it was getting more obvious by the moment that this was no dummy. What a horrible way to die.

I was getting nearly close enough to see who was there when Grace grabbed my arm. "Suzanne, what do you think you're doing?"

"I need to see who it is," I said. It could easily be one of my friends there, or even my ex-husband. Whoever it ended up being, I had to know so I could start dealing with it.

"We need to wait for the police," she replied.

"We can just as easily wait near the tree." I looked at her and saw the sheer terror on her face, and I wondered briefly why I wasn't feeling the same thing myself yet. For whatever reason, I seemed calmer than I ever would have guessed. I suppose that it wasn't real to me at that point. When I saw the body close enough to recognize it, I had a feeling that would change. And then another reason struck me, one that added a sense of urgency to my actions. "Grace, you can stay here if you'd like, I completely understand, but I'm going to see if whoever's hanging there needs our help. For all we know, they may not be dead."

"But they aren't moving," she said, her voice almost a whimper.

"Not that we can see, but that doesn't mean that whoever is hanging there is really dead. Grace, what if there's the slightest chance they're still alive? That's even more reason to check on them, isn't it?"

Grace took a deep breath, and then nodded firmly. "Okay, let's do this."

"You don't have to, you know," I said.

She let out a breath, and then said, "No, I'm all right. Well, I'm not really, but I will be. You can count on me."

I nodded, took her hand, and as we walked toward the tree, as Grace looked up, she asked, "Do you think it's someone we know?"

"I still can't tell from here, but there's a good chance that it is."

I neared the body, being careful about where I stepped in case there were footprints, though the ground was mostly just dirt and gravel.

As I got closer, I could finally tell for sure that it was a man.

I was still ten feet away before I could make out the face.

It was Tim Leander, our town handyman, and there was no doubt in my mind that he was long past any help we might have given him.

The man was clearly dead.

I don't know how long Grace and I stood there looking up at him, but the next thing I knew, there were footsteps behind us.

Chief Martin, still dressed in his best suit, came running up to join us. "The dispatcher just called me," he said as he neared us.

"It's Tim Leander," I told him dully. It was finally sinking in that a man I truly liked and admired was dead, and there was an ache in my chest that felt as though someone had hit me.

Chief Martin approached more cautiously and looked up at the handyman. "Who would want to kill him?" he asked softly. "It just doesn't make any sense. The man didn't have an enemy in all of April Springs. He's done good work for me a dozen times over the years, and I've never heard a bad word spoken against him."

"I still can't believe it," I answered. Tim was a friend, and a frequent visitor to Donut Hearts. I'd miss seeing his smile, but it was going to be a long time until I'd be able to wipe the image of his dead body hanging from that tree branch and replace it with an image from a better time for all of us.

Three squad cars were pulling up now, driving into the park and ignoring the footpaths entirely. I knew they had to do it, but it felt like an added violation of the sanctity of the park.

I'd almost forgotten about Grace when she asked the police chief, "Is there any chance that it was suicide?"

I started to answer when the chief beat me to it. "I don't think it's likely. He would have had to climb the tree, tie the rope around his neck, and then throw himself over. There are easier ways to die."

"I can't think of many worse," I answered.

"Then you're a lucky woman," Chief Martin answered. "I can think of more than I even want to consider. Do you have anything else to add to that 911 call you two made?"

"No," I answered. "We were walking back home after eating at the Boxcar, and we found him hanging there." I glanced at my watch, and suddenly remembered his date with Momma. "What are you doing back so early?"

"Your mother had a headache," he said curtly. It was clear he didn't want to talk about it. "Why don't you two wait back at the house?"

"Will you be stopping by on your way out?" I asked. I wanted to know what he and his officers found out, even if it meant waiting up all night.

"Not tonight," he replied cryptically. I wondered how real my mother's headache had been, or if it had just been an excuse to end a bad date early.

76

"Come on, Suzanne," Grace said as she tugged at my arm.

I wasn't sure I wanted to give up that easily, but I realized that I wasn't going to learn anything else tonight, at least not from the police department. "You're right. Let's go."

We walked back to the house together, and Grace shivered as we neared the front steps.

"Are you cold?" I asked.

"Not from the temperature." She tried to shake it off, and then said, "Listen, if you and your mom want to stay with me at my place tonight, I've got plenty of room at my house."

"Why would we want to do that?" I asked, honestly puzzled by the offer.

"Come on, Suzanne, that tree isn't far from your doorstep, and I don't know how you're ever going to get that image out of your head. I know I'm going to have nightmares about it for weeks, and I live down the road."

"Don't worry about the two of us. We'll be fine," I said, certain that my mother would echo the sentiment. The evils of the world had come close to our home before, but we wouldn't let them chase us away, even for one night. It was more than a house for us; it was our sanctuary, and we weren't about to let anyone spoil it for us.

"Well, don't say I didn't offer," she said. "If you change your mind, any time, even in the middle of the night, you're welcome there."

I stopped and squeezed her shoulder. "I appreciate that so much, and I'm sure Momma will, too. Would you like to come in?"

"Maybe just for a second," she said as her gaze went back to the crime scene.

"Good enough," I said. I didn't want to keep her there any longer than it was comfortable for her, but I also didn't want her leaving with a bad taste in her mouth, with memories of bodies and not the friendship we shared. My home needed to be a place of comfort and refuge for her as well, if I could help make it so.

We walked up the steps of our cottage together and the porch light came on.

"What happened?" Momma asked. She was still dressed in blue, and I marveled again at just how pretty she looked, though she was frowning in concern as she spoke.

"How's your headache?" I asked, ignoring her question for the moment.

"Better," she admitted. "Do you know who was hanging from the tree?"

There was no use in trying to sugarcoat it, she'd find out sooner or later. "It was Tim

Leander," I said.

Momma looked shaken by the news, and Grace and I raced up the stairs to support her. "Are you okay?" I asked her as I helped her to the porch swing.

"I'm fine," Momma said as she settled into it. "It's just shocking, isn't it? Tim fixed a flat tire for me just last week, did I tell you about that? I was about to call the auto club when he offered to change it for me, and when I tried to pay him, he refused to take any money. He told me that friendship was worth more than cash to him." Momma looked as though she might cry at any moment. "Who would want to hurt Tim?"

"The chief just asked me the same thing," I said. "What really happened on your date, Momma?"

She frowned again, this time for my benefit entirely. "We were having a fine time, but I got a headache, so we left, and I don't care to discuss it anymore."

"Does that mean we don't get a minute-by-minute recap, then?" I asked.

Grace tweaked my arm, but I ignored her. I wasn't about to let Momma get away with blowing the chief of police off like that, after all they'd been through setting up their first date. Though it was clear to anyone who knew me that I wasn't the man's biggest fan, he at least deserved better than he'd gotten tonight.

"Drop it, Suzanne." The tone of her voice made it loud and clear that she was finished with the subject, maybe forever.

I chose to ignore it. This was too important to just forget.

"I will, if you promise never to say another word about my love life again," I said. I knew it was an idle offer. There was no way she would ever agree to that, but maybe I could get her to see that it was important we discuss what had really happened that night. The worst thing that could happen in my opinion is that she might just give up and never take another chance again.

Momma tried to stare me down, and I fully realized that look would make most people wilt, but I wasn't one of them. I was pretty immune to it, having been desensitized over the years.

She shook her head finally, and I heard her sigh. When she spoke again, the sternness of her previous tone was gone. "I honestly did have a headache," Momma admitted. "It was crushing."

"And yet it's gone now," I said, making certain there was not a hint of mocking in my voice. I was on thin ice at the moment, and nobody knew it better than I did.

She waved a hand in the air. "Who can explain these things?" she asked.

"Are you going to try again soon?"

Grace looked at me as though I'd lost my mind, but I wasn't about to stop.

"Perhaps in a few days," she admitted. "I truly was having a good time when the headache came on so suddenly." She paused, looked surprised to be admitting it, but then added, "I really was reluctant to end it so abruptly."

I hugged her, and as I pulled away, she asked me, "What was that for?"

"You tried once, and you're going to try again," I said. "There's nothing more that I can ask of you. I'm proud of you, Momma."

She looked puzzled by my explanation. "Nonsense. I've done nothing to be proud of."

"If it matters, I think you did, too," Grace said.

"You two are getting to be too much alike," she said. After dismissing the thought, she asked, "Would either of you have room for some apple pie? I baked one this afternoon."

I smiled at her. "Are you sure you wouldn't rather share it with Chief Martin? He's just over there, and I'm sure he can spare ten minutes for a slice of pie."

"Phillip has his hands full at the moment," she said as she glanced briefly in the direction of the Patriot's Tree. "Don't worry, there will be other times, and other pies. For tonight, I can't think of anyone I'd rather share a slice with than the two of you."

We each got our slices, and as we sat at the front table eating, the lights from outside were an unspoken presence that kept trying to violate the sanctity of our home. Death had come to April Springs again, too close for our comfort, but we would find a way to deal with it, as we did the other troubles in our lives.

Half an hour later, Grace stood and stretched, then said, "I'm going to take off, if you don't mind. Thanks again for the pie."

"You're most welcome, dear," Momma said. She turned to me and said, "Suzanne, you should walk her to her car."

I got up and moved toward the door. "Come on, Grace. Let's go."

"Don't be silly," she said. "I can manage just fine by myself."

"I'm sure you can, but I don't mind."

"Fine. Good night," she called out to Momma as we started out the door.

"Sweet dreams," Momma answered.

Before we could go, she added, "Suzanne, don't linger out there. The police are still working, and they don't need you nosing around in their business."

"I wouldn't dream of it," I said with a smile, and we both knew that I was clearly lying. I suddenly realized that Momma hadn't been all that concerned about Grace getting an escort after all. She wanted to know what was happening at the Patriot's Tree, and it was the only way she could ask me to check things out without openly encouraging me to meddle.

I wouldn't let her down.

Once Grace and I were outside, I said, "See you tomorrow."

As I started back toward the Patriot's Tree, Grace asked, "You're really going back over there after what your mother just told you?"

"Are you kidding? She practically begged me to check things out just now."

Grace frowned at that. "Odd, I didn't hear anything like that."

I smiled. "That's because you don't speak 'Momma.' You're welcome to come with me again if you'd like."

"Why not?" she asked as she changed directions at the last second to join me. I hadn't really meant to offer the invitation, and Grace had surprised me by taking me up on it. Perhaps she was dealing with it okay after all.

As we approached, I was relieved to see that they'd cut Tim down from the tree, and his body was now gone. I'd been fond of the man, and I didn't want or need another image like the one I'd seen earlier sticking in my mind.

Chief Martin was standing to one side watching a pair of his officers scan the scene with bright handheld lights. I recognized one of them as Officer Grant, a good customer of mine and a budding friend, but I made no move to attract his attention. He was intent on what he was doing, no doubt scanning for clues, and I didn't want the police chief to accuse me of distracting one of his officers while he was at work.

When Grace and I walked up to him, the police chief glanced at his watch and whistled softly. "I'm impressed," he said.

"Thank you," I said. "Why exactly are you impressed?"

"It took you forty-seven minutes to come out to see what was going on. I was betting you'd be back in ten."

I offered him a grin. "I would have been, but Momma had baked a pie this afternoon, and you know how hard that is to resist." It may have been mean of me to let him know that there was pie so close, but I wanted him to realize that Momma had originally meant it for him.

"Any chance it's cherry?" he asked, a wistful look on his face.

"Apple," I admitted.

"Even better."

I nodded my agreement, and then I asked, "Have you found out anything about what happened to poor Tim?"

He seemed to consider my question, and then said, "I could give you a line about an active police investigation, but what's the use? We don't know anything new. The doc's called the medical examiner, and we've collected about all the evidence here we can. What ever happened, it's clear that Tim double-crossed somebody, and I'm guessing the killer lives in April Springs."

That assumption was beyond me. "How can you say that?"

He shrugged. "Come on, the significance of the Patriot's Tree hanging can't be lost on you. It's a spot reserved for traitors. It always has been, and I'm guessing it will be until folks forget what happened here someday."

I hadn't even considered that, much to my dismay. Of course the location of the hanging was a symbol. But that begged the question, who had Tim betrayed?

"That's absolutely brilliant," I said, not fully realizing that I'd said it aloud.

He looked equally shocked by my admission. "Are you actually complimenting me, Suzanne?"

I grinned at him. "I'm just as surprised as you must be. Thanks for sharing that, Chief."

"You're welcome," he replied. As Grace and I walked away, he added, "Tell your mother good night for me."

"I will," I said.

As soon as we were out of hearing range, Grace tugged at my arm and asked, "What was that all about?"

I admitted, "The man deserved a compliment, and I gave him one. I didn't see the significance of the tree in Tim's hanging, but his insight was spot on. It's the only reason for taking a chance and doing it out in the open that makes the slightest bit of sense. Somebody was sending a message that betrayal is not acceptable behavior. I just wish I knew who sent it."

"That makes two of us," Grace said as we approached the house.

Momma was standing on the front porch waiting for us.

"I was coming right back," I said. "You didn't have to watch out for me."

"I wasn't," she said. "Suzanne, you have a telephone call."

"Is it Jake?" I asked.

She bit her lower lip, and then said carefully, "Actually, it's Max."

I shook my head. I knew why he was calling. The man hated having anyone upset with him, including his ex-wife. "Tell him I'll call him back later," I said. "I'm in no mood to deal with him tonight after what I've seen."

Momma wasn't buying it, though. She pushed the telephone toward me and said, "You need to deal with him, Suzanne."

If there was anyone in April Springs who was less a fan of my ex than I was, it had to be Momma. She wouldn't urge me to take his call unless she thought it was necessary. "Hand me the telephone."

I took the phone from Momma and said, "This is Suzanne."

"It's Max," my ex said.

"I gathered as much. What can I do for you, Max?"

"Listen, I just wanted to say I'm sorry about what happened this afternoon."

I laughed. "Don't flatter yourself, I was concerned about Emily. We aren't married

87

anymore. You don't owe me any explanations, and even if you thought you did, I don't need to hear them. We're fine, okay?"

"Okay, if you're sure."

"I'm sure. Good night, Max."

"Night."

"What was that all about?" Grace asked, and I could see Momma wanted to hear the answer as well.

"You know Max," I said. "He doesn't like it when anyone's mad at him."

"Boys will be boys," Grace said.

Momma added, "And some of them will never become men."

# SOUR CREAM DONUTS

This is a good, solid recipe that really shows the depth of flavor in these donuts. We like these iced, but they're good plain, too.

## Ingredients
- 2 cups all purpose flour
- 1 teaspoon baking powder
- 1/2 teaspoon baking soda
- 1/2 teaspoon nutmeg
- Dash of salt
- 1/4 cup sour cream
- 1/4 cup buttermilk
- 1/2 cup sugar
- 1 egg, beaten
- 1 teaspoon vanilla

## Directions
First, beat the egg, and then add the sugar, buttermilk, sour cream, and vanilla. Mix thoroughly, then set aside.

In a separate bowl, sift the flour, nutmeg, baking soda, baking powder, and salt together, then add to the egg mixture in thirds until it is all combined. Roll the dough out to 1/4 to 1/2 inch thick, then cut rounds and holes. Fry in 360-degree canola oil for three minutes, turning halfway through, then place on paper towels to drain. Powdered sugar can be applied immediately, but wait until they cool to add icing and sprinkles.

Makes 6–8 donuts and holes

# CHAPTER 5

Momma moved to the couch and picked up the latest mystery novel she'd been reading. She'd gotten interested in crafting mysteries, and was devouring them at an alarming pace. "Don't they all kind of run together if you read them so quickly?" I asked.

"Nonsense. This series is about candles, the last one I read featured quilts, and the next series I'm tackling centers around cardmaking. They couldn't be any different." She set the book aside. "I'm happy that Emily's turned up, but we're still left with poor Timothy's murder. The two of them had a special bond, you know."

"Tim and Emily? I didn't know that."

She nodded. "He's been an honorary uncle to her since she was born. Tim and Emily's father were friends since they were boys, and Tim had looked out for her ever since."

"How did I not know that?" I asked.

She smiled slightly at me. "You don't know everything that happens in April Springs."

"Hey, I'm just glad that one of us does."

Momma sat there for a moment, and then said softly, "I'm going to miss Tim."

"The town's going to miss him, and I am, too," I agreed. "I don't know what we're going to do without someone to take care of things around here."

Momma waved a sheet of paper in the air. "Perhaps we won't have to. I found this in the mailbox when I got home."

I took the flyer from her and read it.

*"Handy Andy at your service, new to April Springs. I'm bonded, licensed, and suited to do any home repair, from wet basements to leaky roofs. If you want a real dandy, it's time to call Andy."*

There was a phone number below it, and a pencil sketch of a man holding a toolbox dashing around.

It was unsettling reading the advertisement after what had happened to Tim. How odd that we learned of a new handyman the same day our old one was murdered. Was Handy Andy's timing one of the biggest coincidences of all time? I couldn't help wondering if there was the slightest chance that the new handyman had decided to eliminate his competition before he got started with his new business in April Springs. On the face of it, it sounded like total nonsense, but Tim was dead, and someone had killed him. I couldn't ignore any suspects in my search for the truth, no matter how trivial their motive might be. Tomorrow, I was going to give Andy a call and see how much he knew about Tim Leander's demise.

In the meantime, I needed to get to bed if I was going to get any sleep at all before it was time to make my donuts yet again. I'd been hoping for a call from Jake before bedtime, but if he was somewhere off the beaten path, he might not even have any cell phone reception. For the moment, I'd have to be content that I had a boyfriend, someone who cared deeply about me, and a man that I cherished in return. I'd gone to sleep plenty of nights with nothing but hopeless despair in my heart, so nodding off now should be a snap.

I was awakened by my telephone the next morning at 1:29, a full minute before I had to get up.

"Good morning, sunshine," Jake said, and I felt the sleep wash away from me.

"Jake. I miss you." His voice sounded a

bit hoarse, as though he'd spent more than a little time yelling the day before. I just hoped he wasn't getting sick.

"I miss you, too," he said after clearing his throat. It was much better now, and I realized that I'd probably overreacted. I had a tendency to do that when we were apart. "Why don't we do something about that?"

There was a happy tone to his voice now, a bit playful. "What happened with your case? I thought you were trying to catch a train robber?" I said.

I could hear his grin even over the phone. "Well, ma'am, we got a posse together and tracked those varmints down," he said in his best western drawl.

This was great news. "How on earth did you find them?"

"We utilized excellent police investigating techniques in our pursuit of the suspects, and took advantage of all the benefits modern science has to offer to today's law enforcement agencies."

"So, you got lucky?" I asked with a laugh.

"Mostly we just followed the trail of broken branches and bushes. Neither one of this pair could be considered an excellent woodsman, so tracking them down was just a matter of time."

"Where were they hiding?" I asked. I loved

it when Jake was in a good mood, and he was practically giddy as he spoke.

"There's an abandoned hunting camp deep in the woods, and we found them huddled around a fire trying to stay warm. All the wood around them was green, and they were so desperate, they were just about to start burning money when we got to them. If I didn't know any better, I could swear they were almost happy to see us when we showed up. They didn't even put up a fight."

"I thought they were on four-wheelers. What ruined their getaway?" I asked, keeping an eye on the clock. It was too precious having time with Jake before work, and if I had to push harder at the donut shop to be ready to open in time, then so be it.

"Turns out they wrecked one of their four-wheelers trying to get back to the highway, and one of the bandits broke his leg in the process. That was bad enough, but then the other machine wouldn't carry both of them and their loot. It broke down, and they barely managed to get to the camp before they wore themselves out. They're both in custody; one in the Buncombe County jail, and the other in the hospital in Asheville, and if you ask me, the two of them needed a little time apart anyway after their big adventure together."

"And you woke up early just to tell me before I had to go to work? That is so sweet."

"Don't give me too much credit," he said, laughing. "I haven't even been to bed yet." He paused for a moment, and then said, "Suzanne, I know you need to get going, but I wanted to ask you something before you headed off for work."

"Fire away," I said as I got up and started making my bed.

"Do you have any plans this afternoon?"

I wanted to tell him about Tim, and my team's impromptu investigation into his murder, but I didn't have the heart to ruin our chat. Besides, we hadn't exactly come up with our next step. "I'm not really sure. Why, what did you have in mind?"

"If you're interested, I'd love to take you out to an early dinner. How about five?"

"That sounds wonderful! It's a date," I said. That could still give me time to look into what had happened to Tim. "Try to get some sleep. I want you wide awake for our date."

"I'm heading off to bed right now. I just wanted to catch you before you got busy at the donut shop." He tried to stifle a yawn as he said the last bit, and I could hear just how tired he was in his voice.

I glanced at the clock and saw that I was already going to be late. "Well, your timing is excellent. I can't wait to see you, Jake. Thanks for calling."

"Good-bye for now," he said.

"Good night," I added, and we hung up.

As I took a quick shower and then got ready for work, I wondered if I had any right to dig into Tim's murder. After all, when I'd been accused of doing something to Emily, I'd had a stake in finding out what had happened to her. No one was pointing a finger at me about Tim's death. Did I have the right, or the justification, to look into it?

Maybe, just this once, I'd take a pass leading an impromptu investigation.

Then again, Tim had been a good friend to me, to Grace, and to the rest of April Springs. He would be greatly missed, and clearly he meant more to some folks than I'd realized. Apparently his relationship with Emily was especially close, and I wondered how she was dealing with the news of her honorary uncle's murder.

As Emma walked into the donut shop at her regular time — half an hour after I arrived — she said, "Good morning, Suzanne." She paused a moment, put on her apron, and then studied me for a second.

"You look really happy today. What's going on?" My employee must have noticed something different about me, though I couldn't have said what it might be. I'd been working on my cake donuts, and had things going at a steady pace.

"Why do you say that?" I asked as I scraped the remnants of flour into the trash from the counter where I'd been working.

Emma laughed. "Oh, I don't know. It could be because there's a grin on your face that you couldn't hide with a mask."

"Guilty as charged," I said as I finished wiping down the kitchen counter. "Jake's back in town, and we're having an early dinner this evening."

"I thought it might be because of our ad in the newspaper this morning," Emma said.

"That's right," I said. I'd nearly forgotten about our plans for the day. Our Take-a-Chance-Tuesdays where Emma offered an offbeat roasted blend and I tried to come up with an outlandish donut to match it hadn't really taken off yet, so we'd decided to put an ad in the *April Springs Sentinel*. Emma's father, Ray, had given us a great deal on it, setting us up with a cheap graphic designer and offering us his best advertising rate. I hadn't seen the ad myself, promising Emma that she could handle everything concerning our experiment herself. I figured it couldn't hurt, and it gave Emma a sense of satisfaction by contributing to the business.

She smiled broadly at me. "Just wait until you see it, Suzanne. It's awesome."

"I'm looking forward to it." I had no idea what it looked like, but Emma's excitement was payment enough. She'd be tough to replace when she went off to school someday, and if I could keep her happy and invested in the donut shop in the meantime, I'd do it.

Emma frowned, and then said, "I'm going crazy waiting for the paper to come out. I can't wait for you to see it," she said, and dug into her purse. "Here's the proof for the ad my dad's running for us today."

She thrust a folded sheet of paper toward me, and I took it and studied it for a few moments. I really liked what I saw, and I had to admit that it had a real sense of fun about it, something we'd agreed we wanted to capture in the ad. There was an image of a donut and coffee cup holding hands, and their legs appeared to be dancing. Song notes hovered around them, and the ad copy said, *"Don't be afraid to take a chance on Take-a-Chance Tuesdays, only at Donut Hearts in downtown April Springs. Try your luck, they're only a buck!"* It may have been a little busy for my taste, but still, there was a whimsical charm about it that I liked.

Then my glance caught the fine print at the bottom of the ad.

Emma and I had discussed it before she got started on the design, and we'd agreed that there would have to be a limit of one per customer. After all, we were losing money selling a small cup of coffee and a donut for a dollar, but we hoped that most folks who came in would want more than one donut.

There was a problem, though. Instead of a limit of one per customer, someone had slipped up, and the limit was now eleven! We could actually sell out today and still lose money.

"Emma, did you check this before it went to your dad?" I asked as I handed it back to her.

She looked puzzled by my question. "Sure I did. It's perfect, don't you think?"

"You didn't make any changes to it at all at the last minute?"

Emma frowned at me. "What's wrong with it, Suzanne? You told me I could do whatever I want. We agreed on the general scope and conditions of the ad, but I got to design it myself."

"Honestly, I love just about every bit of it," I said.

"Then what's the problem?"

"Look at the bottom of the ad," I said as I handed it back to her.

Emma looked puzzled, but after nearly a minute, she finally caught it. Her face was white as she said, "This is just the proof. I'm sure that Dad fixed it. He had to."

"Did you tell him to make any changes to the proof?"

"No," she admitted, and I could hear the tears coming up in her voice. "How did I miss this?"

I touched her shoulder lightly. "We may be worrying for nothing. Call him," I said.

Emma nodded and took out her telephone. After a brief conversation, she hung up, looking as though she wanted to cry. It was clear she hadn't gotten the answer she'd been hoping for. "He said he thought that was what we meant to do to drive in some foot traffic. Suzanne, this is a nightmare. What are we going to do?"

I thought about it, and then said, "Honestly, what can we do? Sure, it was a mistake, but mistakes happen all of the time. Trust me; I've made more than my share myself." I saw her lower lip start to quiver, and I knew that I couldn't deal with a crying employee at the moment. "Don't worry, Emma. It will be fine, but I think we should be prepared for an onslaught, just in case. Let's start making some extra donuts so we won't be caught short."

"My coffee blend is ready. Are you happy with the recipe you've been working on for today?" she asked.

"On second thought, I don't think I'm going to take a chance on that one," I said as I started scanning my recipe book. It not only had the recipes I used every day, but also contained ideas that I wanted to try someday when I got the chance. My gaze settled on a brightly colored confection I'd played with on paper but had never made, and I decided that it would be just right for Emma's Thunder Coffee offering. "Today, I think we'll make rainbow-iced orange cake donuts."

"We've never done those before," she said.

"No, but they should be pretty and festive, and I don't need to do anything exotic to them except decorate them like rainbows."

"That sounds great." She paused, and then added, "Suzanne, I really am sorry about this."

It was time to put what had happened behind us so we could focus on the work we had to do before we could open. "Non-sense, don't worry about it. Come on, this could be fun."

"Thanks for letting me off the hook," she answered, the relief obvious in her voice.

"You know what? As far as I'm concerned, this might be a blessing in disguise. After all, the whole purpose of the ad was to drive folks into the store, and if this doesn't do it, I don't know what will. Let's make it a good day, no matter what, okay?"

"That sounds great," she said, and we dove into work.

"Is it always this crowded in here?" a new customer asked as he finally made his way to the counter so he could order. He was middle-aged, and from his girth, I was pretty sure he'd never passed up a free donut in his life, let alone eleven of them. If I had to guess, I would say that the dollar would just about cover our expenses for the exotic coffee blend, but I was afraid the donuts would be on the house. Emma had suggested switching to a less expensive coffee when we realized what had happened, but I wasn't about to disappoint anyone if I could help it. I had to admit one thing. If the ad's purpose had been to bring folks into Donut Hearts, it was a rousing success.

I'd brought my recipe book up front so I could go over a new donut I'd been thinking about offering, but I hadn't even had time to glance at it. The place had been hopping with customers since we'd opened, and for one of the few times since I'd owned the shop, I had a line before I even unlocked my door. We were moving a great deal of donuts and coffee, but I honestly didn't have a clue where we stood financially. I had hoped that we wouldn't lose too much, although as far as mistakes went, it could have been a great deal worse, and I wasn't about to make any more donuts than we already had. When we were out, we were out, and there wouldn't be any rain checks, which a few customers had already asked about.

I looked at the man who was clutching a dollar bill in his fist and said, "Are you kidding? This is a slow day." I added the last bit on a whim, fighting to keep a straight face as I said it.

"Wow, I'm impressed," he answered as he looked around.

Not a chair or stool was empty, and several folks were standing along the windows and the walls. I'd made one change to our offering; it was now dine-in only. At least that way we didn't have to cater to every office within a hundred-mile radius. No one really seemed to mind once I explained what had happened, and it did make the shop a place full of laughter and smiles. Many of my customers kept their free eleven down to one or two extra, but a few insisted on the full dozen for the price of one. Those folks I made eat at the counter, and more than a few gave up after five or six. My rule became if they ordered, but couldn't eat, the dozen donuts and drink all of the coffee, they had to pay for every extra they ate, so that took care of the rest of them.

I couldn't let this customer think that I'd been telling the truth earlier. I explained, "I'm just kidding. This is Take-a-Chance Tuesday. We had Rainbow donuts, but we ran out of them hours ago. You can take your pick of what we have left. When we ran out of Thunder coffee, we switched to Harmony, and now we're serving Starshine. I'm afraid when that's gone, it's back to our regular blends." Emma loved to give her coffees exotic names, and I liked that it added a little mystery to our selections on Tuesday.

"I'll take one special, and you can pick out two donuts for me," he said as he slid the dollar across the counter to me. Initially

I'd been charging tax to push it over a dollar, but one high roller had come in and tipped me a fifty to cover everyone's tax for the day. It was a sweet gesture, and I'd returned it with two dozen donuts, which he gladly accepted in return, laughing as he said that they could have only cost him a couple of bucks if he'd been a little hungrier.

I chose one lemon filled and a regular glazed donut, got his two coffees, and then handed him the tray. "Enjoy."

"Thanks," the stranger said. He grabbed one of his donuts before he even moved out of line, took his first bite of the lemon, and then smiled at me and said, "That is awesome! Who owns this place?"

"I do," I admitted. "I'm Suzanne Hart."

"Donut Hearts for Hart, I get it." After another big bite, he asked, "Have you ever thought about selling this place? I'd give you a good and fair price for it; fryers, equipment, tables and chairs, recipes, display cases, everything. I'll even buy the name from you."

I looked around the shop, and realized that no matter how much he was offering, I knew I could never give up Donut Hearts, and what it had come to mean to me.

"Thanks, but no, thank you. This is home for me now."

The stranger shrugged, and as he moved on, I called out, "Next."

If nothing else, the newspaper misprint made for an exciting morning for us.

An hour later, Emily Hargraves came into the shop pushing a child's stroller. I was about to ask her whose kid she was babysitting when I saw that she had Cow, Spots, and Moose safely buckled into the stroller together. All three of them were wearing sunglasses and brightly colored caps, and I had to admit, they looked rather dapper sitting there.

I couldn't hide my grin when I saw them. "Taking the guys out for a walk?"

She nodded. "I felt that I owed them at least that after leaving them unprotected and unguarded yesterday."

I laughed out loud. "You know, there are some folks in town who think you've lost your mind. I don't mean me, but you know how people around here talk."

Emily smiled broadly at me. "Are you kidding? Sometimes I think I've slipped over the edge myself, but I'm not about to apologize to anyone. It's fun, and if they don't get it, then they don't get me." She looked down at the stroller and asked, "Right, guys?"

I swear, for a split second, I waited for one of them to answer. Who did that make the craziest one of us? Emily looked at the cases behind me, now nearly empty, even with the double batch of donuts we'd made that morning.

"I'm sorry there aren't many left," I said. "It's been a big day."

"I heard about the misprint. How bad a hit are you going to take?" It wasn't the first time I'd been asked that question, each time by another small-business owner. They knew, better than anyone else, how razor-thin profit margins could be when you owned your own place.

"I don't even want to think about it yet," I answered. "We'll do a rough count when we close, which, judging by this display case, will be after the next few customers. I take it you want our day's special."

As I started to get her coffee, she shook her head and said, "If it's all the same to you, I'd like one coffee, one donut, and one favor."

I turned around and handed her the cup. "A favor?"

She lowered her voice and moved the stroller aside so she could get closer to me. "Suzanne, I need you to find out what happened to Uncle Tim." There were tears in her eyes as she spoke, and her voice quivered a little.

"I'm not really qualified," I answered. I'd been debating the same course of action no matter how many promises I made to myself to butt out, but as much as I wanted to walk away from the murder case, I wasn't sure that I'd be able to do it.

"Come on. You've done it before, Suzanne. I know the police chief can follow up on all of the ordinary leads, but you've got a knack for looking at things from a different angle than he can." She looked frustrated as she continued, "I can't let this go unpunished, but I don't know what to do. Please don't say no to me." She reached into the stroller, and for a second I thought she was going to pull Spots out, but instead, she grabbed an envelope she'd stored there. "He's my watch cow," she explained as she nudged Spots back into his position. Emily held the envelope for a moment, and then slid it across the counter to me. "Take it."

I did as she asked, opened it, and found it was stuffed with twenties, tens, and fives.

I waved the envelope at her and asked, "What is this for?"

"I'm willing to pay you for your help," she said. "It's that important to me."

I pushed the envelope back into her

hands. "You know that I can't take your money."

She looked forlorn. "Does that mean you won't help? I don't know where else to turn." She hesitated a moment, and then asked, "It's because of Max, isn't it? That's over, I promise you."

There. It was finally out in the open, and now we could deal with it. "Emily, you don't have to explain to me how impulsive Max can make you feel; I know better than most. Trust me, you don't owe me any explanations."

"Then why won't you help?"

"I'll do what I can," I said as I patted her hand. "But I won't take a dime of your money. Friends don't do that. I can't promise you anything concrete, but I'll do my best."

The relief on her face was obvious. "Thank you. Thank you so much."

I wasn't sure just how much I'd be able to accomplish, but if I could give Emily some peace of mind by trying to help her, I wasn't about to deny her that.

She started to go when I said, "Hang on a second. You've still got a donut coming to you."

"Thanks, but just the coffee is fine."

The next two customers took care of the

last bit of inventory I had left, and it was barely past ten-thirty. It looked like Donut Hearts was about to set a new record, not for actual sales, but for depleting our inventory in amazing time.

"It's closing time," I announced to the customers remaining in the shop. "Thank you all for coming."

"But you've got another hour and a half to stay open," Maggie Brentwood said as she looked at the hours posted on my door.

"We would, but there's just one problem. There's nothing left to sell," I replied. "The donuts are gone, and the coffee's nearly had it, too. I hope you all enjoyed your donuts and coffee today."

To my surprise, the ten customers left in the shop all started applauding, and I was glad we'd honored the ad, even if it may have cost us a day's sales.

Emma heard my announcement from the kitchen, and as I showed the last customer out and locked the door, she came up behind me. "Suzanne, I've been thinking about this all morning, and I hope you respect my request. I want to forfeit my pay today because of my mistake. It may help the bottom line, at least a little."

I smiled at her and hugged her. "Emma, there's no way that's happening. We both worked harder today than we ever have here. If anything, we both deserve bonuses."

She pulled away, but couldn't meet my gaze. "How bad was it?"

I thought about it, and then said, "In all honesty, I'm not sure, but even if we lost a lot, the PR had to be amazing. I can't imagine folks not talking about this day for quite a while."

She wasn't going to let me get away with that, though. "Suzanne, quit dodging the question. I know you keep pretty close tabs on what things cost, so you have to have a decent idea of what we spent today."

I couldn't deny it. I'd learned early on to be aware of my expenses, so I could probably have guessed within a few dollars how many supplies we'd used catering to the crowds we'd faced today. "I told you before; it doesn't matter, as long as we're careful the next time we run an ad."

She looked at me as though she didn't believe it. "Do you mean that there's actually going to be a next time?"

I hugged her, and then said, "Of course there is. I *would* like to see the ad before it's approved, though, the next time, if you don't mind." I didn't think there was a chance in a million that she wouldn't be ultra-careful when we ran another ad, but

I'd feel better knowing that if we made another mistake, both of us would share the blame equally.

"Consider it done," she said. "You know, I was thinking about a Hawaiian theme next time. You can do some kind of pineapple-coconut combo donut, and the Kona coffees are awesome. We can even decorate the place and give away plastic leis with every purchase."

"Why not? It sounds like fun. Tell you what, since we're both dying to know how we did today, why don't you finish the last dishes, and I'll run the reports."

"It's a deal."

As Emma disappeared in back, I moved to the register and started punching in the report keys.

It was time to see how bad a hit we took.

# CHAPTER 6

I ran the report on the cash register, and then checked the cash against the totals I'd gotten. The two numbers weren't even close, and I didn't have any idea how I was going to reconcile them. I'd had many people tell me to keep the change over the course of the morning, and I'd kept the money in the till without really worrying about accounting for it. I did a rough estimate of what our costs were for the day on the back of a donut bag, and then subtracted that amount from our total take.

I called Emma back up front so I could tell her where we stood.

She joined me with a bright smile on her face, but that quickly faded when she saw the report in my hands.

"How bad was it?"

"They don't come anywhere close to adding up," I said.

She looked shocked by the news. "What

114

happened? Did I mess up again?"

I shook my head. "We both know that you never touched the register, so if any mistakes were made up here, they were all mine. I lost track of how many people told me to keep the change, we were so busy this morning."

"Where do we stand?" It was clear that the suspense was killing her.

"Two hundred and ten dollars," I said solemnly.

She was shattered. "That's all we brought in for everything we sold today? It's even worse than I thought it would be. I'm so sorry."

I couldn't hide my smile any longer. "Are you? Considering everything, I think that's a wonderful profit for today."

Emma couldn't believe it. "We actually *made* money? How is that possible?"

"It appears that a lot more people overpaid and told me to keep the change than I realized. Don't forget, I also charged a few folks who tried to take advantage of us with our special, and we sold other things as well in the course of the day. All in all, I think we should be happy with what we took in."

"Does that total even count the tip jar?" Emma asked.

We'd put one in a few months before after

getting a few requests, and despite Emma's protests, I usually managed to convince her to put whatever was there into her college fund. "Honestly, I'd forgotten all about it," I said.

"That counts, too," she said. "It goes in the pot."

"That's for your college expenses," I said.

"Suzanne, are you really going to fight me on that today after what I did?"

I thought about it, and then realized that she was right. While it's true we all make mistakes, it's also important that we pay for them. How else can we learn from them otherwise?

"I give up. Just for today, we'll put it with the rest of the cash. Count it out for me, would you?"

She did, and then proudly announced, "There's almost a hundred dollars in there."

"Then we had a banner day," I said. How was that possible? There was only one way it could have happened; it was purely through the generosity of our customers and friends. Without them, Donut Hearts would be just another place to grab a donut and run.

As I made out our deposit slip, Emma said, "I may be crazy, but I've got a question for you. Should we do the same thing

116

next time?"

I had to smile at her audacity. "Buy one, get eleven free? Don't kid yourself. We were lucky this time. It could have been a disaster."

"I'm just happy it worked out," she said.

"So am I."

I sent Emma on her way as soon as the dishes were finished and the front was swept and cleaned. I'd tried to help a little, but she'd insisted on doing it all as additional penance, and I wasn't going to fight her on it. If it was a normal day, I'd wonder what to do with myself that early, but I'd made a promise to Emily Hargraves, and I wasn't about to break it. I'd do my best to find out what had happened to Tim, but I couldn't do it alone.

I needed my crew.

It was time to call in reinforcements in the form of George and Grace.

To my surprise, I found them both at Grace's, sitting on the front porch in deep conversation. "I'm not interrupting anything, am I?" I asked as I walked up the steps and joined them.

"Be careful, that handrail is loose," Grace said.

"Is that why you were waiting on Tim to come by?" I asked.

"No," Grace answered. "I wanted to get his opinion on increasing my back deck. But for Andy, George and I just loosened the handrail ourselves."

"Why on earth would you do that?" Had they both lost their minds?

George held a flyer up, exactly like the one Momma had, only printed on bright green paper this time. "We thought Handy Andy could give us an estimate," he said with a grin.

"And while he's here, you can grill him about what happened to Tim," I said, nodding my approval.

"Not me," George said. "I'd probably make him suspicious. I'm going to be inside, and Grace is going to be helpless out here all by herself." He couldn't get over the levity in that statement, and I had to agree. Grace Gauge was many things, but helpless didn't even make the top one thousand items on the list.

"Are you up for it?" I asked.

"Are you kidding?" She batted her eyes at us and added, "You know me. I was born for the stage."

"For you to convince *anyone* that you're helpless is going to take some major-league acting," I said.

"I can do it. Besides, I'd have to be better at it than you would be. You couldn't act helpless if you had a broken leg and a concussion."

"Hey, I'm good, too," I protested. "I was in every school play you had a role in."

"Let's leave it to the judges," Grace said. "George?"

"Sorry, Suzanne," he said as he pointed both fingers at Grace as the winner. "Hey, what are you doing here, anyway?"

"Thanks for that," I said. "It's always good to feel welcome among my friends."

"You know what I mean. You should be open for at least another hour."

I did my best to look sad as I explained, "Ordinarily I would be, but we got wiped out early because of that ad."

"We heard about it," Grace said as both their faces fell.

"That's tough," George said.

"Don't feel bad for me," I said with a grin. "We made out just fine. Now, who's the best actress?"

"Still me," Grace answered with a smile.

I looked around. "Okay, I concede. Where should I be when Handy Andy shows up?"

"Inside with me," George said. "The windows are open, so we should be able to hear everything they say."

"That sounds good," I replied. "Will we have popcorn and soda for the show?"

Grace shook her head. "You know, it's going to be difficult to give my best performance with you two for an audience."

"But you'll manage somehow, right?" I asked.

"You know it."

"When exactly is Handy Andy supposed to show up?"

George replied, "Not for another fifteen minutes. We've got plenty of time to get in position."

I looked down the street and saw a pickup headed our way with a bright sticker on the side. "He's early," I said as I helped George stand. "We need to get inside quick."

George and I had barely made it to our window view when the pickup truck pulled up in front of Grace's house. Normally I liked being in the middle of the action, but for once, it was nice to just sit back and watch someone else at work.

And right now, it was time for the show.

I could see a young man get out of the truck from my vantage point. He wore a red shirt, crisp new blue jeans, and a white cap. It appeared that Andy was going for the patriotic look.

I couldn't believe it when he actually tipped his cap to Grace as he approached. "Good morning," he said. Now that he was closer, I could see that he was barely in his twenties, and I wondered if he really knew how to fix things. Most handymen I'd ever met had been older, but I knew I shouldn't judge him by his age alone.

He studied Grace for a few seconds with more interest than he should have shown a prospective customer. "Are you Mrs. Gauge?" he asked her.

"Actually, it's 'Miss,' but you can call me Grace."

"Grace. I like that. It suits you." He looked at her for a few more seconds, like a shark watching a surfer, and when his smile returned, there was something kind of oily about it. "Grace, I'm Andrew Martin. It's nice to meet you."

"Good to meet you, Andy," Grace said, doing her best to keep him at bay. She took his offered hand, and I wished I could see her face as he continued to hold it a little too long. After a delay that lasted longer than I ever would have believed, Grace finally managed to pull her hand away.

"Now, should we talk about my problem?"

Andy looked at the clipboard in his free hand. "It says here that you need an estimate for your porch rail, is that right? Why don't we have a look?"

I watched as Grace approached the rail that she and George had just loosened. As she put a hand on it, she said, "It wiggles a little, see?"

Andy got down on one knee and studied the bracket that held the rail. After thirty seconds, he frowned, and then stood up. "I'm afraid your problem is a little more serious than you might think."

"It's not just a screw or something?" Grace asked. I couldn't believe how naïve she sounded.

I could see Andy try his best to look solemn as he said, "I'm afraid it's worse than that. The anchor bolts are missing, and you need a cross-brace to keep it all from falling over. I'll need to do some major reconstructive work to get it right again."

"How much would all that cost?" Grace asked, the fear and trepidation clear in her voice. I couldn't believe she didn't tell him what she'd done on the spot, and I wasn't sure I would have been able to keep my mouth shut. It appeared that we'd chosen the right actress for the role after all.

Andy pulled a calculator from his shirt pocket, and started entering figures. As he punched the add button, he explained what he was doing. "Let's see, that's sixty-eight for the anchors and another one-fifty for the bracing." He looked up at her and smiled as he added, "I cut you a break there. That includes tax and labor." As he hit the button again, he finally said, "That's two eighteen, but let's call it an even two hundred dollars."

"I don't know. I'm not sure. That sounds like a lot," Grace said.

"What's your safety worth, or your guests'? A lawsuit because someone falls off your porch would cost you a lot more than that."

"I need to think about it," Grace said haltingly, and I couldn't believe she didn't throw him off the porch then and there.

He jotted a few things down on a sheet of paper, and then presented it to her. "There's your estimate." Andy hesitated, and then added, "If coming up with the payment is a problem for you, I'm sure we can work something out."

"Thank you for coming," Grace said. "I'll let you know."

"Can't wait to hear from you," he said as he went back to his truck.

"You can call him when pigs bark at the full moon," I said, unable to keep my mouth shut a second longer.

"Quiet," Grace said. "He's not gone yet."

Another few moments, and the truck finally drove off. George and I walked outside, and there was a troubled look on Grace's face. "I know we loosened the screws on purpose, but could he be right about my railing? He was pretty convincing."

"He's a con man," George said as he took out a screwdriver and tightened the screws. After he did that, he tested the railing. "It's solid as a rock. The rest of what he said was pure nonsense. Tim did good work when he built this porch. That guy's trying to get you to make it withstand a hurricane."

"We should call Chief Martin and tell him that Andy had a huge motive to kill Tim," Grace said.

George shook his head. "Just because he believes in overkill doesn't mean he had anything to do with Tim's murder."

"It doesn't exactly clear him, either," I said.

George nodded. "Don't worry, I'm not going to give up on him yet; trust me. The chief needs to know what Andy's doing, at the very least."

"Who else had any motive to want to see Tim dead?" Grace asked.

"That's the question, isn't it?" I asked. For as much as Tim was a part of all our lives, it amazed me how little I actually knew about his. "Does anyone have any idea about Tim's love life?"

"I don't think he had one," George said.

"I'm not so sure," I admitted. "There have been rumors for years that he was seeing someone in town. I just never heard who it might be."

Grace asked, "If he kept it a secret from us all this time, how are we supposed to find out?"

I hated to go to the best source I had in town, but there was no alternative. "We have to talk to Gabby Williams. She's more plugged in than anyone else in April Springs, and that includes my mother."

George looked as though he were in pain from my suggestion. "Tell you what. You two talk to Gabby, and I'll deal with our friend Andy."

"He's not exactly our friend," Grace said.

"I don't know," I answered with a slight smile. "It looked as though he wouldn't mind getting a little friendlier with you."

Grace couldn't hide the look of disgust that blossomed on her face. "As much as I'd like a boyfriend right now, Andy doesn't even make the 'maybe' list. He was a little oily, wasn't he?"

"I couldn't believe you didn't give him a

black eye when he suggested you could work out a payment plan together."

George said, "I owe him one for that, if nothing else. If he gets anywhere near me, I'll whack him with my cane."

I glanced at the hard, polished wood, and realized that it could cause a great deal of havoc if used the right way. "That thing's a weapon, isn't it?"

"It can be. You two watch your step," George said as he walked carefully off the porch, hanging on to the rail with a solid grip.

"The same goes for you," I said.

After he was gone, I said to Grace, "Are you ready to tackle Gabby with me, or would you rather I go alone?"

"I don't mind going with you," she said, "but I think you might have more luck without me. Besides, I have a few calls to make for business before we get too far into this. Why don't you swing back by here after you're finished, and we can have lunch?"

"Coward," I said with a smile, and then stuck my tongue out at her.

"You know it," Grace said with a laugh.

I decided to leave my car at her place and walk to Gabby's. That was one of the great things about being so close to everything in April Springs. There were days when I walked everywhere, not even getting into my Jeep at all.

Besides, I was in no rush to see Gabby. It could be a minefield dealing with her, and it took me the entire walk to her shop to get my nerve up for the coming conversation.

I walked into ReNEWed, and was surprised by Gabby's latest offerings in the storefront's window. Where did she get her merchandise? I knew for a fact that little of the gently worn clothing she sold came from April Springs. Did she have some kind of exchange with a merchant in another city, or was there a more mysterious explanation for what she offered? I'd never had the courage to ask, and I wasn't about to bring the subject up now, not when I was looking for information.

Gabby was waiting on a customer when I walked in, so I started browsing through her racks of clothing. Mostly I wear blue jeans and T-shirts, but there were times I liked to dress up, especially when Jake and I were going out. I found a nice blue top on the rack that would jazz up my jeans, and I was thrilled to see that it was my size. I took it to one of the dressing rooms in back, and as I started to try it on, I heard voices coming from the next dressing room.

"I don't care how you feel about him, you've got to stop crying like that," I heard a young woman say in a familiar voice, though I couldn't place it. "What are people going to say?" From the sound of it, someone was having boy troubles.

And then the other voice answered, and I changed my opinion. Now, it seemed as though a daughter was trying to advise her mother. The older woman answered haltingly, "I can't help it. I miss him."

"You and two other women in the county," the younger woman said, not trying to hide her contempt for the situation. "Get yourself together, Mother."

"I still can't believe Timothy was dating all of us at the same time," the mother replied.

What? Could it really be Tim Leander they were talking about? I had a hard time believing that he was some kind of Romeo, but then again, I'd seen stranger things happen in April Springs since I'd opened my donut shop.

I kept my eye on the door, and after a minute, I saw the women leave the dressing room and return to the sales floor to continue browsing. I knew now why that voice had sounded familiar.

It was Penny Parsons, a nurse from the

hospital and a friend of mine, and the older striking woman with her had to be her mother.

I was about to approach them as I came out of the dressing room myself, but Gabby cut me off before I could get to them.

"Did you like it?" Gabby asked.

What was she talking about? Did she have a clue that I'd been eavesdropping? "Like what?"

Gabby pointed to the garment still in my hand. "The blouse, of course."

In my desire to hear the conversation next door, I'd forgotten all about it. "To be honest with you, I'm not sure."

"Why are you hesitating? It's perfect for you," Gabby said.

From the front of the shop, Penny said, "Thanks, Gabby. We'll touch base again later," as the two women walked out. She looked in my direction for a moment, but I'd stepped back into the dressing room, and I wasn't sure she saw me there.

"Don't be strangers," Gabby called out.

When Gabby turned back to me, she studied me a moment, and then asked, "Suzanne Hart, what did you just overhear?"

"What do you mean? I'm sure I don't know what you're talking about." There was no doubt in my mind that she knew I'd been eavesdropping, but I wasn't about to admit it.

Gabby took the blouse from me. "Don't try to lie to me. You were gone nearly five minutes, and you didn't even try this on. The tag is right where I left it, tucked into the front pocket, and you couldn't have taken it off the hanger without disturbing it, let alone be able to try it on. So I'll ask you again. What did you overhear?"

There was no use denying it any longer, and besides, wasn't that the reason I was at Gabby's shop anyway? "Penny's mother was dating Tim Leander," I said.

"I knew that," Gabby said, looking smug.

"Okay, but did you know that Tim was dating two other women in the area at the same time?"

Gabby frowned. "I didn't have a clue. Who were they?"

Ha. It felt good knowing something that she didn't, though I tried my best not to let my gloating show on my face. "I don't know, but I'm going to find out. Gabby, do you have any idea who might have wanted to see Tim dead?"

"You mean besides the three women he was dating? The only other person I can think of might be Orson Blaine. The two of them used to be best friends, but they haven't been able to stand each other for the past two years. Something happened between them, and I'm willing to wager that it was something big."

I didn't know Orson personally, but I'd heard of him a few times over the years.

"Any idea where I might find him?"

Gabby frowned, and then said, "If I had to guess, I'd say he's hanging out at Go Eats." I knew the place was a greasy-spoon hole-in-the-wall diner, but I hadn't eaten there since I was a teenager.

"Thanks for all your help," I said as I tried to hand the blouse back to her.

She wouldn't let me. "Take it home, and if you like it, you can pay me tomorrow. If you don't, bring it by in the morning, but not too early. We all don't keep your ungodly hours, Suzanne."

"What can I say? It's a living," I said.

After Gabby took the blouse off its hanger and put it in one of her bags for me, I began my walk back to Grace's to see if she'd finished her telephone calls.

It was a lovely day, the temperature nearing seventy and no clouds in the Carolina Blue sky, but the weather was lost on me. I had other things on my mind. I'd gone into her shop to get Gabby's thoughts about Tim, but it had quickly turned into more than that. I hadn't known a great deal about Tim Leander while he was alive, and it appeared that it was going to take his murder for me to discover anything deeper about the handyman I thought I'd known so well over the years. It was difficult reconciling the smiling and competent man I knew with what I was uncovering about him as I dug into his life, but when it came down to it, most folks had their own set of secrets.

And whether I liked it or not, I was going to have start digging into Tim's to find out who might have wanted to see him dead.

# Apple Juice Donuts

You can use apple cider as a substitute in this recipe, but we rarely have it on hand, and there always seems to be apple juice in our fridge. Either way, it makes a tasty donut!

## Ingredients
- 1/2 cup dark brown sugar, packed tight
- 1 egg, beaten
- 1/2 teaspoon nutmeg
- 1/2 teaspoon cinnamon
- Dash of salt
- 3 tablespoons butter, melted
- 1/2 cup apple juice (or cider, if preferred)
- 2 1/2 cups all purpose flour
- 1 teaspoon baking powder
- 1/2 teaspoon baking soda

## Directions
After beating the egg, add the dark brown sugar, butter, and apple juice. Set aside, and in another bowl, sift the flour, nutmeg, cinnamon, baking powder, baking soda, and salt. Add the dry ingredients to the wet in thirds, mixing thoroughly. Refrigerate the dough 30 minutes, then roll out to 1/2 to 1/4 inch thick. Cut out with donut round and hole cutter, and fry in 375-degree canola oil for 3 to 4 minutes, turning

halfway through. Drain on paper towels, then add powdered sugar immediately, or wait until they're cool and add icing and sprinkles.

Makes 8–10 donuts and holes

# CHAPTER 7

Grace was just getting off the telephone when I knocked on her front door. She held up one hand to me, and then said into it, "Meredith, I don't care why you aren't in the field today. Just get dressed and start working while you still have a job. I expect you to e-mail me your time sheet at five so I can check it. Are we clear?"

After she hung up, I said, "Wow, you were hard on her."

Grace frowned. "I should fire her, if you want to know the truth, but I don't want to have to do all of the HR paperwork. She works when she feels like it, which wouldn't be a problem if she felt like it more often than she does. I thought I was a slacker at times, but that woman doesn't get out of bed most days, and say what you will about my work ethic, I always got the job done." Grace pointed to the bag in my hand. "Do a little shopping while you were at

Gabby's?"

"I thought it might make things go a little smoother if I bought something," I said, which wasn't exactly true, but it was all Grace was going to get out of me.

"Let's see it," she asked, so I took the blouse out of the bag and held it up in front of me.

She studied it for a few seconds, and then said, "It's hard to tell that way. How did it fit?"

"To be honest with you, I didn't even try it on."

Grace whistled softly. "That's really brave of you. Gabby has a no-return policy."

I'd forgotten all about that. "Actually, she told me I could bring it back tomorrow if I didn't like it," I admitted.

"Wow, she must really like you. Did you happen to have a chance to ask her about Tim?"

I nodded. "I learned some things about him that you might not like, and I know Emily's going to react badly to what I've got to tell her."

"What did he do?" she asked.

"Apparently he was dating three women at the same time."

I wasn't sure what I expected Grace's reaction to be, but it wasn't the whoop of delight I heard. "Tim was an old tomcat, wasn't he?"

"Are you saying that you approve of that?" I asked, not sure why Grace's reaction bothered me.

She shook her head slightly. "I'm not saying I do, and in truth it's none of my business. I was just worried he was lonely all the time."

"That turns out to have been the least of his problems. I just hope he told them all he was dating around." I thought about what Gabby had told me, and then asked Grace, "Have you had much contact with Orson Blaine?"

"Suzanne, that's a pretty abrupt segue, even for you. I know him, but we're not exactly friends. Why do you ask?"

It was time to share what I'd learned. "According to Gabby, he and Tim were best friends for decades, but something happened to turn them against each other a few years ago, something serious enough to ruin a lifelong friendship."

Grace nodded her approval. "So then we have somewhere else to look."

"That's true; they all fit," I said.

"What do you mean?"

"A betrayed friend, a spurned lover, or a shunned competitor could all have a motive for murder, particularly considering the way Tim was found. We can't lose sight of that."

Grace frowned at me. "I'm not sure I follow what you're saying, Suzanne."

"Think about it. A scorned woman, a lost friend or a rebuffed competitor might all have loyalty issues with Tim, and any of them might explain why the Patriot Tree was used to hang him."

Grace nodded. "You're right. I never really thought about it along those lines."

"You didn't have the benefit of the walk over here," I said. It was nearing noon, and my stomach started rumbling softly. I could always count on it to remind me when it was time to eat. "Can you leave for lunch now, or do you have more calls to make?"

"There's nothing I have to do that won't keep," she said. "Where should we go? Is it too soon to go back to the Boxcar Grill?"

"As a matter of fact, I was thinking we might visit Go Eats," I said.

Grace looked surprised by the suggestion. "I haven't been there since my grandfather took me. Is that place even still open?"

"It must be. What do you say? Are you game?"

She looked at me for a moment, and then said, "Suzanne, something tells me that we're not going to that greasy spoon for its culinary offerings. What gives?"

"Gabby told me that it was Orson's favorite place to hang out, and I remember that Tim told me once it was his favorite place to eat, too," I admitted. "I thought we might go and ask around about him."

Grace appeared to consider it, and then said, "If your stomach can take it, so can mine."

"Then let's go."

"Do you know why it's called Go Eats?" I asked as we pulled into the crowded parking lot thirty minutes later. It was off my normal route to anywhere, and I was a little surprised that the place was still open.

"The *O* and the *D* fell off, so instead of fixing it, the owner changed the name from Good Eats to Go Eats. Grandpa told me he helped steady the ladder when the owner nailed the rest of the letters in place."

"Another mystery solved," I said as I found a place to park my Jeep. It was a little out of place with all of the pickup trucks and beat-up cars in the lot, but it looked more at home than Grace's company car would have.

As we walked in, the smells were the first thing that hit me. I didn't even have to see a menu to know that there wasn't a healthy or low-cal item offered by the place. Country music from twenty years ago played in the background, and there was a steady hum of conversation all around us. Light came filtering in through the two large windows in front, but an accumulation of grease over the years had clouded them somewhat with a gentle golden haze. The floors were linoleum, faded and scratched in places, but the whole package presented a place meant for comfort, not class.

There were over a dozen tables in the diner, and all of them were full, except for one.

One chair sat at the table, and instead of the usual salt and pepper shakers, a paper napkin dispenser, and a ketchup bottle, there was a photograph of Tim Leander, smiling with that grin of his that he was so famous for.

A waitress who looked as though she'd been at the job for twenty years saw us looking at the picture.

"Did you know Tim?" she asked.

"He was a friend of ours," I said.

"He was a good man," she said. Her name tag said her name was Ruth, and she looked around the place. "Sorry, but we don't have a table free just now."

An older man with a shock of white hair

called out, "They can sit with me, Ruth. I've got room at my table."

She looked at us, and then said, "It doesn't matter to me where you sit, just as long as it's not at Tim's table, at least not for the next few days." She gestured toward the man who'd offered us seats, and added, "Don't worry about Billy. For the most part, he's harmless."

I looked at Grace to see what she thought, and after she nodded her acceptance, we joined Billy at his table. He stood as we approached, and I couldn't believe it when he actually held out our chairs for us.

As he did, Billy said, "Ladies, I'm glad you could join me. Chivalry and manners may be dying, but they are not dead, at least not yet."

"Thanks," Grace and I said in unison.

After we took our seats, Ruth handed us menus, and then left to get the two iced teas we requested.

I looked at the menu and asked Billy, "What's good here?"

Before he could say a word, Ruth came back with our tea.

Billy said, "The country-style steak plate is good. I have it with mashed potatoes, gravy, and fried apples."

I looked at Grace, and she said, "Why not?

When in Rome and all that."

I told Ruth, "We'll have two."

"Apiece?" she asked, one eyebrow raised slightly.

"I think we'll each start with one and see how it goes from there," I answered. "After that, you never know."

I looked at Billy, who was smiling broadly. "A woman with beauty and a sense of humor is a rare commodity these days. If only I were thirty years younger, I might be able to do something about it besides admire your spirit."

I grinned back at him. "If you were thirty years younger, something tells me that you wouldn't settle for me."

"My dear," he said, "no man who could capture your heart would ever be settling for anything."

"Should I leave you two alone?" Grace asked.

Billy pivoted in his seat to face her. "Forgive me. The only reason I didn't address you directly was because I've been working up the nerve to approach a woman with your abundance of stunning loveliness."

"I thought Ruth said you were harmless," I said with a smile.

He shrugged. "Some say I'm all bark and

no bite, but I may have a few nips left in me yet. Don't worry, though. You two are safe with me."

"Did you know Tim Leander well?" I asked after taking a sip of tea so sweet my teeth started to ache from it.

"For many years," Billy answered. He shook his head as he continued, saying, "He was no saint, like some folks around here are saying today, but I have no interest in being friends with an angel. Tim had his flaws, though they were far outshadowed by his strengths. I'll miss him."

Grace lowered her voice and asked, "Is there anyone who might feel differently?"

Billy frowned. "Why would you want to know that?"

"He was murdered, after all," I said. "It just makes you wonder."

"It does, indeed. Let me see. Stu Mitchell comes to mind. He was always battling Tim about something or other. They never really liked each other, that much is true. Tim used to hate to smell the smoke from Stu's cheap cigars, and he crowed about it when North Carolina banned smoking in bars and restaurants."

"What about Orson Blaine?" I asked.

Billy looked at me with surprise. "I suppose that Orson had more of a right to resent Tim than Stu had, but yes, those are the only two men in the world to my knowledge who had a problem with him."

"How about women?" I asked.

Billy waved a hand in the air. "I believe those are rumors, lies, and falsehoods, every last one of them. Tim liked the ladies, but he never went out with a married woman. I don't care what folks say. He enjoyed female company, much like I do myself, and why shouldn't he? He hadn't had his teeth pulled yet, and he was still playing the field." Billy smoothed his hair down, and then added, "On the other hand, I was always a one-woman type of man in my younger days. The stories I could tell you both."

I didn't want to get diverted to Billy's love life. "I heard there were three women he was dating at the same time. I know one, but not the other two."

Instead of answering, Billy took a sip of coffee. "May I ask why you two are so interested in Tim's life, when I've never seen either one of you before today?"

Grace blurted out, "We're the ones who found his body."

I had been about to tell him that we were looking into Tim's murder, but Grace might have been right with that approach. If we had Billy's sympathy, he might not think we were ghoulish by trying to solve the case ourselves.

"It's understandable, then," Billy said. "I can see how you both might have a stake in this."

Ruth came to the table with our plates, and before I could thank her, Billy asked, "Who was Tim seeing lately? Do you happen to know offhand?"

"I might," she said. "Why do you want to know?" She'd asked the question of him, but Ruth had taken a moment to look suspiciously at each of us as well.

Billy looked long and hard at her before he answered. "These are the ladies who found him hanging in that tree. Isn't it natural they'd reach out to those who loved him to ease the memory of finding him like that?"

She nodded, and I silently thanked Billy for his help. After a moment's thought, Ruth told me three names, and I nearly dropped my fork when I heard the last one that made her list.

I'd already known about Gina Parsons, and I was familiar enough with her daughter, Penny, from George's stay in the hospital, to talk to her about what had happened to Tim. I didn't know the second name that made the list, Betsy Hanks, but the third name she mentioned gave me quite a turn.

It was Angelica DeAngelis, a dear friend and the woman who owned Napoli's, my favorite Italian restaurant.

Though I managed to keep my composure, Grace choked on her tea when Ruth mentioned Angelica's name.

"Girl, are you all right?" she asked her.

Grace was about to say something when I shook my head slightly. I wasn't sure what she'd been about to say, but instead, she replied, "I swallowed a bit too much with that drink."

"That tea is sweet enough to chew," Billy said chiming in. He looked at our plates, and then added, "Come now, ladies, don't you like the food?"

In truth, neither one of us had touched our meals. I took a dutiful bite, not expecting to like it, but if I didn't think about how the country-style steak was made, I really found myself enjoying it. "It's delicious," I said.

Billy nodded his head at the validation. "I told you so. That's enough talk for now; eat up."

Grace and I both started digging in, and I sopped up some of the juice from the fried apples with one of the biscuits Ruth had brought us. It was unbelievable, good enough to qualify as a food group all on its own.

When we were finished, I grabbed our check and Billy's as well.

He wasn't all that pleased by the gesture. "Ladies, I was going to buy you both lunch," he said. "Don't deprive me."

"Please, the pleasure was all ours," I said. "It's only right that we treat you, since you've been so gracious to us."

He mulled that over, and then Grace added, "Besides, think about the bragging rights."

"I don't follow you," he answered.

"You can always say that two young, good-looking women bought you lunch just so they could enjoy your company, and not too much of it would be a lie."

"None of it would, if you ask me," he said. "Given the graciousness of your offer, I'll leave it at saying thank you so kindly."

"You're welcome," we said in unison. I made sure to leave Ruth an especially nice tip, and then we paid the bill and left.

"We got more than we bargained for there, didn't we?" Grace asked once we were out-side.

I nodded. I didn't like saying it, but there was something I had to get out in the open. "I'm not sure I like where it's leading us, but you know that we can't take it easy on Angelica just because she's our friend."

"I couldn't agree with you more, but I have a suggestion. Let's go talk to her right now," Grace said. "I don't like the idea that we're going to just ambush her, so I'd rather get it out of the way first."

I nodded. "Union Square isn't that far away. We can speak with her, and I can still make it back to April Springs in time for my early dinner with Jake. I'm not sure how hungry I'll be, though, after all I just ate." I'd gotten swept up in my meal, and I was afraid I wasn't going to be ready to eat again when Jake came by to pick me up later. I'd manage somehow, though. I still tingled a little at the thought of seeing him again.

Grace agreed with the game plan. "Then we'd better get to Union Square so we can talk to Angelica."

As we drove the twenty minutes to Napoli's, I asked, "Do you know anything about the two men we talked to Billy about?"

"Not really. We'll have to ask George if he knows them. As a matter of fact, one of us should call him right now and bring him up to date on what we've learned."

I reached for my cell phone, but Grace said, "Suzanne, no offense, but you have enough trouble focusing on the road without having a phone conversation about murder. Why don't I call him?"

She probably had a point. "Do you need his number?"

"I've got it on speed dial," Grace said. After a quick conversation where she told him all we'd learned and what we were going to do next, she hung up.

I'd managed to hold my tongue until they'd finished their conversation. Once it was over, I asked, "How did you happen to have George's number so handy?"

"We talk sometimes," Grace said, "especially when we're working on something together with you. Are you surprised?"

"No, when you explain it that way, it makes perfect sense. What did he say?"

"He agreed that it's probably a good idea if he focuses on the two men right now. That way we can focus on the women who were in Tim's life."

After a few minutes, Grace turned to me and asked, "Suzanne, can you really see a woman hanging him in the tree like that?"

I thought about it, and then answered, "Actually, I can, but it might not be the woman herself. It could have been a jealous boyfriend, or even husband, no matter what Billy said."

I hated saying it, and it was clear that

Grace didn't enjoy hearing it. "Do you honestly think sweet old Tim would date a married woman?"

I considered her question, then thought about the way Tim was always so good at what he did, so friendly, and so eager to help when he was needed. Then I tried to reconcile that with the things I'd learned about the man since he'd been murdered. "Not really, but then again, I didn't think he'd date three women at once, either. It was pretty clear from what I overheard in Gabby's that Penny's mother had no idea she wasn't his only girlfriend."

"I wonder if Angelica knew he was dating others as well," I asked.

"There's only one way to find out, but I'm not all that excited about asking her, are you?"

"Not particularly," I answered. Angelica was a close friend of mine, someone who had always gone out of her way to make me feel special when I visited her restaurant, and now I was going to be the bearer of some very bad tidings indeed.

When we got to Napoli's, the first thing I noticed was the lack of cars parked in front of the restaurant. At that time of day, I hadn't expected their business to be booming, but I did think they'd have at least a few customers enjoying their wonderful cuisine.

After we parked and walked to the front door, I didn't have to wonder about it anymore.

The sign said, *"Closed today and tomorrow. Sorry for the inconvenience. The Management."*

"What's that all about?" Grace asked. "Could it be related to what happened to Tim?"

"I can't imagine it's a coincidence," I replied as I knocked on the door. There was no answer.

"No one's here," Grace said.

"I'm not giving up that easily. Come on," I said.

As I started walking toward the back of the strip mall, Grace asked excitedly, "What are we going to do, break in? You know I'm up for it if it helps us in our investigation."

"Stop thinking like a criminal," I said with a laugh. "We're just going to try to see if they'll answer the back door. The last time we were here and ate pasta in the kitchen with Angelica and the girls, I noticed an entrance for deliveries in back."

"But we aren't kicking the door in," Grace said. If I hadn't known better, I would have said she was disappointed by the realization that we were taking a more conventional approach.

"Sorry, but it's not going to be anything as dramatic as all that," I replied. "I just want to be certain that no one is here."

As we came around the back, it was difficult at first to figure out which door belonged to Napoli's, but then I noticed a small sign that had the name of the restaurant on it. It was certainly a lower-profile entrance than the front.

I knocked with authority, waited a few seconds, and then knocked again.

"Come on, Suzanne, no one's here," Grace said as she started to walk away.

I gave it another shot, and this time, I called out Angelica's name. A moment later, the outside door opened slightly.

"No deliveries," Maria DeAngelis said without looking at us. Maria was one of Angelica's daughters, all lovely, and all employed at the restaurant in one capacity or another.

Before she could close the door again, I said, "Maria, it's us."

She looked at us then, and said, "Hi, Suzanne. I'm sorry you drove all this way for a meal, but we're closed."

"We're not here to eat; we want to talk. Please?" I asked. "I wouldn't ask if it weren't important."

"I suppose it would be okay," she finally said as she stepped aside.

"Thanks," I answered. As Grace and I walked in, I saw that Maria was making homemade pasta, one of the specialties of the house.

"Who is that for?" I asked.

"Not for customers; just for the family. I had to get out of the house, so I made an excuse to come here instead."

"How's your mother holding up?" I asked softly.

"Momma's fine," she said as she looked closely at me. I knew we were friends as well, but her first loyalty was to her mother, something that didn't surprise me at all. Every daughter openly talked about leaving Napoli's and their mother's domain, but I knew that it was idle talk. There was too much love there for any of them to ever go. "Why do you ask?"

It was time to lay my cards out on the table. "You're closed, so I know Tim Leander's murder must have hit her pretty hard."

"Murder? He hanged himself," Maria said, not disputing her mother's involvement with the man at all.

I didn't like it, but I was going to have to go into more detail. "It turns out that someone killed him, and then hoisted him up into that tree." There was no delicate way to ask, so I took a deep breath and then added, "How long had your mother been seeing him?"

"I'm not willing to acknowledge that she was," Maria said, her olive-toned arms folded over her chest now.

"Maria," I said, keeping my voice as gentle as I could manage, "we're not with the police. We're just trying to find out what happened to Tim. I know your mother must have cared for him, and there's no doubt she's hurting right now, but he was our friend, too."

Grace added, "Won't helping us find the murderer give your mother some of the comfort she needs right now? She has to want to find the killer even more than we do."

Maria seemed to think about that, and then said, "Excuse me for a moment. I need to make a quick call."

She was checking with her mother, there was no doubt in my mind about that, and I couldn't really blame her. If the roles were reversed, I would be doing the exact same thing.

Maria stepped through the kitchen into the dining room to make her call, and Grace asked, "Did I push her too much?"

"No, as a matter of fact, I think you shoved her exactly the right amount."

"What's Angelica going to say?"

I shrugged. "I don't know, but I have a feeling we're going to find out pretty quickly."

Maria came back out a minute later and joined us.

"What did she say?" I asked.

"Momma's sleeping, and Sophia said no one wanted to wake her."

"So you won't talk to us?" I asked, resigned with the answer I knew I would be getting already.

Maria appeared to think about it, and then said, "I'll tell you what I know, but you should realize up front that this is all new to me as well."

"You didn't know that your mother was seeing someone?" Grace asked.

Maria frowned, crinkling her nose slightly. "We knew there was someone, but up until yesterday, we didn't realize who it was."

"And none of you ever asked?" I said.

Maria smiled sadly at me. "Let me ask you, Suzanne, if your mother decided to keep a relationship secret from you, would you push her about it if you knew you weren't going to accomplish anything but make her upset and angry with you?"

I thought about it, and then nodded. "You're right. Sorry about that, I should have known better than to ask."

Maria smiled. "You're forgiven. Momma's been happier lately than I've seen her in years. None of us were about to question it. I heard that Tim died, and he came here sometimes so we all knew him. I thought it was important to tell everyone what happened." She grimaced, no doubt at the memory. "Momma collapsed when she heard the news, and it took all three of us to get her to a chair. The story came out in bits and pieces, and she told us that she'd been dating Tim for just a month, but that they'd gotten serious in that time, and there was talk of making their relationship permanent."

"That was going to be hard with two other women in the wings."

"Well, Momma didn't know that at the time. She took his death hard, but it got even worse when she found out she wasn't the only woman in his life."

"How did she happen to discover that?" Grace asked.

"She was at the florist ordering flowers for the funeral when a woman named Betsy Hanks came in to do the same thing. As soon as both women realized why they were there, there was pandemonium, from what I heard."

"Do you know anything about Betsy?" I asked.

"Just that she works at Harper's over in Jackson Ridge."

Maria was about to add something else when the phone rang. She took it, and after a quick conversation, she hung up and said, "Momma's awake, and she needs me back home."

"How did she sound?" I asked.

"Better," Maria said with a smile. "She wanted to know where I was, and when Sophia told her I was here making pasta, she insisted I come home with it immediately. Anyway, that's all I really know."

I had a question to ask, but I wasn't sure I had the nerve to voice it, even though I didn't really have any choice. "Do you think she'd talk with us about Tim?"

"Not today," Maria said, "and most likely not tomorrow. I don't know, Suzanne, Momma likes you, but she's in some real pain right now."

"Tell her that we're sorry for her loss," I said.

"I will," she answered, and then Grace and I left her to finish her pasta. I knew from firsthand experience how great that pasta was going to be. If it gave Angelica some kind of comfort, then that was all the better.

"Where should we go now?" Grace asked.

I glanced at my watch. "If you don't mind, we'd better get back to April Springs. I've got a date with Jake, and I don't want to miss a minute of it. Life is short, you know?"

She finished our old saying, I'm sure without realizing it. "And then you die."

There was an unsettling creepiness to it this time, and I wasn't certain I'd ever be able to say it again without thinking of Tim.

But for now, it was time to focus on the living.

I had a date, and I knew that Jake wouldn't disappoint me.

# CHAPTER 8

"Hey, Suzanne," Jake said as I picked up my telephone around five. I'd just dropped Grace off and wasn't even back to the cottage yet.

"Are you at the house already? I'm so sorry I'm late. Hang on, I'll be there in two minutes."

"I'm not in April Springs," he said, and I felt my enthusiasm suddenly die.

"That's too bad," I said, knowing that with the nature of his work, he could be called away at any time. "I was hoping we could have dinner together."

"Don't give up on me just yet. We still can," Jake said. "I'm just a little behind schedule. I've got a great idea. Why don't we meet at Napoli's? I can catch you up with what's been going on with me, and you can tell me what you've been up to while we eat."

"I'm sorry, but we can't do that," I said.

He hesitated, and then said, "Come on, Suzanne, I don't have to pick you up every time we go out, do I? Ordinarily you know I wouldn't mind one bit, but I'm coming back from Dillsboro, and Napoli's is on the way." He paused a second, and then added, "Think of it this way. If you start driving right now, we'll both get to Union Square at about the same time."

"I'd be happy to meet you there, but that's not the problem," I said. "Napoli's is closed."

"For good? I can't believe that." He sounded devastated, and I didn't blame him. If Angelica ever decided to shut down, I'd go into mourning for a year. The pasta was just that good, not to mention the friendships I'd lose with Angelica and her daughters if I couldn't visit with them.

"It's just for a few days. It turns out Angelica was one of the women Tim Leander was dating, and she's not taking it very well."

"Yes, I heard about him from one of my friends," Jake said. "To be honest with you, I was kind of surprised you haven't brought it up yourself yet."

I grinned as I asked, "Jake, you don't have anybody spying on me in April Springs, do you?"

He laughed, and I knew he heard the humor in my voice. "Are you kidding me? I'm not that crazy. There's no way that I would risk it. That's hazard pay if I ever heard of it. No, one of the guys on my posse is dating a girl from Hickory, and she heard about it from her cousin, who just happens to live in April Springs. It's a small world, isn't it?"

"Not that small," I said. "Seriously, though, I know I should have told you about it myself last night, but it was so nice talking to you, and I didn't want to spoil the way I felt. If you want to scold me for not telling you about it then, you have my blessing."

"You found the body," Jake said gently. "I figure that was hard enough on you without me piling it on. That's a real shame about Tim. I only met him once, but he seemed like a really nice guy."

"He was," I agreed. I took a deep breath, and then decided to tell him the rest of it since I was confessing everything. "Emily Hargraves was close to Tim, and she's asked me to look into what happened to him as a personal favor. She disappeared for a while herself, but at least we found her safe and sound, though I admit it had us all scared there for a while."

"Where did she go?" Jake asked innocently enough.

Why did I have to bring that up? Now I was going to have to get into the whole situation, and the part Max had played in it. My boyfriend was not a big fan of my ex-husband, not that I could blame him. "She left her shop to go to Max's place and forgot to tell anybody. Folks got real concerned when they learned that she took off so quickly she forgot to lock up her store."

Jake didn't seem all that surprised to hear that my ex-husband was involved. "Whenever there's trouble with women in your town, Max is usually not that far away."

"Not this time." I had to end this tense situation before things got suddenly worse. "If you can believe it, Tim Leander was dating three women in the area, apparently none of them knew about the others, and to add to it, he had two men who were enemies as well."

"You've been busy," he said simply.

When another question didn't immediately follow, I asked, "Jake, are you going to tell me not to snoop into his murder?"

There was a long moment's pause, and then he said, "No, I understand why you're doing it. I know you've got your reasons."

That was a nice change of pace. Maybe

Jake was starting to come around. "Is there any chance your boss will assign you to the case?" I would love to have Jake's presence in April Springs, and not just because of a murder investigation. I felt fine when he was gone, but the sun seemed to shine a little brighter whenever he was around, as sappy as that might have sounded.

"No chance at all. I'm taking a few days off, and I thought I'd spend them with you, if you were interested."

I couldn't believe my good luck. "Are you serious?"

"As I can be. I'm really excited to see you."

I'd learned long ago that if something seemed too good to be true, it probably was. I had a hunch his decision to take some time off wasn't entirely because of me. "There's something you're not telling me, isn't there?" I asked.

He sighed, and then said, "I won't lie to you, my vacation is not by choice. According to my boss, I might have used a tad too much force apprehending one of our suspects, but the idiot we were arresting took a swing at a deputy, and he connected before we could stop him."

Jake was big on loyalty, to me and to his fellow officers. It was a trait I admired in him, but I knew that it could also get him into trouble sometimes.

"I've got an idea," I said.

"There's no chance we can take a trip, is there?"

"Sorry, I can't leave the shop on such short notice. You could always help me," I said, trying to jolly him out of the darkness that had just crept into our conversation.

"At the donut shop, or on your impromptu investigation?" he asked.

"Why not both?"

He laughed. "Why don't I stick with what I'm good at? You and Emma make the donuts, and I'll help you and your crew dig around a little into Tim Leander's murder."

"You're not going to get into any trouble with your boss or Chief Martin, are you?"

Jake paused, and then said, "Actually, my boss doesn't want to see me or hear from me for the next four days, so that's not a problem. As for the police chief, I'll talk to him. When I'm finished, he'll think I'm working for him. I've got a feeling that if I give him all of the credit once we find the killer, he'll be more than happy to take my help. What about you?"

"What about me?"

"Are you okay with not getting the kudos if we catch whoever murdered your friend?"

"To be honest with you, I'd just as soon not get any more public acknowledgments for a while about my crime-solving skills." Emma's dad had written about a few of my exploits in his paper, and it had brought me some unwanted attention in our community. As an amateur sleuth, I was better off keeping a low profile at the moment.

"Then it's a deal. So, if we can't meet at Napoli's, where can we grab an early dinner? I'm starving, and I'm too tired to do much else but grab a bite and hit the sack."

"How about at my house?" I asked. "Momma and I can whip something up for us."

"Thanks for the offer, but why don't we make it the Boxcar instead," Jake answered.

"What's the matter? Don't like my cooking?"

"It's not that," he said with a laugh. "I just don't want to share you with anybody just yet, including your mother."

I laughed. "That's a very good answer; I'll have to give you that one." I thought about it for a few seconds, and then said, "Tell you what. I'll get a few things to go from Trish if you'll tell me when you're getting close to town, and we can eat at the park."

"You aren't a little spooked to go back there?" he asked, his voice suddenly full of concern.

"It's a part of my home, and my heritage," I said. "I can't let one murder keep me away from it, and I can't think of anyone I'd rather picnic with than you. Honestly, this might be just what I need to replace that bad memory with a nice fresh one."

"If you're sure, then it's a date," he said. "Give me forty-five minutes, and then get the food. I should be there in an hour with no problem."

I was glad for the delay, even if it meant that I had to wait to see Jake. His timetable gave me time to go home, shower and change, and still make it to Trish's before he showed up. "That sounds wonderful. Jake? I really can't wait to see you."

"Right back at you," he said, and then hung up.

I must have still been smiling when I walked into the house three minutes later. Momma was standing near the front door when I came in, and it was clear that she noticed my good mood immediately.

"What was that all about?" she asked.

That could cover so many situations, I wasn't about to confess to anything until I had more specific details. "What do you mean?"

"Helen Crenshaw just called me and said

166

you were broken down on the side of the road. I was just coming out to look for you."

"I was on a telephone call," I said, "so I thought I'd better pull over so I could take it without any distractions. If you ask me, Helen has an overactive imagination."

"She was concerned about you, as am I," she answered. When Momma continued, there was a slight smile on her lips. "Was it Jake, by any chance?"

"It was indeed," I said. "I'm going to grab a quick shower, and then we're having a picnic in the park."

Momma smiled brightly. "Good for you."

"Would you like to join us?" I asked suddenly. "We'd love to have you." It wasn't Jake's first choice, but I hated leaving Momma to her own devices.

"Thank you, but I'm not quite sure that's what your young man has in mind for a homecoming meal. I think I'll heat up that minestrone soup I made the other night. It was delicious, wasn't it?"

Suddenly I wasn't feeling quite so sorry for her. I'd been hoping to get in on the last of that soup myself. "It was outstanding, above and beyond your usual fare, and that's saying a lot. Save some for me," I said.

"Sorry, but there's just enough for one." She must have seen the expression on my face, because she smiled as she added, "Don't pout, Suzanne. I can always make more."

"I'm holding you to that," I said.

As I started up the stairs, she asked, "Jake really makes you happy, doesn't he?"

"You know he does," I replied. "It's wonderful having him in my life. Why do you ask?"

"No reason," she answered. "I just like seeing you like this."

I smiled broadly at her. "Well, get used to it. He just told me that he's staying in town for a few days."

"Excellent." Momma glanced at the clock, and then she added, "Now go take that shower. You don't want to keep him waiting."

"Why not? You've kept the police chief on the hook for a month," I said.

"That's different, and you know it. Our love lives are completely different situations. Go on, now."

I did as she asked, not because I was giving up pushing my mother to start dating again, but because I really didn't want to be late for my rendezvous with Jake.

"Perfect timing," I said as Jake walked through the park to where I'd set up our picnic dinner. "I just got here myself two minutes ago."

Jake was tall and lean, and his sandy hair was getting a little long for his usual short-cropped taste. I watched as his glance went quickly to the Patriot's Tree, but then it came back to me as I stood and wrapped my arms around him. After we greeted each other with a kiss, I pulled back a little, but I stayed in his arms when he didn't release his hold on me. "If you don't let me go, our food's going to get cold."

"Let it," he growled, and then kissed me again.

There was something to be said for cold burgers and fries after all.

After we ate and threw our trash away, Jake asked, "Why don't you bring me up to speed on the case? What have you found out so far?" He was in full-on investigation mode now, and I could see the cop in him coming out. It was as if he had two faces; one professional, and one just for me. At the moment my boyfriend was gone, and the state police investigator was there and ready to dig into the case.

"Should I brief you before you talk to Chief Martin?" I asked as we walked back to my house.

"Already taken care of it. We spoke on my

drive here," Jake admitted. "It turns out that he's all in favor of me pitching in."

I didn't doubt that for a second; Chief Martin knew how good Jake was at his job. "Did you mention that I was looking into the murder as well?"

Jake grinned, and my heart melted just a little. "I may have glossed over some of the details when I mentioned you, but to be honest with you, I think he's just happy to have a helping hand. He gave me a little information about what he's been doing, but I want to hear from you first."

"You're not going to share?" I asked. "What good is it having you as a boyfriend if I can't get the inside scoop?" I asked as I gave him a gentle nudge

"I think we can come up with a few reasons," he said with a smile. "But not right now. Go on, I'm listening."

After I told him what Grace and I had been able to find out, and what George was up to, he stared at the sky and appeared to consider it. "So far you've done a great job, given the limited time and resources you have at your disposal."

I did my best teen imitation as I replied, "Well, I know I'm just a girl and all, but I'm trying real hard, mister. Honest, I really am."

The ditzy-girl act wasn't lost on him. Jake smiled as he said, "That's not what I meant, and you know it. You're just intentionally trying to tweak me now."

"Just as long as you admit that I'm not entirely without skills here."

"I admit it," he said as he held his hands up in surrender.

I was eager enough to accept it. "Good. Now, I've come clean with you. It's your turn to tell me what you know."

"Less than you'd think," Jake said. "The chief believes that the killer is a man because of the strength it had to take to hoist Tim's body up into that tree. I'm not so sure, but if I try to tell him otherwise, we're going to tangle."

"So, you believe the killer could be a woman?"

He thought about that for a moment, and then said, "I'd be sexist not to keep it in mind, wouldn't I? Who knows? Maybe two of the ladies Tim was playing got together and pulled at the same time. One's thing's certain; we can't ignore the women you've collected as suspects, and that includes Angelica, no matter how much we don't like it. For now, I think the best thing we can do is split up."

"The caseload, you mean," I said.

"Suzanne, that's the only part of me that you're going to get rid of."

I smiled up at him. "Good. What did you have in mind?"

He said, "If you're okay with it, I think I'll help George. We can deal with the men, and you and Grace can keep focusing on the women. Do you think George would be upset if I butted onto his turf?"

"Are you kidding me? He's a retired cop. He'll love hanging out with you so you two can swap old war stories." I leaned forward and kissed Jake soundly after I said it.

"What was that for? Not that I'm complaining."

"One, for not scolding me about looking into Tim's murder, and two, for volunteering to help out with the case."

He smiled at me. "The way I figure it, I should get two kisses, then, right?"

"You can have as many as you want, after you answer one question."

He laughed. "There's a fee now? When did that happen? Whatever it is, I'll gladly pay it. Go on, ask away."

I stared into his eyes, because I wanted him to know that I was serious. "Why the sudden change of heart, Jake? You've been upset with me in the past when I dig into murder cases around here."

Jake rubbed my shoulder gently before he spoke. "Suzanne, I'm beginning to understand that trying to get you to do what I want is just going to frustrate us both. This is important to you, you don't have to tell me that, and I happen to be free at the moment. If I can lend a hand without stepping on too many toes around town, why shouldn't I? Isn't that what boyfriends do? I have a particular skill set that you can use, and thanks to my boss, I have the time to pitch in." He hugged me, and then added, "Besides, why should you have all the fun? I love what I do. Sharing it with you just makes it that much sweeter."

"But there's another reason, isn't there?"

He wouldn't meet my gaze when he finally answered. "Okay, I admit it. I have an ulterior motive. If I'm nearby, maybe I can keep you safe if something happens." Before I could reply, he quickly added, "I know you are perfectly capable of handling yourself in ordinary circumstances, but you're going after a killer here, and you could use the backup, whether you're willing to admit it or not."

"You're absolutely right," I said quietly.

Jake leaned forward. "I'm sorry. I didn't catch that. What did you say?"

I pushed against his chest. "You heard me.

I'm not going to feed your ego anymore," I answered with a grin.

We were at my porch now, and I asked, "Would you like to come in for a few minutes? I'm sure Momma would love to see you."

"Can I take a rain-check? I was up most of last night, and I'm dead on my feet. I'll catch up with George in the morning, and we can come up with a game plan."

He noticed my grin and asked me, "Why the smile?"

"Usually I'm the one going to bed early. It's nice for it to be someone else for a change. Good night, Jake."

I kissed him good-bye, and then watched him as he walked to his car and drove away. For more reasons than I could count, it was good having him back.

I only wished he didn't have to go away again so quickly.

Momma was reading a new mystery when I walked in. "How's your book?"

"Excellent," she said as she put it aside, but not before carefully placing a bookmark at the page she was reading. Momma had raised me to believe that books were sacrosanct. There was never any underlining, highlighting, or worst of all, dog-earing book pages in our household. She had raised me to treat books with respect, and it was a lesson I'd learned well.

She frowned as she looked at the door and added, "Is Jake gone already?"

"He had a long night, so he's going to Cam's to get some rest." Hotels had become too expensive for him on a regular basis since he was coming to April Springs so often, so Jake had found a place where he could sleep in town for a rock-bottom price. Cam Jennings was a retired bachelor who rented rooms on an extremely select basis, more for the company than the money, and he and Jake were fast becoming friends. I dreamed of the day when my boyfriend might actually live in April Springs full-time when he wasn't on the road, but he hadn't mentioned the possibility of moving to our town, and I wasn't about to bring it up myself. For now, I was just glad he was here when he could manage it.

"Good enough," Momma said.

"He sent you his regards," I said, "and he asked me to tell you that he'll see you soon."

"I should bake a pie in the morning to celebrate his arrival," Momma said. "What kind do you think he would like?"

"I'm sure he'd love anything you'd make for him. I know the police chief's eyes lit up when I told him about your baking the other evening. By the way, when are you two going out again?" I hated to pass up any chance to keep her thinking about another date. After all, it was the only way she'd ever find out if someone was right for her.

"As a matter of fact, we're going out tomorrow night," she said. "Since Jake's in town, I don't have to worry about leaving you here all by yourself."

I couldn't believe what I was hearing. "Hang on one second. You don't have to wait until my boyfriend's in town to go out on a date. I think I can manage on my own for one evening."

"I know that," she said. "It just makes sense this way."

I knew it was probably not the best time to pick a battle with her. "It's fine with me. Does that mean you're going to make two pies, then? I expect each man would appreciate the gesture."

"You know what? I might just do that," Momma said with a slight smile. "I probably owe him one."

"I'm sure Jake will love it, but you shouldn't feel obligated to make him a pie."

Momma shook her head. "I'm not talking about him, Suzanne, and you know it. I ended our date rather abruptly the last time, and I've felt guilty about it ever since."

I leaned over and hugged my mother. "I'm sure he'll be happy you're rescheduling, with or without the pie." I glanced at the clock and saw that it was past my bedtime, though I knew many folks were just finishing up their evening meals around town.

I stood, stretched, and then said, "If you don't mind, I'm calling it a night. Sleep tight, Momma."

"And the sweetest of dreams to you," she said.

As I walked up the stairs, I glanced back down at her. There was the whisper of a smile on her lips, and I had to wonder if the prospect of her second date with Chief Martin was on her mind. Whatever its source, the smile was gone just as quickly as it had appeared, and she picked her book back up and started reading again.

It appeared that the Hart women were both thinking happy thoughts about the men in their lives, and that wasn't a bad thing at all.

The next morning, Emma came into the donut shop with a package wrapped in brightly colored newspaper flyers.

"Did someone give you a present?" I asked as I worked on the batter for my apple spice cake donuts.

"It's for you," she said.

I finished the batter, and then washed my hands. "Why on earth would you get me a present, Emma?"

"It's not from me," she said as she handed the package to me. "It's from Dad."

"That's even odder," I said as I took it. "Why would your father do that?"

"Come on, Suzanne, you must realize that he feels bad about the ad."

"I shouldn't take this," I said as I tried to push it back at her. "We ended up making money from the deal, so as mistakes go, it wasn't bad at all."

Emma smiled slightly. "Do me a favor and don't tell him that, okay?"

I didn't understand her grin. "Why shouldn't I?"

"Because the more he thought about it, the more Dad felt as though it was as much his fault as it was mine that the ad was wrong. This is his way of saying that he's sorry, and it's important to me that you take it. After all, I haven't had the upper hand with him many times in my life, and I'm not about to throw it away this time."

"Let's see what it is before I make a decision," I said as I unwrapped it.

Inside the box, I found an envelope buried

in a mound of shredded paper. "Your dad's a fan of recycling, isn't he?"

"It's not that as much as he's too cheap to buy anything he can cobble together himself. Go on, open the envelope. I've been dying to see what he gave you."

I did as she asked, and grinned when I saw it.

Emma said impatiently, "Don't hold out on me. What is it? A coupon for a free massage? A weekend getaway to the mountains? What?"

I held the printed letter up for her to see. "It's a coupon for a free quarter-page ad. How thoughtful."

"A weekend away would have been better," she replied.

"I think this is perfect. Should we run another ad next week?"

Emma smiled. "You were really serious when you said we could try Take-a-Chance-Tuesday again?"

"Of course I was. But remember, I get to see the ad before you turn it in this time."

"I'm not about to forget."

I put the coupon away, and then said, "Why don't you grab your apron and we can get to work. I've got an idea for lemonade donuts with real iced tea in the batter."

She looked at me as though I'd temporarily lost my mind. "What made you think of trying that?"

"Haven't you ever had an Arnold Palmer?" I asked. "The golfer invented them, and they're really delicious. I thought, why not try it in a donut and see how it works out."

"I suppose it's worth a try," Emma said.

Later, when the first donut came out of the fryer, not even the glaze could help the new creation I'd come up with. Emma took a taste herself, and she couldn't hide her unpleasant reaction to it.

"That's just awful," she said as she drank a quick swallow of coffee to get the taste out of her mouth.

"I agree," I said as I threw out the rest of the test batch. "Hey, it was worth a shot."

"You never know until you try," Emma said.

I looked around for my recipe notebook so I could add this failure to it so I wouldn't repeat the same mistake, but it wasn't in its usual place in the kitchen. I hadn't used it that morning, since I could make my cake and yeast donuts practically by heart, but that didn't mean I could function without it. It held the sum total of my experience as a donut maker, successful recipes and failures alike.

I looked everywhere in back, but I couldn't find it.

Emma looked alarmed. "Suzanne? What's wrong?"

"My recipe book. I can't find it," I told her as I kept hunting through the bags of ingredients and the invoices stacked up on my desk.

"I'm sure it's got to be here somewhere," she said. "Calm down and take a deep breath. Don't worry, we'll find it."

Half an hour later, we had to acknowledge that the recipe book was gone. That book was so much more than directions to the concoctions I made. It was the operating manual for my donut shop, and I wasn't sure that I could run Donut Hearts without it. That didn't even cover the history it represented, the trial-and-error approach I used in making donuts, and my thoughts and dreams since I'd first opened Donut Hearts. It was, simply put, a part of me.

Had I just carelessly misplaced it? I couldn't see how. Emma and I had practically torn the place apart looking for it, and I was confident that it wasn't anywhere in the shop. Then I remembered bringing it to the front with me so I could play with recipes.

We searched the entire front area even

181

more thoroughly, but finally, I had to admit that it was gone.

That just left one other option.

During the frantic rush yesterday when three-quarters of the town had been in my shop, someone must have seized the moment and deliberately taken it.

# CHAPTER 9

"What are we going to do?" Emma asked as we stood there staring at each other. It was a disaster of epic proportions, and we both knew it.

"I should have made copies," I said, my heart sinking as I spoke the words. "You kept telling me to, and I ignored you. I just don't get it, though. Who would take it?"

Emma looked surprised by the idea. "Do you really think it's been stolen? We could have just as easily thrown it away by accident. That's what I was thinking, anyway."

"Do you honestly believe that there's the slightest chance that happened? One of us would have noticed something as big as that recipe book in the trash."

"Maybe so, but I like that idea better than the thought that someone took it on purpose from the donut shop," Emma said. "Has the trash run yet?"

"I don't think so." We both headed for the

back door where we kept our trash cans. It was pickup day, but I knew the truck didn't come by until seven, so if the recipe book was there, we'd be able to find it before they came.

I opened the back door as I flipped on the outside light. Emma was right behind me, wearing a pair of gloves, and holding another set. "Here, put these on."

I did as she asked, and then I lifted the first lid. "This is going to be messy."

It wasn't, though.

Our trash cans, every last one of them, had already been emptied.

"How is that possible?" I asked, getting more distraught by the second. "I would have heard Sam coming down the alley if he'd been by." Sam Winston was our chief refuse and recycling engineer, a title he'd given himself when he'd first taken the job of working on the town's garbage truck.

Emma looked as though she wanted to cry, and I felt the same way myself.

I walked over to Gabby's back door, and on a whim, I lifted her lid.

It was still full.

"This is odd," I told Emma.

"What did you find?" she asked as she joined me.

We both stared down into the full trash can, and Emma said, "That just doesn't make sense. Why would Sam take ours and leave Gabby's?"

"I'm beginning to wonder if it was Sam at all." Was I making any sense, or just being paranoid?

"Come on, Suzanne, nobody's stealing our trash."

"How else do you explain it? Maybe they didn't want to be seen walking out with my book, so they stashed it in the trash so they could come back when we were gone and retrieve it."

"There aren't any military secrets in it," Emma said. "Why would someone go to that much trouble?"

"I don't know, but if they did it to get my attention, it worked. We might be able to limp along without it, but it's not going to be easy." I dreaded the thought of re-creating the recipes in that book. It would be a real nightmare, and in the end, I still wouldn't have my book back. In baking, the difference between a teaspoon and a table-spoon could mean success, or complete and utter failure.

"You can do it," Emma said. "I'll help you."

"How do we even know where to begin?"

I tried to hide the hopeless feeling in the pit of my stomach, but it was no use. I was beaten, and I knew it better than anyone else.

"You start on the basic batter mix we use for cake donuts, and I'll sit down and try to write down as much as we can remember."

"Do you honestly think that's going to work?"

She shrugged. "At this point, I'm not sure what else we can do."

Emma had a point. If someone was trying to distract me from Tim's murder by stealing my recipe book, they couldn't have found a better way to do it short of burning Donut Hearts to the ground.

By the time we were ready to open, we were both exhausted, and I'd written down as many recipes as I could remember. Emma and I had worked frantically trying to put out our donuts, but about a third of them didn't pass our taste test after they were finished. Under the stress of not having the recipe book as a safety net, I'd somehow managed to mess up several of the recipes that I made all the time. We had plenty of plain cake, frosted, and glazed donuts for sale, but our specialty section was kind of sparse.

This was clearly not going to do, but I wasn't sure what other options I had until we could figure something out.

Just before opening, I tacked a hand-lettered sign to the cash register for all the world to see.

Emma whistled, and then read it aloud.

*"Lost, one recipe book, handwritten in a plain black and white notebook. $500 reward for its safe return. No questions asked. See the management for more details."*

"Five hundred dollars?" Emma asked. "Isn't that a lot of money for a book?"

"How much is the shop worth?" I asked her. "I want those recipes back by midnight, and I'm willing to do just about anything I have to do to get it."

"I guess so. Don't worry, Suzanne. It will turn up."

"I hope you're right," I said, though I wasn't at all sure the offered reward would work. If someone took it out of spite, maybe we'd get a taker, but if the purpose of the theft was to distract me, I doubted I'd ever see the book again.

For the first time in months, I wasn't excited when I opened my doors to the public.

It was going to be a long day, and there wasn't a thing I could do about it. If only

I'd made a copy one of the dozens of times I'd thought about it, I wouldn't be in this mess.

Emma had made a mistake yesterday with her ad, but mine had made it look insignificant by comparison.

I just hoped it turned up before I had to shutter my windows and lock my doors forever.

"Morning," Jake said a few hours later as he came in. "George is finding a place to park, so he'll be here in a few minutes."

"Hello," I answered, trying my best to put a bright smile on for him. I didn't get to see him all that often, and I wasn't about to let the loss of my recipe book ruin it for either one of us.

I didn't have to say another word, though.

Jake read the sign with the reward notice, then looked sadly at me. "What happened, Suzanne?"

"That says it all, doesn't it? My recipe book is gone," I said.

"Do you think someone actually took it?" Jake asked.

"There's a possibility that we could have lost it," I answered, "but I don't think so. I think someone stole it to keep me from looking into Tim's murder." Saying it out loud sounded a little ridiculous. I wasn't sure what use that book would be, even if they made donuts for a living. Emma had said it a hundred times when I'd had her look up a recipe. My handwriting was tough enough to read when I knew what it said. For an untrained eye, it would be impossible to get more than general ideas about how to make the donuts I offered.

"You don't think it was lost by accident, do you?" Jake asked. He tapped the sign. "You never take it out of the shop, right?"

"No," I admitted.

"And it's a little big not to notice if you accidently throw it away. I'm assuming you've already checked your trash."

"It was empty before we got to it," I said. "There's something curious about that, though. Gabby's trash cans were still full when we checked them, but there wasn't anything in ours. I can't imagine Sam taking ours but leaving hers."

"Has anyone shown any interest in what you've been doing here lately?"

"Just idle talk," I said. "I get an offer for the place at least once a month, but nobody is ever serious about it. I know it might sound crazy, but I honestly think it was stolen to keep me from digging into Tim's murder."

"You said that before, but I'm not sure how it connects," Jake said as I poured him a cup of coffee.

"What better way to distract me than to steal my book," I said as George walked in.

"What book? Who stole it, and why?" George asked us.

"My recipes are missing," I said softly. Jake and I were keeping our voices low. I wasn't sure George had that volume level in his repertoire. He was the type who announced a great deal of what he said.

"That's serious business," he said as I handed him a cup of coffee.

"What kind of donuts do you two want?"

"I'll take a plain cake donut and a powdered one," Jake said.

I grinned at him. "You don't have to impress me with your appetite. I know you're fond of my offerings."

"I'm not trying to impress you. I'm holding back. Suzanne, your donuts are great."

George agreed. "I'll take a glazed donut to start."

"I'm glad you ordered things I know how to make by heart, but then again, I'm guessing it wasn't a coincidence, was it?" I asked as they moved to the counter and I got their donuts for them.

"It's too early in the day for you two to

have made any progress, isn't it?" I asked after I served them their food.

George grinned at me. "Are you kidding me? This guy of yours is unbelievable. I thought I had connections. Man, he just has to make a call, and the information's there at his fingertips."

"I have a few friends; that's all."

"So, what did you find out?" I asked. It was clear George loved being able to hang out with Jake, but we still had a murder to investigate.

Jake shrugged. "Not a lot we can use, unfortunately. Most of it was negative information at this point. The reason we came by is that I have to wait until a few folks get into work so I can pick their brains. I figured there was no better place to wait than here."

"I'm glad you decided to come by," I said as I got them both coffee.

After Jake took a bite of his powdered cake donut, I asked, "Tell me the truth. Is it as good as you remember?"

He considered it for a few moments, much too long for my taste, and then said, "I can't be sure. I may have to take another bite before I can say one way or another."

George laughed. "Stop making her squirm. Suzanne, they are great, as usual. If you ask me, you don't need that book."

"I'm not sure if I agree with you, but there's not much I can do about it at the moment." I sensed that they were both trying to spare my feelings, holding back so I wouldn't run sobbing back into the kitchen. Maybe they had a point; I was pretty fragile just then.

A young man from the high school who looked vaguely familiar came in with a grin on his face. "I'm here for the reward," he said as he patted his backpack. "Great news. I found your book."

"Let me see it," I said. I couldn't believe it had turned up so quickly, and I felt my heart racing.

He took a step back. "Not so fast. Show me the money, and then I'll show you the book."

Jake stood and moved silently behind the young man, blocking any possibility for an exit. "You heard the lady. I suggest you do as she says. Now show her the book before you dig yourself into any trouble."

He spun around, surprised by Jake's sudden appearance. "Who do you think you are?"

Jake flashed his badge, and the young man paled. That's when I knew where I'd seen him before. "Tommy Grace, if you have my notebook, give it to me. You don't want me to call your mother, do you?"

"You know me?" he asked. "I've never been in here before in my life."

"Your mom has, though. She was in this morning, as a matter of fact, and bought a dozen glazed donuts for her knitting club. What happened, did she tell you about the reward when she got back home?"

Tommy just nodded.

Jake stepped in, and I knew Tommy could feel his presence, like heat coming off a fire. Jake said in an icy voice, "You don't have the book, do you? You never did."

Tommy looked at his feet, and Jake nudged him a little. "I asked you a question, and I expect an answer."

"No, I don't have it," he finally admitted. "Never did."

I suppose I should have been expecting something like that to happen when I offered the reward. Still, it hadn't taken the vultures long to come down from the skies. "What were you going to do, grab the money when I showed it to you?"

Tommy's face went white, and I had a feeling I'd scored a direct hit. He stammered, "No, I don't know, it wasn't like that."

I was about to scold him when Jake

stepped in even closer and said, "You and I need to have a talk outside."

Tommy nearly crumpled on the spot as my boyfriend put a hand on his shoulder, getting a good grip on it, from what I could see.

I wasn't about to let him do anything he shouldn't on my behalf. "Jake, he was stupid, but it's okay. You can let him go."

Jake looked surprised by my intervention. "Are you sure?"

"I am," I said.

Jake shrugged, and then released his grip on the high schooler. Tommy nearly flew out the door, saying that he was sorry as he hurried out.

"You were too soft on him," Jake said. "I was just going to talk to him, Suzanne. He needs to learn a lesson, and now he's not getting any punishment at all."

"That's what you think." I looked up a name in the telephone book, and then dialed the number I found. "Mary? It's Suzanne from Donut Hearts. Tommy was just here. He tried to extort money from me."

I held the phone away from my ear so Jake could hear what Mary was saying. After she finally wound down, I said, "There was a state policeman here at the time, but I convinced him not to arrest your son. I thought you'd rather handle it yourself. Was I wrong? Good, I'm glad you'll take care of it. Of course. You're welcome. See you later."

After I hung up, Jake said, "I'm having second thoughts. It might have been more compassionate to let me scare him a little than turning him over to his mother."

"Who said I wanted to show mercy? Mary will take care of him."

"I don't doubt it for a second," Jake said. "You're probably going to get more of these cranks, you know. Should I stick around and help you weed out the bad ones?"

I raised an eyebrow as I looked at him and asked, "Did I appear to have any trouble with Tommy?"

Jake laughed as he shook his head. "I rescind the offer. You can do fine on your own."

I smiled softly at him. "It is good having you around. You know that, don't you?"

"Sure, but don't be afraid to tell me again," Jake said. "I love hearing it." He glanced at his watch, and then called out, "George, are you ready to go? We should be able to make those telephone calls now."

"On my way, sir," George said. He got off that stool so fast I was beginning to wonder if he even needed the cane anymore. It was clear hanging around Jake was the best tonic he could ask for.

I didn't doubt it; I found the same remedy was true for me, too.

"Sorry again about your recipes," Jake said as they started to leave. "Don't worry. They'll turn up."

"I hope so," I said.

"Trust me, I know these things," he said with a wink, and then the two men were gone.

I was still watching them leave when the phone rang.

I reached for it and said, "Good morning, Donut Hearts," and I heard Grace on the other end.

"I'm going to have to bail on you today. I'm sorry, but something came up."

"That's okay," I answered. "What happened?"

"My boss, and her boss, are in Charlotte. I have to drive down for a surprise meeting this afternoon."

"Maybe they're going to give you a raise," I said.

"Getting fired is more likely. We're really downsizing, and there have been rumors that some of the sales teams are being consolidated. I just hope they let me go back to my old route so I can still work."

"Is it that serious?" I knew how much Grace loved her job, and I hated the thought that it was going to change for the worse.

"No, it's probably nothing. Sorry I'm deserting you."

"I just wish I could go with you and offer some moral support."

"I don't think the Grimms would like that."

"The Grimms?" I asked.

"The last time I saw them together, they looked grim and grimmer, so I've started calling them the Grim Twins. That got shortened to the Grimms, with two *m*'s for some reason."

"You don't say that to their faces, do you?" I knew Grace had spunk, but there was a line that I didn't think she'd cross.

"Of course not. I'm the very image of propriety when I'm with them. Don't worry, Suzanne. It will all work out in the end."

"I certainly hope so," I said, and then wished her luck and told her good-bye.

Emma came out an hour later. "Has anybody tried to collect the reward yet?"

"We've had one false alarm, but that's it so far," I said. "It's tough being patient like this, isn't it?"

"I must have washed the same glass three

times," she admitted. "It's driving me nuts thinking that someone just walked off with your book."

"How do you think I feel? I'm the one who refused to make a copy of it, even though you told me a hundred times to do it."

"Have faith," she said, and then vanished into the back again. Since Emma's mother worked at the shop on the rare occasions I was gone, maybe I'd ask her to look over the recipes I'd tried to reconstruct and see if she caught anything that I might have missed. She'd worked a shift for me a few weeks before when I'd taken a day off to spend time shopping with Grace in Charlotte. If the book didn't turn up soon, I'd have to ask her, in the hopes of salvaging at least a part of what I'd lost.

Even with the complaints that our selection was less steller than normal, we still managed to sell donuts at a pretty good pace. At least we wouldn't lose money. Yet. But I knew that if I couldn't come up with that book by the end of business today, I was going to have to spend a lot of time and money I didn't have testing and trying to re-create what had taken me so long to come up with in the first place. That meant that my investigation into Tim's death wasn't going to happen, at least not until I could get my own house in order. If Jake and George and Grace had to do it without me, I couldn't help it. No matter what I'd promised Emily, my first priority was to keep Donut Hearts open. It was a great deal more than just my livelihood now; it had become a big part of my life.

I was taking stock of what we had left to sell for the day when the door chimed, and I turned to greet a new customer.

It was Emily Hargraves, and from the look on her face, I had a feeling that she wasn't stopping by just to say hello.

# CRULLER ROUNDS

These are good hot, or after they're cooled as well. They are a little dense, so they go great with coffee or cocoa.

## Ingredients
- 3 eggs, beaten
- 2/3 cup sugar
- 3 tablespoons butter, melted
- 1/4 cup whole milk
- 1 teaspoon baking soda
- 3 cups flour
- 1 teaspoon nutmeg
- 1 teaspoon cinnamon
- 1 teaspoon cream of tartar

## Directions
Beat the eggs, then add the sugar and butter. In the whole milk, dissolve the baking soda, then add it to the wet mix. In a separate bowl, sift together the flour, nutmeg, cinnamon, and cream of tartar. Add the dry to the wet ingredients in thirds, stirring well as you go. Roll the dough to 1/4 inch thickness, cut out rounds and holes, and fry for three to four minutes in 375-degree canola oil. Drain on paper towels, and then dust with powdered sugar.

Makes 10–12 donuts and holes

# CHAPTER 10

"Suzanne, we need to talk."

Why were those words never good to hear? "Was there anything in particular on your mind, Emily?"

"I had to come by and tell you again how sorry I am about dating Max. What was I thinking?"

Better women than her had fallen for my ex-husband's lines. I didn't call him the Great Impersonator for nothing. "Emily, I keep telling you, don't apologize. Max can be smooth as silk when he wants to be. I don't blame you for a second, and you shouldn't blame yourself, either."

"I should have used better judgment," she said with a long sigh.

"I'm not one to comment on that, since I've had a few lapses myself when it comes to my former husband." It was clear that she felt terrible about what she perceived as a betrayal, but I wasn't about to let that cloud our friendship. She meant more to me than Max, and I wasn't about to let him continue messing up my life, even after we were divorced. "I don't know about you, but I'm sick of talking about it. Let's drop it, okay?"

"Are you sure we're good?"

"I'm positive. Hey, where are the guys this morning?"

"Back on their shelf in the shop," she said. "Don't worry, I checked three times to make sure I locked the place up tight before I left them."

"Have you had any thoughts about their next outfits?"

"It's starting to get cooler, so I think I'm going to hold out for Halloween," she said. "The costumes are excellent, and I can really let my imagination go wild. It's my favorite time of year."

"Mine, too," I said, and it was true. "We offer pumpkin donuts, spiced cider, and ghost éclairs. The decorations are tremendous, too."

"I love the nip in the air. I know some folks think I've lost my mind, but I actually enjoy taking the three amigos out for a walk in their stroller. You should see how kids react to them."

"You don't have to sell me; I'm a big fan

myself. I can't wait to see how they're going to dress up."

Emily leaned forward as she spoke next. "Don't tell anyone, but I've been thinking about making Cow an astronaut, Spots a robot, and Moose a pirate. What do you think?"

I thought she'd just ruined a surprise I looked forward to every year, but I wasn't about to tell her that. She thought she was doing me a favor by giving me a sneak peek, and I wasn't going to tell her otherwise. "I think it's brilliant, as always," I said.

"Good. I'm glad you approve." She hesitated, and then asked, "Have you made any progress finding Tim's killer?"

"I've got some friends in town working on it with me," I said, "including my boyfriend, who happens to be a state police inspector on vacation. I'm hoping that one of us will be able to find something out about what really happened to him." I just hoped that was true, even if it wasn't going to be me. I didn't have the heart to tell her that I was busy trying to save my business. We each had our own priorities, after all.

"I can't tell you how much I appreciate all of your hard work," she said.

"Don't thank me yet. We haven't done anything."

"Don't kid yourself," she said with a sad smile. "I've asked and asked, but the police chief won't tell me a thing about what's happening."

"He has his own set of problems and pressures," I said. Now why on earth was I defending Chief Martin? That was something I'd never expected to find myself doing.

"I know, but Tim was so dear to me." She glanced at the clock over the donut case, and then added, "I've got to get back to the shop. The guys will wonder where I ran off to."

"Do you want any donuts while you're here?"

She slapped her forehead. "I can't believe I forgot. Give me two chocolate glazed donuts with star sprinkles, candy corn, and an extra dollop of frosting each."

That was more like the Emily I knew. "Coming right up."

I grabbed a pair of donuts and took them in back.

Emma was still washing dishes when I showed up in the kitchen. "Do you need me to watch the front?"

"No, I just need a second," I said. As I adorned the donuts, Emma smiled brightly. "Emily's here. Mind if I go say hello?"

"Go right ahead. You can take these with you."

I handed her the donuts, and as she went up front, I decided to give her a hand in back. Sometimes washing dishes could be soothing, and I've managed to come up with some pretty good ideas while I've been doing it over the years. I'd read somewhere that Agatha Christie had claimed the same thing, and if it was good enough for her, I am certainly not one to contradict the patron saint of the traditional mystery.

Emma came back a few minutes later, and in that time, I'd managed to finish up her dishes. "Suzanne, I feel bad. You didn't have to do that," she said.

"I didn't mind," I answered. "How's Emily doing?"

"She's still pretty rattled about disappearing like that and alarming everyone in town," Emma said. "Evidently her mother is driving her crazy. She has to check in if she goes to the post office or the grocery store, or even down the driveway to get the newspaper. I guess that's just one of the perils of living at home."

"We can both relate to that, can't we?"

She bit her lip, and then said, "In a way, but at least Emily went to college. At the rate I'm going, I may never get away from

April Springs." She must have realized how that sounded, because she quickly added, "Not that I don't love working here, but you know I want to see the world."

"I know," I said. "At least you're taking some classes at the community college. That will help when you transfer to a university."

"That's something, I guess," she said.

I knew, better than most, the wanderlust my employee and friend felt. "Just not the bright lights of the big city, right?"

"Right," she said. "I knew you'd understand."

I nodded as I said, "I might get it, but I don't agree with it. The lights in April Springs are just fine with me, Emma."

She started drying dishes as she said, "I know you feel that way. It's just something that I don't get about you."

I laughed as I said, "Give it a few years and then we'll talk again. I'd better get back up front. We're heading down the home stretch," I said.

As I was about to walk back out front, I asked casually, "Emma, do you think your mother might remember some of my recipes? She's helped you out here a few times in the past, and I can't afford to ignore any help I can get."

"I don't know," Emma answered. "Should

I ask her?"

"If you wouldn't mind, that would be great. Do you have any plans for this afternoon?"

She frowned, and then said, "Nothing I can't cancel. Why? What did you have in mind?"

I hated to intrude on her personal life, but I really was in trouble. "I'm going to have to start re-creating my recipes, and I was hoping you'd be able to stick around and help. I'll pay you double time if you do."

Emma laughed. "Suzanne, you don't have to bribe me to help."

"But you won't say no to it, either, will you?"

"I'm not exactly in a position to turn it down," she answered. "Don't worry; we'll make it fun."

I couldn't imagine what we were about to do could be entertaining in any sense of the word, but if she felt that way, it was fine with me. "I'm glad you're willing to stay. Thanks, Emma."

"Glad to help out whenever I can, boss."

It was nearly closing time, and the dishes were clean and put away, the donuts were nearly gone, and ordinarily I'd start thinking about what I was going to do with the rest of my day.

But unfortunately, not today.

I had a recipe book to re-create, and I was dreading it. Not that I had any choice in the matter. I could skate by on my basic fare just so long before my customers began to complain, or worse yet, stopped coming in, but as much as I loved donuts, there could be too much of a good thing, and I'd already had my fill of donut-making for one day.

Just as I was about to evict the last few customers and close up shop, I was startled to see Angelica DeAngelis coming toward Donut Hearts.

From the look on her face, it appeared that we had something to talk about.

"Angelica, how are you?"

"The truth?" the older, but still quite attractive, brunette asked. "I'm devastated. How could Timothy do this to me?" She sounded as though she was about to cry, but I didn't want her to do it in front of an audience. "Give me one second and then we can chat, okay?"

"Fine," she said as she dabbed lightly at her soulful brown eyes.

"We're closing shop a little early today," I announced to the three customers still there.

"Hey, we've still got nine minutes," said a

young man who was typing something on a laptop computer.

"Sorry. Would a free donut make it up to you?" He'd been milking a coffee for the last hour, and had bought a pair of donut holes to go with it, but I'd seen him eyeing the case more than once.

"Two might," he said with a grin.

I could live with that. "Two it is. Would the rest of you like them as well?"

It's been my experience that no one already in a donut shop will pass up two more free treats, no matter what the circumstances. After all, these were my kind of people.

After they were gone, Angelica said, "I didn't mean to cost you money. Let me pay for those donuts you just gave away."

"I was just going to toss them anyway, so we're good," I said. "Angelica, how can I help you?"

"I don't want any donuts today, but thank you for asking."

I smiled gently at her. "I wasn't taking your order. I want to be your friend and help in any way that I can."

"If only you could," she said, dabbing at her eyes again.

"There's something I've been dying to ask you. Did Tim lie to you?" I asked softly.

She looked at me, a startled expression on her face. "What do you mean?"

"Did he ever say or imply that you two were in an exclusive relationship?" I needed to know, for my own sake, whether Tim had been playing the women, or just playing the field.

"No, he never came out and said it in those exact words, but he cared for me. Anyone could see it."

"I'm sorry for your loss, and I mean that with all of my heart, but you can't let yourself keep feeling like the wronged woman, or you'll never be able to get past this. It's not good for you, and I suspect it's not fair to Tim's memory. I could never date three people at once, but some folks seem to enjoy a variety of loves in their lives. We both know there are lots of women who do it. So why was it so wrong for Tim? Were you happy when you were together?"

She didn't even hesitate to answer that one. "Very much so."

"Then you had something special," I said.

"I thought so."

She hadn't said it with much warmth, but I decided to accept it at face value and ignore the implied sarcasm. "Then you should be thankful you could find some joy in life, and sad that Tim's gone, but you shouldn't feel betrayed. At least that's how I feel."

It was touch and go for a few moments, and I could see Angelica start to say something, and then bite it down again. She must have reached some kind of conclusion, either from my words or the emotions they had sparked in her. Suddenly Angelica started crying, and I offered her a hug for comfort. After nearly a minute, she pulled away. As she did, she took my face in her hands. "Suzanne, how did you become so smart in the ways of love?"

I had to laugh. "Are you serious? I've made just about every mistake in the book. I'm no expert; trust me."

"And yet what you say makes perfect sense," Angelica said. "I've been a real fool, haven't I?"

I wasn't about to respond directly to that, but I knew how to answer her. "Can anyone be anything else when it comes to love?"

Angelica took my hands in hers. "You must come to my restaurant tonight. We are going to reopen, I'm sure much to my daughters' surprise, and you and Jake will be my honored guests. He is in town, isn't he?"

I nodded. "He is, but I didn't realize anyone knew it."

"Trust me, my sources keep me informed. So, you'll come?"

How in the world was I going to get out of this invitation graciously? "I really appreciate the offer, but I have a thousand things going on in my life right now."

She jutted out her chin, and I knew that this conversation wasn't over. "Suzanne, protest all you want to, but I won't accept no for an answer. You may think your life is busy right now, but there is always room for a little handmade pasta and a touch of romance, am I right?"

"Right," I said. She knew my weakness, and how to strike home to get what she wanted. "I can see I don't have a chance arguing with you. We'll see you at six."

"Six? That's too late for you. Make it five."

"See you this evening," I said.

"Thank you, Suzanne."

"I didn't do anything special."

"You were my friend when I needed one, you told me a truth no one else would, no matter how much pain it might have caused, because you care about me, and that's the most special gift I could ever receive."

I didn't want to ruin the moment, but I had to ask her something else about Tim. "Angelica, Tim was a friend of mine, too, though not as special as he was to you, and you're probably aware that I'm looking into what happened to him. I know it might be painful for you, but I have to ask so I can tell the police they can cross you off their list." It was a stretch thinking that Chief Martin cared about what I thought on any topic, but I couldn't let that stop me.

"Go ahead," she said, and I could see her steel herself. "I'm ready."

"Where were you the night Tim was killed?"

She didn't even have to think about it. "Oh, I already told this to your Chief Martin. I was in the kitchen with my girls. We were filled to capacity, and I didn't leave the kitchen from five until ten that night."

"That's all I need to know. I'm sorry that I had to ask."

"Find the person who took Timothy out of my life so he can be brought to justice," she said as she clasped both of my hands in hers.

"We're all doing our best," I promised.

After she left, I locked the door behind her, and then told Emma, "That's it. We're shut down. Are you ready to start making donuts?"

If Emma felt any reluctance to start our day all over again, she didn't show it. "Let's get busy."

■ ■ ■ ■

Jake called sometime around three, but I had my hands full of dough, so I let Emma answer it.

After a few moments listening to him, she put a hand over the telephone and said to me, "He wants to know how long you'll be."

"Tell him to pick me up at four-thirty at the cottage. We're going to dinner at Napoli's, but I can't talk right now."

She relayed my message, and then grinned. "Okay, I'll tell her." After Emma hung up, she said, "He wanted you to know that you could be as mysterious as you want to be, but if you keep him in the dark, you're paying tonight."

"I can live with that," I answered. "Now, do we add three tablespoons of orange extract to the orange cake donuts, or is it three teaspoons?"

"I don't have a clue, but if you ask me, I thought it was two," Emma said.

"You may be right. Let's divide the dough into two equal parts and try it with each."

"But won't they all be too strong, then?" she asked.

"Not if we scale them back by half," I answered.

"This is going to take a while," she said as we started adding the proper amounts of extract to the dough.

"And that's the best-case scenario. I'm worried we won't get the book back and we won't be able to duplicate the recipes we've been using at all."

"What will we do if that happens?" Emma asked, the concern clear on her face.

It wasn't time to panic yet. At least that was the message I wanted to convey to her. "Don't worry. We'll manage somehow. Were you ever able to get hold of your mother and ask her what she remembered?"

"Sorry, she's shopping in Hickory," Emma said, "but I expect her home by six-thirty. Should I call you after I speak with her about it?"

I thought about it, and then decided against it. "No, with any luck, I'll still be having dinner with Jake. It will wait until tomorrow morning."

"Are you sure?"

"As I can be." I looked at the array of donuts that we'd already made, and realized that over three-quarters of them were not even good enough to give away, let alone sell in our shop. "I think we need to stop and call it a night as soon as we test that orange donut recipe. I'm going to try to grab a twenty-minute nap before my date with Jake. Let's just toss all of these," I said as I pointed to the donut discards.

"Really? Are you sure?"

"You can take them home with you if you want to, but just don't give any away to anyone. I don't want our reputation tarnished with second-class donuts."

"Okay, if you say so," she said reluctantly. I wasn't that eager to do it either, but we really had no choice. Emma looked around the kitchen, and then added, "Tell you what. We're nearly finished here. Why don't you go home, and I'll take care of the rest."

"I can't do that to you," I said, looking around at the dirty dishes and the piles of bad donuts we had on hand.

"Trust me, I can handle it," she said. "Besides, you clearly need a nap. I don't know how to tell you this, but you look exhausted."

I tried to muster a smile. "I've heard better compliments, but I'm going to take you up on your offer, if you're sure. I really do hate to saddle you with this, though."

She grinned at me. "Hey, at least one of us has a love life at the moment."

"I thought you were seeing someone new," I said.

"He didn't work out, and to be honest

with you, I think I need a little break from men for a while. Now go and enjoy yourself, and Suzanne, for one night, forget about murder, recipe books, and most importantly of all, donuts."

"I don't know if I can keep from thinking about any one of those things," I replied honestly, "let alone all of them."

"You never know unless you try. Now scoot, before I change my mind."

I didn't need to be told twice. "I'll drop the deposit off on the way home. It's the least I can do. See you in the morning." Before I made it out the door, I added, "Why don't you sleep in tomorrow? That way I won't feel so guilty tonight."

"Really? Do you mean it?" I knew how much Emma cherished the mornings she got to sleep in instead of coming to the donut shop in total darkness.

"Sure, why not? Don't come in until three-thirty."

She laughed. "Wow, you're a real sport."

Emma had a point. I thought about it, and then said, "You know what? I've got a better idea. Take the day off, with pay, for your hard work these past few days. I can handle things here by myself tomorrow."

"I don't have the heart to do that to you," she said. "But I will sleep in."

"It's your call, either way. And Emma?"

"Yes?"

"Thank you."

"You're most welcome," she said.

As I drove home to catch a quick nap, I realized yet again how lucky I was to have Emma in my life, both as an employee and a friend. I wasn't sure I could run Donut Hearts on a full-time basis without her, and not just for the help she gave me in the kitchen. It was wonderful having a friend working side by side with me, and if she ever broke free and went off to college as she'd long threatened, I knew I'd miss her more than I could even imagine.

It felt as though I couldn't have been asleep on the couch in our cottage for more than ten minutes when Momma came in. "Suzanne? Are you here?"

"Right here, Momma," I said as I waved a hand in the air.

"I woke you, didn't I?" she asked as she walked around the couch to face me.

I sat up and rubbed my eyes. "It's fine. It was nearly time for me to get up anyway." I looked her over, and then added, "Wow, you look nice. Don't tell me you're already set for your date tonight?"

"And why not? You know I hate leaving

things until the last second."

"What are you going to do for the next three hours until he gets here?" I asked.

"It's not going to be that long."

"What time is it?" I asked as I stared blearily at the clock.

"It's nearly four-thirty," she said.

"No! I've got to get ready. When Jake shows up, stall him."

"When is he coming?" Momma asked.

There was a knock at the door. "Unless I miss my guess, he's already here." I ran up the stairs two at a time, not even waiting for Momma to greet him.

In nine minutes, I'd taken a shower and gotten dressed, but my hair was less than ideal. At least I'd had a chance to put a little makeup on. I'd needed every second of that nap, but Jake was going to have to deal with a less-than-perfect me.

At least it wasn't our first, or even our second, date.

"You look great," Jake said as I walked down the stairs. "I don't even mind waiting when that's the result I get."

I stopped where I was. "Maybe I should have made you wait a little longer, then," I said with a smile. I was wearing that rarity for me, a real dress. Jake was in his best suit, and I was glad we were going to a place as special as Napoli's.

"I called the restaurant while you were in the shower," Jake explained. "They said it wasn't a problem if we showed up a little late. Angelica herself got on the line. She said they had our table reserved, so we should take our time. What happened today?"

"We can talk about it in the car on the way," I said.

As we headed out the door, I called out, "Momma, I'm leaving now."

She came out of the bedroom, and I was relieved to see that she was still dressed up. Knowing her, I wouldn't have put it past her to chicken out already.

"You're still going on your date, right?" It didn't hurt to confirm that her plans were still solid.

"Of course I am," she said shortly. "I'm actually looking forward to it."

"You don't need me to hang around until he gets here, do you? I can, you know. It's no problem if we're a little late."

Momma gave me the look she reserved for the times she thought I was being at my most difficult. "Suzanne, I'm a grown woman. I'll be fine."

"Where are you two going tonight?" Jake

asked. Momma had asked him to call her Dorothy, but he still had trouble managing it. I found it amusing that now he just avoided calling her anything at all if he could help it.

"I'm not quite sure," she said with a frown.

"Hey, if you make it Napoli's, we can double date," I said with a grin.

She laughed at that, and I was glad to see her good nature was back. "I believe we'll choose another restaurant, if it's all the same to you."

"Be that way," I said as I hugged her. "Did you take some aspirin as a preemptive strike?"

"There's not a headache in sight," she said as she hugged me back. "You two have fun."

"We will," I said.

"Have a pleasant evening," Jake said.

"You, too. If she gets too difficult, call me."

"Don't worry. If I need backup, you're first on my list."

As we got in the car, Jake said, "You know something? I really like your mother."

"That's good to know. Truth be told, I like her, too. It's different from loving her, you know? She can give me grief sometimes like no other person in the world, but she's always there for me if I need her."

"What more can you ask? So, are you hungry?"

"I'm starving," I said, suddenly realizing it was true. "I can't believe I fell asleep like that. Emma and I stayed after work and tried to replicate my recipes."

"Have any luck?"

"Not much, I'm afraid," I admitted. "Whoever stole it has really put me in a bind."

"Have you come up with any new ideas about who it could have been?"

I thought about it, and then said, "The only thing I can figure is that it had to be one of my customers yesterday. Three-quarters of April Springs was in my shop because of that ad, so it could have been anyone."

Jake nodded. "Then you probably had the killer as a customer."

I wasn't entirely certain I liked the sound of that, but it was true. "I can't believe Tim could inspire such anger and spite in someone. Then again, Angelica was pretty torn up when she came by Donut Hearts today."

"What happened? She seemed almost eager to have us there tonight."

I didn't really want to go into much detail. "We had a chat about love and loyalty, about how it's easy to mistake attention for devotion, and how to look at the world."

"Wow; that must have been some chat. I'm sorry I missed it."

"Don't be."

Jake hesitated, and then asked, "Did you come to any conclusions about any of those subjects?"

"Just that love is hard at any age, but it's almost always worth the risk you take in opening your heart to it." I touched his shoulder lightly, happy for his presence beside me.

We drove on in silence, and after a few minutes, Jake asked, "Who would have thought you were that wise?"

"Hey, be careful there. I get one right now and then," I said.

"You do more than that, and we both know it," Jake said. He touched my hand lightly, and I could see a tear in his eye. I knew my boyfriend was a man's man, a tough state police investigator who had faced down more than his share of criminals, but I also knew there was another side to him that most folks never saw.

He was a man who'd loved and lost, but he'd been willing to take a chance again with me.

And I just hoped I wouldn't ever do

anything to make him sorry for his decision.

# CHAPTER 11

"Welcome, Suzanne," Angelica said as she met us at the door of Napoli's. Dressed elegantly in a sparkling black dress, Angelica looked as though the burdens she'd been under earlier had been lifted, or at the very least, eased considerably, since the last time I'd seen her. "We've been waiting for you."

"Sorry we're late. I took a nap and over-slept," I explained.

"We're just all glad you've come tonight," she said. "If you follow me, I'll show you to your table."

"If you're out here, then who's cooking?"

"My daughters are handling the kitchen tonight, and what a wonderful job they are doing!" She leaned close to me and added, "But no worries. I'll be taking over as soon as you're seated."

"Were you waiting for us?" I asked as she led us to my favorite spot in the restaurant. There was a mural of Italy on the wall, and we were within the sound of the fountain in the lobby, out of sight, but still very desirable.

"It was my pleasure. Maria and Antonia are handling the orders, Sophia is nearby taking notes, and we've all been working hard preparing a feast for you. I hope you two are hungry. I've taken the liberty of planning your menu tonight."

I lowered my voice and said, "Angelica, you really shouldn't have gone to so much trouble for us." I felt bad taking up so much of her time and attention.

She said proudly, "If I can't treat my friends with a special dinner when I please, what kind of woman am I? Suzanne, you were there when I needed you, and I won't forget it."

"They were just words," I said.

"Words that have helped heal my heart," Angelica said.

She left us, and Jake whistled softly. "Wow, I'm really glad we came here tonight."

"She's making too much of a fuss," I said.

Jake grinned. "Suzanne, she is clearly enjoying it. Whether we deserve it or not, let's just accept it all with a smile."

"Okay, you've convinced me," I said.

Maria came out with our salads, and she smiled brightly as she placed them on the table. "Thank you, Suzanne. I don't know what you said to Momma this afternoon, but she's a different woman since she got back from April Springs."

"I'm just glad I was able to help," I said. "I'm a big fan of your mother."

Maria winked at me. "And it's safe to say that we feel the same way about you."

"What's in store for us tonight?" Jake asked.

Maria smiled brightly at him, offering a dazzling display of her real beauty. "That's a secret, but I'd brace myself if I were you. You might want to pace yourself, Momma may have gotten a tad carried away."

After Maria was gone, I said, "She's really quite beautiful, isn't she?"

"Really? I hadn't noticed," Jake said, carefully looking down at his salad so he could avoid eye contact with me.

"Then you're either blind, or you're a liar," I said gently as I touched his hand lightly. I was so happy to be there, with him, and among friends. "Which is it?"

He grinned at me as he answered, "I'm the biggest liar you ever saw in your life, but no man ever won any points answering that question honestly."

I touched his cheek. "Jake, it's okay to admit the truth."

He seemed to consider that, and then said, "She's a little young for my taste. To be honest with you, I can admire her from afar, but I'm kind of smitten with you."

"And I'm glad for that," I said with a smile.

Sophia came out next with a platter full of enough food for six people. When she came straight to us, I grabbed Jake's hand.

"Brace yourself."

"For what?"

"More food than even you and I can eat."

He turned around and looked, and I could see that the broad smile he had was more about the food than the lovely young woman bringing it. "Try me."

"Enjoy," Sophia said as she put the platter down. There was pasta adorned with parmesan cheese and butter, some with Alfredo sauce, and some with a rich and meaty red sauce. There were butterfly shapes, ziti, rigatoni, and shells, and my favorite of all, ravioli.

"We can't possibly eat all of this," I protested.

"Speak for yourself," Jake said, the gleam in his eyes strictly for the food now.

"Don't forget to save room for dessert," Sophia said with a smile.

"You are a wicked, wicked woman," I said,

returning the grin.

"So I've heard."

As Jake and I sampled each offering, one just as exquisite as the next, I felt myself quickly growing full, though we'd barely made a dent in all of the offerings.

Jake pushed his plate away and put his fork down. "I hate to admit it, but I don't think I can go on much longer if I'm going to drive us back to your place. What is she going to say about all of this food that's left?"

"I'd say we'll pack it up and send it with you," Angelica said from behind me. I hadn't even seen her approach.

"It's all so wonderful," I said. "I feel like royalty."

Angelica looked pleased by my response. "That is all the praise I need. Did you enjoy it?"

"More than I can express," I said.

"Good. I'm happy, then."

I touched her hand lightly. "I can see that you are. I'm just glad I could help."

"You did, more than I can ever express."

Jake added, "I don't know about that. I think you've done a pretty spectacular job of it."

She leaned over and kissed his cheek. "You are most welcome, sir." Angelica had a gleam in her eye as she asked, "Are you ready for dessert?"

Jake groaned. "Don't do that to me. You're killing me."

She laughed and patted his shoulder. "Don't be silly. We'll put it in the bag with the rest. I don't want you to be miserable."

Angelica nodded toward the kitchen, and Maria and Sophia came out and whisked the plates away. Jake said, "I hate to bring this up, but we still need our check."

Angelica smiled as she said, "No checks for you, not tonight."

A heavyset man at another table must have overheard her. "Does that go for us, too? If it does, I need to change my order."

Angelica looked intently at him for a moment before she spoke. "Did you save my life today?"

"Not yet, but the night's still young."

"Then we'll wait and see," Angelica said.

"You can't just give us a free meal," I protested.

"And why not?"

"Because it's not fair."

Angelica frowned for a moment, and then smiled brightly. "Send someone here with a dozen donuts tomorrow at nine, and we'll call it even."

"Four dozen wouldn't even cover the tip," I said.

"One dozen, no more, no less. Is it agreed?"

I could see I wasn't about to win that battle. "Agreed, with my thanks."

The boxes came out then, and Jake took them, though he was loaded down by the delicious burden.

"I'll get the door," I said.

When we got out to his car and stowed the boxes on the back seat, he said, "I hope you're planning to share this with me. It will feed us for a week."

I laughed, amazed by my friend's extravagance. "I've got a feeling it will be gone by tomorrow night. We'll put it all in my fridge, and you can come over and help raid it tomorrow. How does that sound?"

"Too good to be true," he said. "Do we have a little time before we have to get this back to your place?"

I looked at my watch. "A little. Why?"

"I thought we might do a little sleuthing on the way back, if you're up to it."

I had been feeling guilty about not helping lately, so I wasn't about to miss this opportunity. "I'd be delighted. What are we going to do?"

As Jake started the car and began to drive,

he said, "We're going to see if one of our suspects has an alibi for the night Tim was murdered."

"Which one?" I asked.

"Orson Blaine," Jake said. "When George and I spoke with him today, he claimed that he was at Lanskey's Bar from six until midnight the evening Tim was killed. I don't know if he was nervous, or if it's just a habit, but he chewed through three toothpicks during the short time we spoke with him. If that's a bad habit, it's not his worst one. I can't imagine how much alcohol he must have consumed."

"Six hours leaves time for a lot of drinking."

Jake nodded, and I caught a hint of sadness in his voice as he said, "He lost his wife three months ago, and from what I've been able to discover, he goes to the bar just about every night these days."

"How did she die?" I asked, suddenly aware of the fact yet again that Jake had lost his wife and child in a car accident. He was usually pretty good about hiding the pain that stayed with him, but I'd been trying to encourage him to talk about them more. Not necessarily the accident, but more about the good times they'd shared. I had no desire to ever replace his wife in his heart, but I knew I could carve out a place of my very own.

"She didn't die, Suzanne; she left him."

"It couldn't have been for Tim, could it?" I asked. That could very well give him a motive for murder, and using the Patriot Tree would be a fitting final touch.

Jake shrugged. "Nobody around here thinks that's even possible but Orson. He married a woman thirty years younger than he was. I know some of those marriages work out, but not many, especially since she cheated with him when she was married to someone else. It's been my experience that if they cheat with you, there's a good chance that someday they'll cheat on you. His ex, Jillian, thought he had money when she married him, and evidently Orson did a good job of hiding the fact that he was living paycheck to paycheck. I've heard that the second she got a better offer, she took off."

"How is Tim involved in all of this?" I couldn't see my friend being involved with that kind of woman, no matter how much I tried.

"It appears that he's one of the few men who ever turned away Jillian's advances. Tim was there putting a covered roof over their deck, and every day he came to work, she'd push herself on him more and more. Orson came home early, spotted her behavior, and immediately blamed Tim for it."

I looked over at him in admiration. "How did you get all that in one day? You must be some kind of investigator, sir."

"Well, it's not my first rodeo, but today wasn't that hard. George and I started talking to Orson's neighbors, and a woman named Mrs. Gunderson told us all of that over iced tea and lemon bar cookies. Talk about your Neighborhood Watch. It's like living under a surveillance camera all of the time."

"If you just got it from one source, how can you be sure that it's true?" I asked.

Jake shrugged. "We got bits and pieces of it confirmed later, but the main thing at the moment is his alibi. I need to talk to the bartender there and see if what Orson told us is true."

I had a sudden thought. "Jake, if Orson's there almost every night, won't he be there right now?"

"I expect so," Jake admitted.

"So he'll know you're checking out his alibi."

Jake smiled broadly at me. "Why do you think I wanted to wait until after Orson got there? There are times when it's good for your suspects to know what you're doing. If you rattle enough cages, you can get more results than if you play nice. If I can scare him, maybe he'll do something stupid, and we'll get him."

It was a dangerous game my boyfriend was playing. "What if he didn't do it?"

"Then he doesn't have anything to fear from me."

Five minutes later, we pulled up in front of the bar. Jake stopped the engine, and then turned to me. "You can wait out here if you'd like."

I laughed. "Jake, believe it or not, I've been in a bar before. Let's go talk to Orson's bartender and see what he has to say."

"Suit yourself," Jake said. He got my door for me, and we walked into the place. It wasn't much, with several dark tables and a long bar littered with worn stools. A mirror lined the back of the bar, and it was the only thing in the place decently lit. Music played softly in the background, but it was turned so low that it was hard to hear. There were maybe seven people in the place, and Jake squeezed my shoulder slightly. "There on the end. That's Orson."

I looked at the man, slumped forward with both hands around a glass, staring into the bottom of it as though it held the secrets to the universe. There was a shredded tooth-pick in his mouth, and a two-day growth of beard on his face. I felt a little bad for him, truth be told, and then I thought of Tim. If he'd killed my friend, he didn't deserve one ounce of my sympathy.

Jake walked to the bar with me on his heels, shook his head when the young bartender asked if he'd like a drink, and then showed the man his badge. I worried that he might get in trouble doing that, since he wasn't working on an official police investigation, but I left that in his hands. One thing was certain; I doubted Jake would do it if there was a hint of impropriety to it. He believed, first and foremost, in rules. Sometimes that drove me a little crazy, but most of the time I admired him for it.

"Do you know him?" Jake asked as he pointed toward Orson.

The young man laughed. "It would be hard to miss him, sitting there every night." He clearly had no problem with Orson hearing his end of the conversation.

"Was he here on the tenth?"

The man considered it, and then said, "I couldn't say."

"You didn't see him?"

"Not from my couch. I wasn't working

236

that day," he said with a smile.

"Do you happen to know who was?" Jake asked, his voice always level, ever patient.

The bartender seemed to think about that for a moment before answering. "Laney Myles. She works the two nights a week I'm off."

"Where can I find her?" Jake asked.

"Besides here? I don't have a clue," the bartender said. "This is just a way for me to pay my way through school. I did a hitch in the service, and now I'm going after something that lets me sit at a desk all day. Standing here night after night really makes you appreciate getting off your feet, you know?"

Jake just shrugged and slipped the man his card. "If you hear from her, have her call me."

The guy took the card and put it behind the bar. Whether he'd give it to his substitute bartender was beyond me.

Jake saluted Orson with two fingers as we walked past him, but he most likely didn't see it. He certainly didn't react to it.

After we left, I said, "That was one big fat dead end."

"Maybe, maybe not."

"He was here tonight, though," I said. "Wouldn't that bolster his story that he never misses a night here?"

As Jake held my door for me, he said, "I do my best not to jump to conclusions. I'll come back and talk to this woman, and then we'll go from there."

"You don't take anything at face value, do you?"

"I've learned my lessons the hard way," he answered. "Check, and then double-check."

As we drove to April Springs, I said, "I couldn't do your job."

"Are you kidding, with as much practice as you've been getting since we met?"

I wasn't going to let him joke about it. I was perfectly serious. "Don't laugh at me. I mean it. You have to think the worst of everyone you come in contact with, don't you?"

Jake shook his head. "You're missing the point. I give everyone an even break when I meet them. I don't start feeling one way or another until I have a reason to suspect that something's wrong."

"I still don't know how you do it."

He drove a few more minutes, and then asked, "Do you think just anyone could open your donut shop and do what you do? Let's put the skill set required aside for a second and just consider your work hours. Getting up at one-thirty every morning has to be some kind of brutal experience. You

work hard until twelve-thirty, by the time
you close and clean up, seven days a week. I
don't know how you do it."

"Okay, you made your point. We each have
our own special talents."

"True, but yours are delicious, as an
added bonus." He glanced in back for a
second. "Speaking of delicious, that's still a
lot of food."

"We could always heat some of it up when
we get back to my place."

He looked at me quickly to see if I was
joking. "I honestly don't think I could eat
another bite. Could you?"

"Probably not, but I won't let you down if
you want company while you snack."

"No, I'd better not, or I'll never get to
sleep."

I smiled over at him. "At least we don't
have to worry about dinner tomorrow night.
You *are* coming over, aren't you?"

"With all of that waiting for me? You bet I
am."

I tweaked his arm a little. "I'd like to think
that you're coming over more for me than
the food."

"That's what I was talking about," he said
with a grin. "The food is just a bonus."

"Good answer," I said as we drove through
town and up to the cottage. I felt happy be-

ing with him, full and warm and most important of all, safe.

It was dark out when we pulled up to the front of the cottage, but there was something flickering on the porch that gave off a dancing light.

Something was wrong.

Fire!

# DONUT PUFFS

We like these puffs because they're easy to make, and the drop donuts go great with coffee or hot cocoa on a cool day. One tip, though: use a cookie scoop. They drop a beautiful and perfect ball every time.

## Ingredients
- 2 eggs, beaten
- 1/2 cup sugar
- 1/2 cup whole milk
- 1 teaspoon nutmeg
- 1 dash of salt
- 1 1/2 cups all purpose flour
- 1 heaping teaspoon baking powder

## Directions
Beat the eggs, then add the sugar and whole milk. Set aside, and sift together the flour, salt, nutmeg, and baking powder. Add the dry to the wet, stirring thoroughly.

Use a small cookie scoop to add the dough to 375-degree canola oil for two to three minutes, turning the balls halfway through. Dust with powdered sugar or add icing after they are cool to the touch.

Makes about a dozen puffs

# CHAPTER 12

Jake must have spotted it the same time that I did. He slammed the car to a stop, then rushed out, with me close behind.

As we raced up the steps, I could see that the fire was confined to a small rectangle on the porch. I went for the garden hose, but Jake grabbed an old blanket we kept on the porch swing and beat the flames out before I could get to it. I doused it just to make sure it was out, and then Jake said, "Turn on the porch light."

After I did as he asked, in the glow from the light I looked down to try to see what had been destroyed.

With a sick feeling in the pit of my stomach, I knew instantly what it had been. There was just enough left of the cover for me to know beyond a doubt that someone had just destroyed one of the things I prized most in the world.

It was my recipe book, and it was clear

that I'd never retrieve another thing from it ever again.

"Look at this," Jake said, his voice bringing me back to reality.

"It's my recipe book," I said, feeling dull and listless all of a sudden. I couldn't even meet his gaze. All I could manage to do was stare down at what had meant so much to me, now destroyed. "I can't believe that it's gone."

"Suzanne," he barked at me. "Look."

I did as he asked, and pulled my gaze upward to him.

He was pointing to something that I hadn't seen in my haste to get to my book.

It was a note taped to the railing.

*Back off, or more than your precious book will be on fire next time. Wood siding burns with the brightest flames. Just give me a reason to light the match.*

"This is serious," Jake said.

"You don't have to tell me. That book held more than recipes. Every idea I had for the donut shop was in there. There's no way I'll ever be able to reproduce a tenth of it. I don't know what I'm going to do."

Jake shook his head. His voice had an angry edge to it as he said, "Suzanne, there's more at stake here than Donut Hearts. The killer is threatening your life."

243

I looked at Jake and did nothing to disguise my attitude in my voice. "I'm not going anywhere, Jake, and I'm not backing down. I'm going to catch whoever did this, and I'm going to make them pay for it."

"Take it easy," he said, his voice suddenly more calm and reassuring. "Is it really worth dying over?"

I had to make him understand. It was important for me that he knew just how deep a blow this was to me and my business. "Jake, let me ask you something. If a bad guy threatened you, how would you react to it? Don't try to appease me with your answer, either. I want the truth."

He scratched his chin a second, and then said, "I'd try twice as hard to catch him, and make him pay."

I looked up at him earnestly. "What makes you think I'm any different?"

He nodded. "I get what you're saying, but I'm a cop."

"And I'm just a donut maker."

He shook his head. "You're not 'just' anything, Suzanne, but I've been trained for this."

I nodded. "That may be true, but do you honestly think there's one chance in a thousand that I'm going to just roll over and quit because of this?"

244

"No," he replied, without pausing to think about his answer. "Not even one in a million."

"And are you the least bit surprised I feel that way?"

"Again, no," he said with a slight grin this time.

He got it; I could see it in his eyes. "Good."

Jake hugged me as he said, "In that case, we'd better find the killer before he can make good on his threat."

"Now you're talking," I said. "Stay right here."

I went inside and grabbed a broom and a dustpan, but I couldn't bring myself to use them. Instead, I got two clean sheets of paper, and when I got back outside, Jake was kneeling by the ashes. He looked up at me with the saddest expression on his face. "I'm really sorry, Suzanne. There's nothing left to save. I tried."

I touched his shoulder lightly. "It's okay," I said with more spunk than I felt. "I'll start over. Emma and I have already been experimenting with old recipes, and I'm asking her mother to give us a hand, since she helps out at the shop sometimes when I'm gone." As I swept the ashes onto one sheet of paper with the other, I added, "I just hope she has a better memory than I do."

Once I had the remnants of my book on the paper, I folded the sheet carefully so nothing would spill. I couldn't bear to just toss it all in the trash can like some sort of discarded filth.

Jake must have noticed my hesitation. He said softly, "You know what? Maybe we should give this a proper sendoff."

"I know you must think I'm crazy for being so sentimental about it, but when I left Max and bought the shop, the first thing I did was buy that notebook so I could start making plans. It's a part of my life I never want to forget."

He nodded. "I get it. Come with me."

I followed Jake to his car, and he popped open the trunk. He disappeared for a second, and then stood up holding a shovel. "We need to treat it with respect. Is there any particular place in the park where you'd like to bury it?"

"I know just the spot," I said as I walked to my Thinking Tree, a place I'd gone to contemplate love, life, school, and marriage. Once we were beneath it, I pointed to a spot where I could see it as I sat on the down-stretched branch of the tree that I favored. "Right there should be perfect."

Jake, even though he was dressed nicely in

a suit, started digging, and after he got down a few inches, I said, "That's enough."

I pulled my dress up a little, and then knelt down in the soft earth and carefully placed the paper holding the ashes into the hole.

"Do you have a lighter?" I asked him.

"I've got one in the car," he said. To his credit, he didn't ask why. A minute later he was back, and he handed a disposable lighter to me. I reached down and lit the edge of the paper. It flared up and burned quickly, and soon the fire was out. As I filled the hole back up with dirt with my hands, I said softly, "Thank you, for everything. You will be truly missed."

As I stood, Jake took me in his arms and held me. I hadn't realized how emotional I really was until that moment. I quietly sobbed into his chest, sad for what I'd lost, and more than that, what it represented. There was a part of me gone now, something I could never get back, and it merited the emotion I gave it.

After a few minutes, I felt the strain and weight of the destruction slip off me, and I pulled away from Jake.

"Thanks for not thinking I'm just a silly fool," I said.

He touched my cheek with a soft caress.

"Never," he said, and then he lowered his head and kissed me.

After a few moments, I heard someone calling my name. "Suzanne? Is that you? What on earth are you doing?"

It was Momma, and it looked like her big date with the chief of police had ended early yet again.

Jake and I walked up onto the porch, and I saw there was an area that still had soot from the fire. Jake said, "I'll put some water in that bucket by the hose and take care of that."

As he walked around the cottage, I asked Momma, "What happened with Chief Martin?"

She shook her head. "That can wait. What happened here?"

"Someone burned my recipe book on our front porch," I said, the words sticking in my throat somehow. Saying it aloud brought the pain back, but I fought it down.

My mother, an excellent cook and baker, knew exactly what that meant without any need for explanation. "Oh, no. That's just awful. Who would do such a thing?"

Jake came back, and I said, "Show her the note."

He'd tucked it into a plastic bag after we'd

discovered it, and Jake pulled it out of his pocket and showed it to her.

As she read it, I watched her reaction.

Instead of fear, I saw anger and determination, and I was never more proud of my mother than I was at that moment.

"You both have got to find who did this," she said, her voice full of steel.

"Don't worry. We're going to, Momma," I said.

She nodded, and then looked at Jake. "You're going to continue helping her, correct?"

"That's right," Jake said, meeting her gaze squarely.

"Good," she said. "If there's anything I can do to help, I expect you both to let me know. The only way we fail is to let this bully win."

I got the leftovers out of Jake's car, and Momma noticed the boxes were from Napoli's. She said, "I've interrupted your dinner. I can make myself scarce while you eat."

As she started into the house, I touched her arm. "That's just the leftovers. Actually, we already ate."

She looked at the boxes of food again, and then asked, "What did you order, if this is just what's left?"

"You wouldn't believe us if we told you," I said.

"Try me. I could use a good story."

"Fine," I said. "Let's get this all put away, and then we can chat. We have more to talk about than food, anyway. How was your date?"

Momma frowned. "It barely got started."

"Did you get another headache?" I asked her.

"No, it was nothing like that. Things started off badly, and then just got worse from there. We went to Mountain View, and he hired a horse-drawn carriage to take us around the lake before dinner."

"That sounds romantic enough."

"You'd think so, but you'd be wrong. The horse had a bad case of flatulence, and then the wheel came off the cart. We had to walk back to his car just as it started to rain. Then, after we went to a fancy restaurant that Phillip clearly wasn't comfortable being in, he was called away on an emergency before we even got to order our food. I'm not at all certain that dating someone in law enforcement is the best idea in the world."

"I don't know," I said as I grabbed Jake's hand. "It's working out so far for me."

Momma realized what she'd said, and looked in horror at Jake. "Jacob, you know I wasn't talking about you. I'd never dream of questioning your suitability for my daughter."

"Relax, Dorothy," he said, saying her first name with a newfound ease. "I couldn't take it personally, mostly because you're right. You shouldn't hold his job against him, though. To serve and protect isn't just a motto; if you take your job seriously, it's a way of life."

She seemed to consider that for a moment, and then said, "Perhaps you're right. Still, the two of us seem to be doomed before we even get started."

"Are you just giving up?" I asked as we started unloading the boxes in the kitchen.

"No, we're going to give it one more try. We both agree that it's worth at least that much of an effort." Momma looked at the food displayed on the table, and then asked, "Would it be presumptuous of me to make myself a plate?"

"Go right ahead," I said. "We'll keep you company while you eat."

As she put together some food, she looked at us and asked, "Would you like to join me? There appears to be plenty."

"No, thanks," I said. "You wouldn't believe how much we ate at Napoli's."

As Momma heated the food up, she asked,

"What on earth made you order this much food?"

"Well, I was feeling peckish when we sat down," I said, trying to keep a straight face.

Jake wouldn't let me get away with teasing her, though. "Don't let her pull your leg. Suzanne had a talk with Angelica today. I don't know what she said, but when we got to the restaurant, the woman practically smothered us with food."

Momma removed her plate from the microwave, took a bite, and smiled. "Angelica has a magic touch with pasta. Suzanne, what exactly did you say to her?"

"We talked about love, and the many ways it expresses itself."

Momma looked confused, so I explained further. "Tim's death hit her hard, but finding out that he'd been seeing other women hurt her even more. Angelica felt betrayed, but as we talked, it turned out that Tim never promised, or even implied, that she was the only one in his life. She never asked for anything exclusive, and he never offered it. Once she realized that she'd created her own perception of things that had no basis in reality, she felt much better about their relationship, and she accepted it for what it was and not some fantasy she'd concocted in her head."

Momma put her fork down on the plate and stared at me. "Let me ask you something. Are you saying that you condone the way Timothy behaved?"

Jake looked as though he'd rather be any place else on earth, but I didn't back down. "Momma, it's not like he was engaged to any of them. Sure, Tim dated more than one woman at the time, but I don't see anything wrong with that if he didn't lie to any of them. Not everyone is monogamous by nature. I don't mind that. It's lying about it that I can't, and won't, accept."

Momma still sported a frown as she turned to my boyfriend. "Jacob, what is your opinion of all of this?"

He didn't even flinch; I had to give him that. Jake looked Momma in the eye, and said, "I've never been able to balance a checkbook, let alone juggle two women in my life. I was born for one woman at a time."

"There, he agrees with me," Momma crowed.

"Not so fast," Jake said, startling both of us. "On the other hand, I know plenty of men like Tim who enjoy seeing different women at the same time. As a matter of fact, I know a few women who like to date multiple men. It's all just a matter of personal preference, as far as I'm concerned. There's no right and wrong here, there's just what it is."

I wasn't sure if Momma was going to respond to that, but after a few seconds, she shrugged and went back to her pasta. "To each his own, then."

A few moments later, Jake said, "Ladies, it's been fun, but I need to get out of here so you can both get some sleep."

I looked at the clock and realized that he was right. "I'll walk you out."

"Good night, Jacob," my mother said.

"Good night," he replied.

I walked him out onto the porch, and we paused there for a moment. "I don't think she liked my opinion about dating," he said after giving me a kiss.

"Are you kidding? You stood up to her, and lived to tell the story. She likes you more than you realize."

"Then it's good I decided to quit while I was ahead." He kissed me again, and I started to lose myself in it, when he pulled away.

In a hoarse voice, he said, "Suzanne, if I don't go now, I might not go at all."

I laughed. "I have a feeling Momma would be able to convince you to leave."

He grinned in return and intensified his

hug. "Maybe, maybe not." The smile vanished as he added, "Suzanne, be on your guard. That fire was a warning you need to heed."

"I'm not going back on my word to Emily," I said. "A promise is a promise. I refuse to stop digging into what happened to Tim."

He nodded. "I know how you feel, and don't worry, I'm not giving up, either. George and I have a big day planned tomorrow."

"So do Grace and I. We should meet up around four tomorrow and compare notes."

"It's a date," he said, and then got in his car and drove off.

When I walked back inside, Momma was rinsing off her plate. "That was wonderful. Thank you again for sharing."

"I'm just sorry your date didn't work out," I said.

"To be honest with you, so am I. I was nearly ready to quit, but I think Jacob makes a good point to give it another chance. He's a good man, isn't he?"

I wasn't entirely certain I could say that about our police chief with a straight face, given our history. "You could do worse," I said, which was the complete truth.

"I'm not talking about Phillip. I meant Jacob."

"That I can agree with you on wholeheartedly," I said. "But don't forget, we had more than our share of problems getting together at first. A wise woman once told me that anything worth having is worth working for. Ring any bells?"

"Don't throw my own bromides back at me," Momma said with a grin.

"Why not, when it's so much fun?"

She glanced at the clock. "Isn't it past your bedtime?"

"When isn't it?" I said with a smile. "I'd go to bed, but I'm having too much fun talking to you right now."

"I feel the same way myself, but we both need our sleep," she said as she hugged me. "Good night, Suzanne. Sweet dreams."

"To you, too," I said, and then headed upstairs.

Maybe tonight I'd be able to catch up on some of the sleep I'd been losing lately.

As my head hit the pillow, I thought about Jake, and how he'd been there for me tonight, helping me deal with my loss, holding me as I'd wept, and kissing me good night.

Even though the danger had escalated tonight, I was happy. After all, Jake was here!

That had to account for the smile on my face as I drifted off.

# CHAPTER 13

I had just flipped on the lights of Donut
Hearts the next morning when I heard the
telephone ringing. Ordinarily I'd just ignore
it and let the machine get it, but it might be
a big order, and I wasn't in any position to
turn one of those down at the moment.

"Donut Hearts," I answered automatically
as I picked up the telephone.

"It's Chief Martin," I heard on the other
end. "Got a second, Suzanne?"

That was odd. "Sure. Is there something
wrong?"

"No. Yes. I'm not sure," he said.

"Well, as long as you're clear about it."

He hesitated, and then said, "Forget it. I
shouldn't have called."

"Hang on," I said. "It's clearly something,
or you wouldn't have bothered calling. Go
on, I've got time."

There was a real heaviness in his voice as
he finally said, "It's about your mother. I

need some advice."

I nearly dropped the telephone. Seriously? He was asking me for help in wooing my mom? I wasn't at all certain I wanted to give dating tips to the chief of police. "Anything specific you wanted to know? She loves yellow roses."

"No, it's about this whole dating business. I don't know why, but it's just not working. I'm trying everything in my power to make an impression on her, but it fails miserably every time I do something special."

"That's your problem, then," I said, without even taking a moment to filter what I was saying. Normally I'd never speak to the chief like that.

"Go on. You've got my attention. I'm listening."

I took a deep breath, and then said, "Stop trying so hard. Be yourself the next time the two of you go out. If she doesn't like you the way you are, it's not going to work anyway, and taking fancy carriage rides and eating at hoity-toity places aren't going to matter one way or the other."

"So you're saying that I should be myself," he replied softly. "The sad thing is, that never even occurred to me. I guess it's worth a shot. Thanks."

"You're welcome," I said.

Emma must have let herself in while I was on the telephone, because she was standing in the doorway when I hung up.

"Who was that?"

I had no real desire to go into it with her. "You wouldn't believe me if I told you." I looked at her and added, "I thought you were sleeping in today, and instead, you're here early."

"What can I say? I'm crazy about making donuts."

I loved Emma's enthusiasm, and her clear desire to help me save the shop. "Then let's get started, shall we?" I told her about the recipe book, and she was just as upset as I was. There was nothing we could do about it, though, so we did our best to forget the bad news.

By the time we were ready to open, I'd come up with a game plan. It wasn't for Chief Martin's goal to romance my mother, or even a way to save the donut shop, but it was an idea about how we could tackle Tim's murder case. Jake and George were still working on Orson and Stu, so that left Gina and Betsy for Grace and me. My best friend had made it clear that she'd help, something I counted on. I was so glad she hadn't taken the job in San Francisco. Having her close by meant more to me than piles of gold in my bank account would. It was a shame we couldn't get started until after noon, but Donut Hearts had to come first. Besides, it would give Grace a chance to at least take a stab at doing her job. I knew her hours were flexible, and even more so since she'd become a supervisor, but I didn't want her to ever get in trouble because of me.

As I opened the front door and flipped the sign over, I found an older woman dressed in an elegant suit waiting impatiently for me. Her purse alone was probably worth more than a week of my receipts at the shop.

"Good morning," I said.

"You've got to help me," she said as she came in, clearly frazzled by something.

"Should I call the police?" I asked as I reached for my cell phone.

"What? No, it's not that kind of crisis. I need donuts."

I smiled at her. "Then you've come to the right place. We happen to have a few on hand."

"How much do you want?" she asked.

I quoted her a price for a single donut, but she just shook her head when I told her the amount. She shook her head as she reached for her checkbook. "No, you don't understand," she said as she waved her hand around the cases. "I want them all."

"*All* of them?" I'd never had a request like that in my life.

"That's right. I have an important meeting this morning, and my caterer quit without warning. This is the best I can do at the spur of the moment."

I thought about chastising her for her commentary on my donuts, but I couldn't really afford to run her off. Besides, my donuts were perfectly capable of defending themselves.

"You can have half of them," I said.

"Why not everything?" she asked petulantly. This was a woman who was clearly used to getting what she wanted. "Let me assure you, cost is not an issue."

"It may not be, but my regular customers are important to me. I'm not about to disappoint all of them just because you're in a bind."

She frowned at me, and then nodded. "I can respect that. My late husband was a businessman. He had a soft heart for his clients, too."

"I'm glad," I said.

"I'm not," she said with a scowl. "It took years for me to stiffen his backbone enough so that we could live comfortably." She bit her lower lip, and then nodded. "Very well. How much for half of your inventory?"

Her attitude was really starting to bother me. Normally I would give a nice discount on the volume she was buying, but the imp inside me quoted the price as though she'd bought them one at a time, and then I added a hefty inconvenience surcharge to the order as well for the aggravation and implication that my donuts were anyone's second choice.

She didn't even flinch as she wrote the check. As she pressed it into my hand, she said, "That includes delivery, of course."

I was tempted to say yes, especially having that check in my hand, but I had to tweak her one last time. Evidently her comment about my donuts having to "do" was bothering me more than I'd realized. "I have to hire someone myself for that. For another fifty, I'll have them delivered anywhere within a thirty-mile radius in under an hour."

She nodded, and then pulled a fifty out of her purse. "I need them in thirty minutes at the Oakmont Country Club."

"Done," I said.

After she was gone, I locked the door behind her, and went into the kitchen to tell Emma the news. "Can you borrow your dad's truck?" I asked.

"Sure, I guess so, as long as I fill the gas tank back up. When do you need it?"

I glanced at the clock. "Right now."

"Where are you going?"

"One of us is making a donut run," I said. When I brought her up to date on what had happened, she said, "Good for you for not selling them all."

"Don't think too highly of me. I charged her enough to give the rest of them away free if I wanted to."

"But you don't want to, do you?" she asked with a smile.

"Not on your life, but unless I miss my guess, we'll be closed before ten."

"And that's a bad thing how, exactly?"

I grinned at her. "I'm not complaining. Now go get your dad's truck and I'll start boxing up donuts. As soon as you're back, we'll start loading."

Emma smiled. "Are you coming with me? It could be fun."

"No, somebody's got to stay and run the shop. You can always stay here and work the front, if you'd like."

"And miss getting paid to drive donuts around? You're kidding, right?"

I just made it as Emma came back with the truck, and we got her loaded in no time.

Once Emma was on the road, I looked at our sparse display cases and thought about making another batch of cake donuts, but there really wasn't time, with customers coming in. Today, this was just going to have to do.

Emma came back an hour later, and our offerings were already running low. At the rate we were going, Donut Hearts would shut down by nine. I'd probably disappoint a few folks, but I'd made the best compromise I could, given the circumstances. For today, the early bird got the donut, and the others would have to wait for another day.

Emma waved a twenty in the air. "She tipped me, can you believe it?"

"I wouldn't expect anything less."

As she started to put the money in our tip jar, I said, "You earned it. Keep it."

"So I can go to the movies this afternoon?" she asked with a grin.

I smiled. "You can go wherever you want to." I took the fifty I'd charged for delivery and handed it to her as well. "You can have whatever's left from this, too, after you fill your dad's gas tank."

As she took it, she said, "Won't he be surprised? I just hope he doesn't think I'm going to make a habit of it."

■ ■ ■ ■

As the donuts dwindled to nothing, Emma kept up with the dishes, and true to my prediction, we were out of things to sell just before nine. I made a sign and put it on the door.

*"Sorry, folks. We ran out of donuts today, but come back again tomorrow. Donut Hearts."*

"I hate to do this," I said as Emma and I left the shop. "I feel as though I'm playing hooky skipping out like this."

"You deserve some time off," she said. "Want to go to the movies with me later?"

I laughed. "Sorry, but I've got plans."

"More crime-busting, I'm sure," she said, absolutely giddy from the combination of freedom and money in her pocket.

"Did you happen to ask your mom about the donut recipes?" I asked as we stood on the sidewalk in front of Donut Hearts.

"I never got a chance to," Emma said. "She's left to visit her sister for a few days in Virginia. I can call her right now if you want me to."

We'd limped along okay without any outside help so far, though I sorely missed having my recipes at hand. "No, it can wait until she gets back."

"She's coming home tomorrow night. I'll ask her then, I promise."

"What are you going to do until your movie starts?" I asked as we split up.

"Are you kidding? I'm going back to bed for a few hours. Where are you off to?"

"I'm going to Grace's," I answered. "I just hope she's free. See you tomorrow."

"Bye," Emma said as she got into her dad's truck and drove away.

I got into my Jeep, and then drove to Grace's place. With any luck, she'd already be up, but I wasn't counting on it. There wasn't much my friend liked more than sleeping in, and I knew if she had the chance, she wasn't going to pass it up.

I was surprised to find her awake when I knocked gently on the door. She was dressed casually, but that didn't mean she matched my blue jeans and T-shirt. Casual for Grace usually meant nice pants, a stylish top, and shoes that didn't have rubber soles like mine.

"What are you doing here?" she asked curiously as she opened the door.

"The donut shop closed early," I said as she led me inside.

"What happened, Suzanne? Is something wrong?"

"No," I said as we moved into her living

room. "I had a customer waiting at the door when I opened this morning, and she bought out half my donuts on the spot."

"Wow; that is one big sweet tooth."

I explained what had happened, and Grace grinned when I got to the point where I charged the woman an irritation fee. "I don't blame you a bit," she said. "I would have charged her double, myself."

"I pushed it hard enough. Do you have time to do a little sleuthing?"

"I'm free until one," she said. "My supervisor canceled our meeting before, so she wants to get together in Charlotte this afternoon."

"That can't be good," I said, remembering the time they'd wanted to move her to San Francisco. Grace had also recently told me about possible layoffs, so I wasn't sure why she sounded so cavalier about it.

"Don't worry, Suzanne," she said with a laugh. "It's nothing that dire."

"I thought you were worried about layoffs."

"That? It turns out our regional manager was the one getting downsized. Everything's good on my level, and the one right above me. My boss had promised a visit to her family, so if we have a brief meeting today, she can write off her trip as a business expense. I imagine we'll go to lunch at Ruth's Chris and then do a little shopping. It's not what I'd call a high-pressure situation, anymore."

Eating for free like that sounded wonderful to me, but my job had its own set of perks. "Are you sure you can spare a few hours for me?"

"Absolutely. Who are we going to tackle today?"

"I thought we'd visit the other women on Tim's dating roster," I said.

Grace frowned. "Let's just get this clear from the start. Do you mean the women besides Angelica?"

"She has an alibi," I said firmly, "so as far as I'm concerned, she's off our list until someone proves to me that her story doesn't hold up."

"Easy there," Grace said. "I don't think there's one chance in a million that Angelica did it, either."

"Good," I said with a smile. "So, what do you say? Should we go do a little inappropriate questioning ourselves?"

Grace grinned at me. "You know me; I'm always game. Can I be a contessa this time? I've always wanted to be a contessa. Maybe I could be his long-lost cousin. I could wear a disguise and everything."

I laughed. "If you can come up with a legitimate reason why a contessa would be looking into Tim's murder, sure, why not? I'll play along."

Grace appeared to think about it, and then frowned. "No, as much as I thought of him, I can't see Tim as royalty. I suppose we could be reporters again. It's worked before."

Grace and I had posed as different reporters in the past, and why not? It gave us a perfect cover snoop without appearing just plain nosy. "You know what? I think you had the right idea before."

She brightened considerably. "I get to be royalty after all?"

"No, but we can both be Tim's nieces. In a way, it's kind of true. I always thought of him as a kind old uncle," I said.

"So did I. Who knew that he'd ever turn out to be such a ladies' man."

"Since he confined his dating to women outside of April Springs, it's not that hard to imagine that we didn't know about it. Grace, who would you like to talk to first?"

She thought about it for a few seconds, and then said, "We should go to Jackson Ridge to see Betsy Hanks, and then hit Iron Forge so we can talk to Gina Parsons."

"Good. We know that Betsy works at Harper's, so at least we have easy access to her, since she'll have to be available to wait on customers."

"Have you ever been to Harper's before?" Grace asked.

"No, it's a little too classy for my taste," I answered. "But I'm willing to bet that you've shopped there a time or two."

"Just once. To be honest with you, I wasn't all that impressed with their selection, and the prices were a little higher than they should have been, even with a healthy markup."

"Then it's a good thing we're not buying anything," I said. "Let's go."

As we drove to see Betsy, I said, "I'm not all that thrilled that we need to talk to Gina Parsons. Her daughter, Penny, is a friend of mine."

"So is Angelica," Grace reminded me. "You weren't exactly delicate with her, were you?"

"I know we can't play favorites here, but it's not going to be easy. Penny knows me. What excuse can we come up with to justify talking to her mother about Tim?"

"We can always use the truth, if all else fails," Grace said. "We were both fond of Tim, and we *were* the ones who found his body. That should be reason enough to want to find out what really happened to him, and what his true relationship with these women was."

"Why am I surprised to find that you're backing the 'honesty is the best policy' approach?" I asked with a smile.

Grace glanced at me and returned my grin with one of her own. "It's fun being inconsistent sometimes. Being mysterious is just one of my charms."

I laughed at that, and she asked, "What's so funny, Suzanne?"

"I was just trying to imagine what would be on my own list of charms, if I had to make one up," I admitted.

"Don't sell yourself short," she said. "I could name quite a few of them myself."

"Go on, I'm listening," I said as I looked over at her.

Grace shook her head and smiled as she reached to turn on the radio. "I'm not going to spend the drive stroking your ego. Suffice it to say that we're both highly desirable women out on the open road and leave it at that."

"You've got a deal," I said.

When we got to Harper's, Grace looked at my outfit with a little more scrutiny than I was comfortable with. "Suzanne, maybe you should wait out in the car while I talk to Betsy."

I couldn't believe what I was hearing. "Are you telling me there's a dress code just to shop there?"

"Don't you remember *Pretty Woman*?" Grace asked.

I wasn't sure I was all that flattered with being compared to a prostitute. "I'm dressed like a working woman, not a hooker. I'm sure what I've got on will be fine."

"We could always say we're giving you a makeover," Grace suggested with a smile.

I knew that she was kidding, but it might not be a bad idea at that. "You're absolutely right. While Betsy's helping us, we can grill her about Tim."

Grace shook her head as she said, "Suzanne, I was just teasing. I think you're nearly perfect just the way you are."

"I'm not buying anything. It's a way to get our feet in the door, though. Go on, use your imagination when you talk to her, and I'll try to keep up."

The smile on her face was the broadest I'd seen in some time.

When we walked into the shop, I started to regret my suggestion. The clothes were from *Vogue* and *Elle,* not Sears and Wal-Mart. What had I gotten myself into?

A lovely young woman approached us, and I knew without seeing her nametag that this wasn't Betsy Hanks, not by several years.

"May I help you?" she asked without completely sneering at my wardrobe. It didn't add to my comfort level that I noticed when she looked at Grace her expression softened considerably.

"We're looking for Betsy Hanks," Grace said.

The young woman, whose name tag read CYNTHIA, frowned for a split second. "I'm sure I'll be more than able to assist you myself."

Grace wasn't backing down, though. "Sorry, but she comes highly recommended. I'm afraid we must insist."

The pout returned for an instant, and then Cynthia plastered the fakest of smiles on her face. "Of course. One moment, please."

As she disappeared into the back room, I asked Grace, "What was that all about?"

"She must work on commission. I've seen enough poaching of other people's clientele to recognize it. That's why I love that we're all on straight salary at my job. Having to claw every month for your salary tends to bring out the worst in most people."

A stylish older woman came out of the

back and smiled as she walked toward us. There was a hint of frost in her hair, and she wore a suit that showed off her fitness. What caught my attention from ten paces, though, was the way she smiled. It brought life to her entire face, and I could see why Tim had wanted to be with her. There was something oddly familiar about her, and I wondered if she'd ever been in my shop.

"I understand I've been recommended," Betsy said in a voice that was a tad lower than I'd been expecting. It was clear she was waiting for the customer's name, but I didn't have an answer.

Apparently, neither did Grace. "I'm afraid we've got a bit of an emergency on our hands," she said as she completely ignored the implied question of who had sent us there. "My dear friend needs a new outfit for tonight, and it must be in black. Tragic circumstances, really. Can you help us?"

Betsy studied me with a gaze that made me feel more than a little uncomfortable, and as she walked around me, I could have sworn her stare was burning holes in me. "I believe I have some selections that might do," she said.

"Thank you," Grace said. "You're a real life-saver."

As Betsy disappeared to make her selections, I whispered to Grace, "Am I really all that bad?"

"For this store, you'd better believe it. You're their worst nightmare. For the real world, though? I think your style suits you just fine."

"I'm not sure there was a compliment anywhere in there," I said.

"Nor should you be," Grace replied with a slight smile.

Betsy came back with three dresses and a suit, and I didn't have to see the price tags on any of them to know they were more than I could ever afford. I hadn't particularly enjoyed playing dress up as a child, and my taste for the game hadn't improved over the years.

As I was led back to the dressing room, I said, "Sorry for the short notice, but we're going to a private memorial for someone very close to us."

Did she flinch a little at that? "I'm sorry for your loss," she said automatically. "Do any of these catch your fancy?"

I chose one of the dresses, and then was ushered into a dressing room. Before I closed the door, though, I said, "Actually, the man we're mourning was our uncle. Tim Leander will be sorely missed in our lives."

Betsy dropped one of the dresses on the

floor, and the rest were sure to follow.

"There's a service for him tonight?" she asked in a halting voice.

"Yes," I said.

Grace stared at Betsy for a moment, and then stated what was obvious to anyone within a hundred yards. "You knew Uncle Tim, didn't you?"

"Actually, we were dating when he died," Betsy admitted.

Grace frowned, and then said, "Forgive me for being so blunt, but I was under the impression he was seeing two other women."

"I knew that. There were no secrets between us," she said. "I was happy for the time we got to spend together. This service tonight, do you know if Angelica or Gina were invited to attend?"

"Not as far as I've heard," I said. It appeared this woman was being open and honest with us, and I didn't want to take advantage of her good nature if I didn't have to.

She seemed to accept that. "That's fine, then. I'll be there at the service tomorrow. Now, about this dress. Why don't you try it on and see how it fits."

I closed the door, but left it open a crack and watched them as I tried on the dress.

With the top and bottom of the dressing room open, I could still hear the two women talking.

Grace said, "We found the body. Did you know that?"

I saw a look of horror on Betsy's face. "How horrible for you both. It must have scarred you for life."

"We were both shaken by it," Grace said. "Something like that isn't easy to forget. I'm willing to bet you remember where you were the night he was hanged."

It was the perfect leading question, and I was proud of Grace for slipping it so effortlessly into the conversation.

"It's too painful to think about," Betsy said.

Grace wasn't about to let it go, though. "It will help if you talk about it. Trust me."

My best friend was doing beautifully, but I hated being on the sidelines. Then again, I couldn't go out now, even in the dress that fit me so beautifully. I'd interrupt the flow of their conversation, and I knew that if I broke that spell, it would be impossible to recapture.

Betsy choked a little, and then said, "I keep beating myself up about it, but I know in my heart that there's no reason I should. I just can't get over feeling guilty because I was with another man the night it happened."

That was a real bombshell. So much for her being madly in love with Tim, and filled with jealousy because of his other paramours. It was hard to imagine this woman in a rage strong enough to kill.

"Who was it?" Grace asked softly.

I had to see her reaction, so I cracked the door open slightly. As I did it, I held my breath, but neither woman noticed. I wasn't at all sure Betsy would answer, but when she did, I had to keep myself from gasping aloud. "I was with Orson Blaine. It wasn't anything serious between us. He finally got up the nerve to ask me out, and Tim had just broken our date for the evening, so on a whim, I accepted. Orson and I just went out once, and when I found out what happened to Tim, I ended it before it could really get started. I still feel so guilty, like I betrayed him."

Grace said, "How could you have known? Do you know what Tim was doing that night when he canceled on you?"

"He didn't want to say at first, but he finally told me that he broke our date so he could be with Gina Parsons."

Grace looked at me, and I hadn't even realized that she knew the door was open. I could see in her eyes that she wanted me to come out, so I did.

As I stepped out, I asked, "How do I look?"

Grace whistled. "Like a million dollars. What do you think?"

"I think if I could afford it, I'd buy it on the spot. I'm sorry, but I just can't swing this."

Betsy looked at the tag, and then said, "I'd offer you a discount, but we just got this in. I could put it on layaway for you, if you'd like."

I shook my head sadly. "By the time I could afford it, I wouldn't fit into it anymore. Thanks anyway."

I quickly changed, and after a few final parting words, Grace and I left.

"You heard it all, didn't you, even before you opened the dressing room door?" Grace asked as we got into the car and began our drive to see Gina.

"I caught every word of it. I'm beginning to think that I'm slowing you down. You handled that situation beautifully all by yourself."

She looked pleased by the praise. "Thanks, I learned from the best. You could have gotten everything out of her that I did," she said.

"It's nice of you to say so. Can you believe he actually admitted to breaking a date with her so he could be with another woman?"

Grace shrugged. "So Betsy says. I'll feel better once we confirm it."

"I agree." As we drove on, I added, "I can't imagine what our conversation with Gina Parsons is going to be like."

"You don't have to imagine it much longer; we'll be there in ten minutes. What did you really think of Betsy's story?"

I considered what she'd told Grace, and then I said, "I'm leaning toward it being the truth. After all, it's too easy to check up on, and besides, what woman would lie about something that puts herself in that kind of light. I still want to talk to Orson, or at least have Jake and George do it, but for now, they're both off my list."

"That makes things easier, doesn't it?"

I thought about it, and then answered, "In some ways. In others, it makes it much harder. I don't know how I'm going to go after the mother of one of my friends," I replied.

"Delicately, I'd say."

# BANANA DROPS

We love these with a touch of icing and a few sprinkles. The donuts stay soft, since the cooking bananas give off steam during the frying process. You might be tempted to eat these hot, but the banana flavor really bursts out if you let them cool first.

## Ingredients
- 1 1/2 cups all purpose flour
- 1 teaspoon baking soda
- 4 teaspoons confectioner's sugar
- dash of salt
- 1/2 cup whole milk
- 1 egg, beaten
- 2 medium bananas, mashed, then add a dash of lemon juice

## Directions
Sift the flour, baking soda, confectioner's sugar, and salt together, then set aside. In a separate bowl, beat the egg, then add the whole milk. Combine the flour mix with the egg mix, and mix thoroughly. The final step is to stir the bananas in. The lemon juice keeps the banana from turning brown. Take a small cookie dropper and deposit balls of batter directly into hot canola oil (375 degrees). Cook for two to three minutes, and then remove and drain on a paper

towel. Let cool, then enjoy.

Makes about a dozen banana drops

# CHAPTER 14

"How exactly are we going to find Gina?" Grace asked as we drove into Iron Forge. I hadn't been there in years, but it hadn't changed much, just gotten older and rustier. I knew that in the days of the American Revolution, Iron Forge was a bustling community, but I had a feeling they'd reached their population apex sometime in the late 1700s. Since then, everything had gone downhill, and it was barely a spot on the map now.

I pointed to the combination hardware store/post office/lunch counter. "Someone there is bound to know where she is, or where she lives."

"You're probably right, but will they tell us?"

"That's another story altogether." I knew that many small Southern towns were tight-lipped about their residents, particularly when strangers were involved. Though we lived less than an hour's drive away, Grace and I were still outsiders. Our accents might give us a little boost in our investigation, but we couldn't count on it.

"I have an idea," Grace said.

"Let's hear it."

"You could tell folks you are friends with Penny. It's true."

I considered that approach, and then said, "It is, and I mean to keep it that way. It's bad enough that I'm going after her mother. I'm not going to drag our friendship into it, too."

"It was just a thought."

"Then keep thinking," I said with a smile.

She pulled up in front of Friendly's, the name of the combination establishment, and said, "Let's just ask someone and see where that gets us."

We walked into the store together, and I was preparing my story when I spotted Gina herself sitting at the luncheonette counter alone. I motioned to Grace to browse around while I had a conversation with Penny's mother by myself. It might go over a lot better if she didn't feel as though we were tag-teaming her.

Grace appeared to get it all with one look, and she changed tracks and started searching through postcards on the desk by the mail clerk's window.

"Excuse me, is this seat taken?" I asked.

"No, it's free," she said, so I slid next to her. I pretended to study her for a moment, and then I said, "I know you. Penny and I are friends. You're her mother, aren't you?"

That brought a smile to Gina's face. She was stoutly built, had short dirty-blond hair, and wore thick glasses. From the looks of her, I had no trouble seeing her hoisting Tim's body into the air, but I had to banish that thought. I had to keep an open mind as we spoke, or I'd tip my hand; I just knew it.

"Are you a nurse, too?" she asked me.

I could lie, or I could tell the truth. Since Penny would find out about this conversation sooner or later, I decided to come clean with her from the very beginning. "No, ma'am. I run Donut Hearts."

"Penny's mentioned you," she acknowledged. "It's Suzanne, right?"

"Suzanne Hart," I said as I offered her my hand.

"What brings you to our little hamlet?" she asked.

It was time to decide how I was going to pursue my line of questioning, and I didn't have a great deal of time to consider it before I answered.

Finally, I came to the conclusion that when all else fails, tell the truth, so I did.

"Actually, I'm here looking for you."

Gina looked surprised by that response. "Me? Whatever for?"

"I was good friends with Tim Leander," I said softly. Just because I was about to ask her some potentially embarrassing questions, there was no reason for her neighbors to hear our conversation.

Gina paled significantly at the mention of his name. "Sure, I knew Tim, but then again, I know a lot of people."

"I understand you were closer to him than that." I hated pinning her down like that, but what choice did I really have?

Gina looked flustered, but she was saved, at least for the moment, by a young woman wearing an apron who approached us from the kitchen. She slid a plate in front of Gina, and then asked, "Are you okay?" As she did, she gave me one wicked look.

"I'm fine, Chrystal," she said. "This is Suzanne. She's a friend of my daughter's."

"What can I get you, Suzanne?" the waitress asked, though it was clear she wasn't all that interested in serving me at all.

There was a club sandwich in front of Gina that looked delicious. "I believe I'll have one of those."

"And what about your friend?" Chrystal asked.

"My friend?" What was she talking about? Had she put Grace and me together so quickly?

"The woman you came in with," Chrystal said as she pointed to Grace, who was doing her best to make herself invisible.

"Would you like a club sandwich, too?" I turned around and asked Grace. "You can join us."

"I just need to buy these postcards first," Grace said as she grabbed a few at random.

Chrystal said, "You can pay with your meal."

Grace sat beside me, and away from Gina.

Gina said, "I'd really like to have my lunch in peace. Can we discuss this later?"

"How about after we finish?" I asked. "I'm sorry, but we don't have a lot of time."

"I was thinking more like next week," Gina replied.

I didn't doubt for one second that she wanted to postpone it as long as she could. I tried to smile as I said, "Don't worry; it won't take long. We can do it right now, if you'd rather go ahead and get it over with." I said the last bit a little louder than I needed to.

"After lunch," she said firmly.

Gina ate her club sandwich without any conversation, and our sandwiches arrived while she was still eating. It was good, but none of us wanted to linger over our meals.

"Where should we talk?" I asked Gina as I paid for the sandwiches. I'd offered to get hers as well, but she'd declined.

"Let's go to my house."

"Is it far?" I asked.

"I'm just across the road and down the block. It's close enough that we can walk."

"That sounds good."

Gina looked at Grace and asked me, "Does she have to come, too?"

I was saved from answering when Grace spoke up. "Not at all. Find me when you're ready to leave, Suzanne."

After Grace left, Gina seemed more comfortable.

Outside, the air was getting a bit chilly, and I pulled my jacket a little closer.

As Gina and I walked to her house, we talked. "Have you known Penny long?" she asked.

"For a few years now," I admitted. "I'm a big fan of hers."

I saw Gina smile. "So am I."

"I would hope so." I hated pushing this woman into talking about something she'd rather forget, but I had no choice. "Gina, I don't want to cause you any more pain than I have to, but we need to talk about Tim."

"I've already spoken with the police," she said. It appeared that our chief of police was on the ball after all. "Do I really have to go over it all again?"

"It would help me understand more about what happened to him," I said. "I can't make you talk to me, but put yourself in my place. I'm the one who found his body, and he was close enough to my front porch to give me nightmares." That much was true. Every time I closed my eyes, a brief flash of Tim clouded my dreams before I managed to fall asleep. I wasn't sure if I'd ever be able to wipe that vision out and replace it with one of him smiling and laughing as he worked on one project or another.

"I understand," she said finally. "How can I help you?"

"When did you find out he was dating more women than just you?"

"The day after you found him," she said sadly. "I was with Penny near your shop, as a matter of fact. She tried to get my mind off it by pulling me into a used clothing shop near your donut stand."

I didn't mind her calling my store a "stand," but I knew Gabby would have a fit if she heard her place referred to as a used clothing store. She was very proud of the reputation she'd built up over the years, and Gabby wasn't very shy about defending it if she felt she needed to. More importantly, Gina's story matched what I knew to be true personally. I'd overheard her and her daughter discussing Tim's murder, but she had no way of knowing that I'd been there. That gave her a point for honesty.

"You must have been shocked when you found out he was seeing other women."

"That doesn't begin to express how I felt," Gina said, her footsteps suddenly slowing on the sidewalk. "I thought we were in love. I was, at any rate."

"Didn't he tell you about anyone else?" Tim Leander as a player still didn't fit my image of the man.

"He made a few casual references to going out with other women, but I had the feeling at the time that he was just trying to get me jealous."

I chose my next words carefully. "And did it work?"

Gina nodded slightly. "Sure, I took the bait. I wanted him all to myself. I'm not afraid to admit it. But I didn't kill him, Suzanne."

She'd shown a flash of anger when she'd said it, which she'd quickly brought under control, but I'd seen it, and wouldn't forget it. I wouldn't have guessed the woman I'd been talking to moments before would be capable of a surge of jealousy, but I would have been wrong. Gina must have realized how it must have sounded to me. She continued, "I would have broken up with him if I'd had the chance, but I never would have hurt him, not like that."

"Not under normal circumstances, but you were angry. You just admitted it."

To my surprise, she smiled. "Suzanne, I was angry, not homicidal. I've had my heart broken before, and it could easily happen again. If you're not willing to put yourself out there, how will you ever find love again?"

It was a lesson I was glad Jake had learned, and Momma was struggling to master. I'd been burned by Max, but I mostly blamed him, not all men, as a general rule.

"Are you going to the service tomorrow?" I asked, wondering what her answer would be.

"I was going to miss it," she admitted, "But the more I think about it, I believe that would be a mistake. I need some closure, and this will be the only way I'm going to have any chance of getting it. You'll be there, won't you?"

"Yes, ma'am," I said. "He was my friend."

Gina nodded, as though the words gave her some comfort. "And in the end, I believe that he was mine, too. Would I have liked for things to have been different between us? Of course I would, but there's nothing anyone can do about that now. He's gone, and I'm not about to lose my last chance to say good-bye to him."

Gina stopped walking and pointed to a nice ranch house with flowers hanging from the front porch. "This is my place. I'd invite you in, but I've got a thousand things to do. We're finished, aren't we?"

I had one more question to ask, one that I'd been saving for the end. It was now or never.

"Gina, do you happen to remember where you were the night Tim died?"

She frowned at me a moment before she spoke. "I do, but I can't prove it. I was here alone, watching an old movie on television."

I had to push a little harder. "Did you happen to talk to anyone, or did anyone come by? Perhaps you spoke with Penny on the phone."

She shook her head. "No, I tried to talk to my daughter, but she was working a double shift that night, and no one else came around or called."

That didn't match something else I'd been told. Gina started to climb the steps when I said, "Funny, that's not what I heard. Someone told me that you had a date with Tim that night, and that it came up at the last second."

"Who on earth told you that?" she asked as she turned to face me.

It was time to put it out there and see what she had to say for herself. "Betsy Hanks said that she had a date with him that night, but he broke it to go out with you, instead."

Gina wasn't at all happy about that. "Then Betsy Hanks is a liar as well as a fool. It's simply not true. Now if you'll excuse me, I really do need to go."

Gina was inside before I could say another word.

That was certainly interesting.

One of Tim's lady friends was lying to me. But which one?

That was the real question, but unfortunately, at the moment there was no way to prove it either way.

I found Grace sitting in her car on Center Street in front of the hardware/post office/diner when I got back. She was deep into a trashy tabloid magazine when I opened her car door.

"Doing a little light reading?" I asked.

"Hey, I was bored, and this was the best thing I could find, sad to say. As soon as I get home I'm going to stuff a few books under my seat in case it happens again. So, don't keep me in suspense. What happened with Gina?"

"She denied killing him," I said simply. "Why don't you start driving back to April Springs? We can chat on the way back home."

"That sounds good to me. I've had about all I can take of this town, and I've got to get to Charlotte for my second lunch of the day."

"Sorry about that," I said. "I hope I don't make you late. This was my fault. We started talking, and I just lost all track of time."

"Don't worry about it," Grace said. "I just ate half my club, so I'll have a light bite when I get there. My boss will be so impressed with my restraint on her expense account, I might even get a raise. What happened?"

"It's not good. I want to believe that she's innocent, but Gina doesn't have an alibi, and she claims Betsy was lying about her having a date with Tim the night he was murdered."

Grace took all of that in, and then asked, "Who do we believe?"

"At this point I'm not sure," I said. "We need to do a little more digging."

"Oh, good, I like snooping around," she said. "I'm just sorry I have to bail out on you this afternoon."

"Don't worry about it at all. I'll just tag along with Jake and George while they're working, if they'll let me. I've been meaning to see how Stu and Orson react under more of Jake's scrutiny. I'm hoping to pick up some Junior Investigator tips so I can get that merit badge."

"Good. When you're finished, you can teach me. Do you have any idea where you can find them?"

"Hang on a second and I'll find out."

After a hurried conversation with Jake on the phone, he told me where we could meet, but he couldn't talk, so he hung up on me rather abruptly.

"What was that about?" Grace asked.

"It sounded as though they were busy, but I got what I wanted. After you drop me off at the donut shop, I'm going to the Boxcar to wait for them. Don't worry, I'll bring you up to date as soon as you get back."

"You'd better," she said with a smile. "I want pictures, and video, if you can get that for me, too."

"How about if I just tell you what I find out?"

"That'll do just fine," she said.

When we got to Donut Hearts, Grace barely slowed down long enough for me to get out. "Sorry, but I've got to run," she said.

"Drive safely," I answered as she sped away. I doubted she even heard me.

As I walked toward the Boxcar Grill, Jake pulled into the donut shop parking lot. I pivoted around and started back, expecting to see George as well, but he was alone.

"Sorry, I can't face another lunch today," he said. "I hope you already ate."

"It's taken care of. Where's your partner?"

"George insisted that we eat before his physical therapy class, and I just dropped him off there. He's graduating tomorrow, did you know?"

"I'm glad," I said.

"About lunch, or the graduation?"

"Both," I answered with a grin. "Grace and I just met with Gina Parsons over sandwiches, and I'm thrilled that George's therapy is coming along."

Jake smiled at me, and I felt my heart skip a little. "It sounds like it's just you and me this afternoon," he said.

"I love it. Did you two get to speak with anyone yet?"

"No," he admitted. "We chased some bad leads all morning, but I have hopes for this afternoon."

"We went two for two," I said. "I've got some interesting things to share with you."

"Share away," he said.

Once I brought him up to speed, I asked, "So, who do we believe, Betsy or Gina? It's crucial that we find out who Tim was supposed to see, but I don't know how we can prove it either way."

Jake nodded and took a moment to consider what I'd told him. "It's a shame he didn't keep a journal, or at least a chart to keep track of his love life."

"How do we know he didn't?" I asked. If Tim had kept any sort of record of his love life, it could be a goldmine helping us figure out what had happened to him.

Jake just shrugged. "I asked Chief Martin about it, and he said they didn't find anything but an old wall calendar with all of his jobs listed on it. There wasn't a thing there about his personal life."

"How nice that he shared that with you," I said.

Jake grinned. "Hey, remember, I do have official standing."

"I'm glad one of us does," I said. "We're not going to wait for the others to keep digging, are we? I want to take advantage of every second we've got."

"I agree. There's just one thing, though."

"What's that?"

Jake looked at me intently before he spoke. "I take the lead, Suzanne. Feel free to interject if you feel as though I'm missing something, but my badge and my title carry some weight here. The less we admit that our investigation is unofficial, the better chance we'll have of getting answers. Agreed?"

"Got it. You're the boss," I said.

He kissed me, and then said, "We both know better than that, but let me have my delusions, at least for now, anyway."

I could keep my mouth shut. At least I hoped I could. "So, who do we speak with first?"

"I'd like to talk to Stu," Jake said. "I'm still trying to check up on Orson, but I'm having trouble tracking Laney down."

"The errant bartender," I said. "Was she one of your tasks this morning?"

He nodded his agreement. "George and I decided that if we could come up with an alibi for Orson, we wouldn't have to pursue that angle anymore."

"And what did you find out? Did you discover any leads about where she might be?"

"As a matter of fact, she'll be at the bar in two hours," Jake answered. "We can talk to her then. I swear, we tracked that woman all over three counties, but she was one step ahead of us the entire morning."

That didn't sound good. "Do you think she was purposely trying to avoid you?"

"No, I doubt she even knew we were that close behind her. I think it's just a coincidence that we kept missing her."

I smiled at him. "You told me once that you didn't believe in coincidences, Jake."

He shrugged. "I stand by it as a general rule, but there has to be an exception sometimes."

"Like never dating a suspect?" I asked with a smile. That was indeed what we'd done when we'd first met, though I was still under a cloud of suspicion at the time.

"You weren't always a suspect," he said.

"At least I'm not at the moment," I replied. "Where do we find Stu?"

Jake glanced at his watch as he pointed up the abandoned railway path. "According to my sources, he should be coming out of the Boxcar any minute now."

"So that's why we've been hanging around

in my parking lot." I started to get out of the car as I said, "We don't have to wait until he's finished eating."

Jake put a hand on my arm. "Take it easy, Suzanne. Things will go smoother if we do this without any witnesses around."

"We're not going to rough him up, are we?" I asked as I got back into the car. "Why does it matter if anyone else sees us talking to him?"

Jake let out a deep breath, and then said, "Just being seen with me carries an air of guilt." He rushed to finish the thought before I could interject. "I don't mean with you, and you know it, but as a state police investigator, I have to be aware of the ramifications of what I do to the innocent as well as the guilty."

I'd never looked at it from his point of view before. "You're right. I'm sorry. I know I have a tendency to fly off the handle sometimes. This way is better."

"Would you mind speaking a little louder into my lapel pin?" he asked me with a smile. "I want that on the record."

I covered the pin with my hand as I said, "If I thought you were actually taping us, I'd say something entirely different."

Jake was about to comment when he pointed up the path. "Speak of the devil, and he appears. That's Stu himself." I looked up and saw the man light one of his cheap cigars once he was outside the restaurant.

"Let's go," I said as I got out of the car.

"I'm taking the lead, remember?"

"Sure, as long as you're doing a good job of it."

"And I'm guessing you're the sole arbiter of that, right?"

I winked at him. "Hey, you're getting better at this. You got it on the first try."

We got within ten feet of Stu Mitchell before he noticed us approaching him. Stu tried to step out of our way when Jake stood squarely in his path.

"Stewart Mitchell?" he asked as he pulled back his jacket, revealing his badge. Again, I wasn't sure how kosher that was, since he wasn't officially on the case, but it must have passed his own internal test of what was right.

"Folks call me Stu," the man corrected. He was dressed neatly in a suit, but it was well worn around the cuffs and sleeves, and the shirt that poked out hadn't been cleaned or ironed in quite some time. Stu's shoes, though polished, were also well worn. Hang on a second. Was he a little off balance as he stood there? Trish didn't serve alcohol in our dry county, but unless I missed my guess, Stu had been partaking, anyway.

"Stu it is," Jake said amiably enough. "We need to talk."

"I didn't have anything to do with killing Tim, and that's the honest truth," Stu said, his words rushing out at us. "You can't pin it on me, so don't even try."

"Who are you talking about, Stu?" Jake's voice had gotten soft, and it might have been interpreted as friendly if you didn't know him. He seemed to be onto something, and it gave him a calm presence that I admired.

"It's Tim Leander you're here to talk to me about, and we all know it." He gestured at me. "Who's that?"

"An acquaintance of mine," Jake said.

I wasn't sure I cared for that description coming from my boyfriend, but then again, I knew that he had to be careful of exactly what he said.

"I didn't do it," Stu repeated. "You can gang up on me all you want; my story isn't going to change."

Jake shook his head, as though he was disappointed with a small child. "Stu, there's a very easy way to make me go away for good."

"What's that?" Stu asked, his reddened

eyes squinting at Jake carefully.

"Where were you the night Tim was murdered?" Jake asked.

"I was entertaining a lady friend all evening," Stu said.

"Really?" I asked.

"I have lady friends," Stu said defensively.

"I'm sure you do," Jake said. "What was this one's name?"

He looked around as he scratched his chin, and it was clear Stu was debating whether to tell us or not. All it took to convince him was for Jake to pull back his jacket slightly so Stu could see his gun. It wasn't a threatening move, but it made a statement nonetheless.

"Okay, fine, it wasn't a lady." He looked around, though there wasn't a soul nearby, and finally admitted, "If you've got to know, I was at the plasma center donating some blood. I was a little hard up, and I needed the cash."

"And you're trying to tell me that you were there all night?" Jake asked. It was clear that he didn't believe him. "Come on, Stu, we both know that it doesn't take that long."

"I had some problems afterward," Stu said. "They kept me for hours. Go on, ask the nurse who volunteered there. She stayed with me the whole time."

"Do you happen to remember her name?" Jake asked.

"Yeah, sure I do. It was Nickel. No, hang on a second, that doesn't make any sense. It was Penny. That was it, I'm positive."

"Nice try," I said, "but Penny Parsons was at the hospital all night."

Jake looked surprised when I volunteered the information. He turned back to Stu and said, "Are you lying to me? I don't like it when people lie to me."

"It's the truth," Stu said, the anger clear in his voice. "Ask her."

Jake seemed to take that in, and then he nodded. "Trust me, I'm going to. Don't go far, Stu. I may need to talk to you again."

"I've got nothing to hide," he said, his anger fading away and his tone becoming more defensive.

"Let's hope that's true, for your sake."

Stu walked past us and headed for the bus stop. I wasn't exactly sure where he lived, but I didn't envy him the wait. Our bus system wasn't exactly known for its promptness. In fact, some folks built in a buffer of half an hour or more, and they got upset when the bus actually ran on time.

"How do you know Penny was working?" Jake asked me as we walked back to his car.

"Gina told me when I spoke with her today."

Jake nodded. "We still need to confirm that it's true."

As Jake got into his car, I followed suit. "Let me guess. We're going to the hospital right now, aren't we?"

"The sooner we can take his name off our list, the better. You don't have a problem with that, do you?"

I shook my head, thinking about how my friend might react to the fact that I'd been a little hard on her mother. "I'm just hoping Penny hasn't spoken to her mother since I did."

# CHAPTER 15

"Suzanne Hart, how could you? I thought we were friends."

It wasn't the greeting I'd been hoping for when I first saw Penny. So much for the chance that she hadn't spoken to her mother yet. We were in a crowded ER with victims from a car crash and an accidental stabbing, and Penny's voice still managed to get us more attention than any of them had garnered.

"We are," I said, trying to keep my voice calm. "Penny, I had to talk to your mother to see if I could somehow clear her with the police. There was no other choice, and I was trying to help her out, not do her any harm."

"She said you accused her of murder," Penny said. Wow, was she angry.

"Penny," I said, snapping her name out like a whip. "She seemed happy enough to talk to me, especially at first. I didn't accuse her of anything, and that's the truth."

"You asked her for an alibi," Penny said, her tone of voice leveling out somewhat as she glanced over at Jake. He'd decided to let me handle this myself, and he didn't say a word as Penny and I talked.

"I told you, I'm trying to help her clear her name," I said. "Trust me, you don't want folks around this county thinking your mother might be a murderer. I've been painted with that particular brush before, and it's no fun."

Penny seemed to take that in. "Let me get this straight. You wrecked her day, but you were really just trying to help her, is that what you're saying?"

"I'm sorry if I upset her. I had the best of intentions," I replied. I really didn't want to make Penny angry again.

Jake finally decided to step up. "There's something we need you to clear up, and then we'll get out of your hair."

"If it's about my mother, I'm not at all sure I care to talk to you."

"It's not that," I said. "I'm really sorry about interrupting. We know you're busy."

Penny shook her head. "Not particularly. We're overstaffed at the moment, so I just punched out."

"Then you have a second," Jake said.

"Just that, but I've got plans."

"Of course you do," he said. "I understand you worked a double shift here the night Tim Leander was murdered."

She frowned before answering. "No, that's not right."

"Penny, your mother told me you did," I said, also supplying the information for Jake's save.

The nurse shook her head. "She was mistaken. I worked my regular shift here in the ER, and then I pulled one at the plasma bank. It's a way to bring in a little extra income from time to time, so I do it when I'm not busy. Why, am I a suspect now?"

"We're just trying to clarify things," I said.

Jake asked, "Did you treat a man named Stewart Mitchell?"

"Oh, yes, Stu was there most of the night. He started hitting his flask the second we were through, and he fainted before he got to the door. We had to keep him here to make sure he was all right."

"He didn't slip out anywhere when you weren't looking?" Jake asked.

"No chance, and I'll swear to that in court."

Jake nodded, and as he turned to go, I realized that I wasn't going to get a better opportunity to talk to Penny about her mom than right now.

I took a deep breath, and then asked her, "As far as you know, did your mother have a date with Tim that night?"

"No, of course she didn't," Penny answered a little too quickly. "She was home all alone watching a movie."

Okay, that was exactly what her mother had told me. That didn't mean that it was the truth, though. "Is there any way she can prove it?"

Penny scowled openly now. "I'm still not sure she should have to, but she left me half a dozen messages that night on my cell phone. She does that when she's feeling lonely and I can't answer my telephone. Can't you check that out?"

"She could have called you from anywhere with a cell phone," Jake said.

Penny laughed. "You don't know my mother. She won't go near one, no matter how much I beg and plead. All of her calls were made from her home. Check the records. It should clear her."

I thought of half a dozen ways that could have been faked, but I didn't say anything. "It's clear that you love your mother. We're just trying to get to the truth."

"Well, you won't find it by digging into my mother's life, or mine, either."

"I understand," I said.

"I hope so."

I couldn't just leave it at that. Her friendship meant too much to me. "Penny, can we put this behind us? I didn't mean any harm by it." I didn't want to lose a good friend, especially if her mother was really innocent. I knew if she wasn't innocent, and Jake and I found out, I'd lose Penny forever, but we hadn't come to that yet, and I hoped we never would.

Penny shrugged. "I just don't like seeing her ambushed like that."

I took her hands in mine. "Penny, I'll make you a deal. If I speak with her again, I'll call you first and you can go with me. How does that sound?"

She started to smile, then bit it back down again. "Okay, I guess that would work. Now if you two will excuse me, I've got to go. My shift at the plasma bank starts in an hour, and I want time to grab a quick bite first."

After she was gone, Jake and I went out to his car. On the way, he asked, "Why did you tell her you'd let her go with you next time?"

"Because it probably won't be me, anyway," I said. "I have a feeling if Gina Parsons merits a return visit, you'll be doing it alone, or with George. It was an easy

311

promise to make, and if her mother's innocent, I don't want our friendship to be dead by collateral damage. Do you understand?"

"Perfectly," he said as he reached out and squeezed my hand for a moment before releasing it again. "You wouldn't be you without doing something like that."

"I'm not sure I'd want to be," I said. I glanced at my watch, and then added, "It looks like our bartender should be starting her shift any minute."

"Then let me buy you a Coke," Jake said.

The bar was nearly empty again when we walked in, and I wondered what kind of crowd they must have at night to justify staying open at all. There were a few stragglers at the bar, but Orson Blaine wasn't one of them.

A tall brunette with piercing blue eyes and a full figure was working behind the bar, though.

"You must be Laney," Jake said as we approached.

"If you say so, handsome, then I must be. What can I do for you?" At that moment, she seemed to recognize him somehow, and after she hesitated a second, the bartender reached for a baseball bat behind the counter. "Go on. Get out. You're not welcome here."

"Slow down," Jake said as he held his hands up in the air. "What's the problem?"

"I heard you were following me around all day. I've had a stalker before, so believe me, I know how to deal with you creeps." She glanced at me and added, "That's a nice touch, bringing another girl along as window dressing. Now, are you going to walk out of my bar on your own, or am I going to have to make you crawl out on your hands and knees? It's your choice, sport. I honestly don't care."

Jake pulled back his jacket slowly and showed his badge. "I'm working on a case."

The bat lowered when she saw his shield. "So, tell me. What's so urgent that it couldn't wait until now?"

Jake shrugged. "I didn't know you'd be here until I got to the last stop this morning. I'm not shadowing you, trust me."

"I will, for now," she conceded as she put the bat back under the bar. From the way she'd held it, I was pretty sure no one ever bothered her more than once. "A girl can't be too careful. What can I do for you after I serve you both drinks?"

"We'll take two Cokes," Jake said, and after she poured them, he paid, leaving her a tip worth more than the sodas had cost.

"You know what? Suddenly I feel like talking," Laney said as she pocketed the change.

"It's about Orson Blaine," Jake said.

"Him," Laney responded as she rolled her eyes. "That man's clearly in love."

"With you?" I asked. If it was true, it ran counter to everything we'd learned about the man so far.

Laney laughed at the suggestion. "Hardly. It's with whoever's pouring him his next drink."

So much for that angle of our investigation.

"Do you happen to know if he was here the night Tim Leander was murdered?" Jake asked. "You were working that shift, I already checked."

"I was here, and so was he. Orson kept drinking, and by the time he left, he was too broke to order another, which was just as well, since I was getting ready to cut him off, anyway."

"How can you be so sure he was here all night?" I asked.

Laney frowned. "It wasn't all that tough. In fact, it was a pretty memorable night. I don't know where he got it, but Orson paid me with a hundred-dollar bill, and when I told him I didn't have enough change, he bought a dozen friends a drink."

"Was that unusual for him?" Jake asked.

"About like a lunar eclipse on a Tuesday," Laney replied.

"Do you happen to know any of his drinking buddies?" I asked.

"I've never seen them before, or since, but they sure were a rowdy bunch. I had to run one of them out of the women's bathroom, and when I finally got him out, another one was behind the bar helping himself to our Scotch," she answered, as she poured a beer and served it to a man at the end of the bar without missing a beat.

"This part is important," Jake said. "Did he ever leave the bar for anything that night?"

Laney frowned, and then pointed to a booth in back by the door. "He moved his little party over there, and I couldn't swear he never slipped out when I wasn't watching him. Things were nuts that night, and I barely had time to look up. I can't swear to it, but my gut tells me he never left. Is that it? It's insulting to the bartender not to take at least one drink of your sodas," she added as she pointed to our glasses.

I hadn't touched my Coke, and neither had Jake. We both took small sips, and then Jake said, "If you think of anything else, I'd

315

appreciate it if you'd give me a call," he said as he slid a card across the bar.

"How about if I don't, and I just want to chat?" she asked with a full smile, giving him every ounce of her charm. A quick look of irritation must have crossed my face, because she instantly pulled back and addressed me directly. "I'm sorry, I assumed you two were partners, not partners, you know what I mean?"

"No harm, no foul," I said.

Jake laughed softly under his breath, and we walked out of the bar.

"What was that all about?" I asked.

"It's funny, but I've never had two women fighting over me before."

"You still haven't," I said, and gave him a light kiss on the cheek.

"Are you kidding? Wait until you hear the way I tell it."

"Dream on, my friend," I said. "Do we believe her?"

Jake shrugged. "What do you think?"

"She wasn't exactly unequivocal about her answer, but I think she's telling the truth, at least as much as she knows it. What about you? Do you have an opinion?"

Jake shook his head. "I'm troubled by what she said, I'll admit it. Laney told us how she saw it, but I still think that it left time for Orson to slip out, kill Tim and string him up, then get back before anyone noticed he was gone. What if he wasn't really drunk at all that night? He could have paid those guys to cause a distraction so he could get away."

"Tell me, do you trust anyone?"

Jake surprised me and took me in his arms, and after a rather nice kiss, he pulled away and said, "I trust *you*."

"That's all you need then," I said.

"You can say that again." After we got back to his car, I asked, "Do we go looking for Orson now so we can ask him more questions?"

Jake glanced at his watch. "Not tonight. I'm afraid that we're going to be late as it is."

"Where are we going?" I asked.

"We have leftovers planned at your house, remember?"

I smiled. "Maybe I should give Momma a heads-up that we're on our way."

"You can do it in the car as we drive. I'm starving."

Momma greeted us at the door with a smile. "Jacob, so nice you could join us."

"Happy to be here, Dorothy," he said. Jake inhaled deeply, and added, "You made garlic bread. I love it."

"Then I'd better have some, too," I said with a smile.

Momma clicked her tongue. "You know, I never even thought about that."

"It's fine," I said. As we walked into the dining room, I saw that she'd already set the table. It was a pretty elegant way to eat leftovers. "I'm suddenly starving."

"I am, too," Jake said. "Can I give you a hand with anything?"

"Thank you, but it's taken care of. Suzanne, if you'll serve the salad, I'll get the main courses ready."

"I'd love to," I said as Momma and I walked into the kitchen together. "You really pulled out all the stops, didn't you?"

"Jacob isn't here that often. I want to make him feel at home," she said.

"That's just one of the reasons I love you," I said as I gave her a quick hug.

She looked surprised, as well as pleased, by the compliment.

I wasn't sure which was better, the first time Jake and I had that meal, or this one. It was delicious, that much I knew.

We were just starting to clear the table when there was a knock at the door. I saw Jake instinctively put a hand on his gun. I looked out the side window and saw Chief

Martin's squad car out there. "It's okay, it's the chief."

Jake nodded, and Momma asked, "Would you mind getting the door? He's probably here for you anyway."

"I'd be happy to," Jake said.

I followed, and he grinned at me as he opened the door.

"Hey, Chief," he said.

"Hello, Jake, Suzanne."

"What can we do for you?" Jake asked. "Are there any new developments?"

"Not in the case," he said. "I was wondering if I might have a moment with your mother, Suzanne."

"Hang on a second. I'll go get her," I said.

"Could Jake do it?" the chief asked.

"Certainly," Jake answered. He looked as puzzled as I'd been by the request.

Once he was in the kitchen, the chief said, "I just wanted to thank you again for the advice."

I'd nearly forgotten what I'd said when I remembered that I'd told him to be himself. He was certainly doing that, showing up unannounced and still in uniform.

"I hope it helps," I said as Momma came out of the kitchen, drying her hands on a dish towel.

"Phillip? What is it? Is something wrong?"

"May I have a second of your time on the porch, Dorothy?" he asked. "I promise, I won't keep you."

"Certainly," she agreed, handing me the towel as she passed by me.

The second the front door was closed, I ran to the window to see if I could make out what was going on outside.

Jake looked at me and said, "Suzanne, you're not spying on your own mother, are you?"

"Not if you keep talking I can't," I said. "I can barely hear them as it is."

"That's not what I meant, and you know it. Come on, we need to give them both some privacy."

I shook my head and moved back away from the window. "What fun is that?"

Jake laughed, and I had to smile at him as he said, "I've got an idea. Let's finish up those dishes. The two of them might be a while."

"You think?" I asked.

"You never know," he said.

He was actually right. We were nearly finished with the dishes when Momma came back in. There was a smile on her face that I hadn't seen in a long time.

"What was that all about?" I asked.

"We're going out again tomorrow night,"

she answered. "I must say, something's changed in that man since the last time we spoke."

"What exactly is different?"

"He seemed so sure of himself. It was rather nice," Momma said. "We're going to the Boxcar Grill tomorrow so we can have a pleasant conversation along with our meal."

"It's not really a grand romantic gesture, is it?" I asked.

"That's exactly why I'm looking forward to it," Momma answered, and then she noticed that we were working on the dishes. "Heavens, I meant to do those myself before I got distracted. Why don't you two go into the living room and I'll finish them up myself."

"We've got it," I said, and Jake agreed. "You go relax."

She nodded, and said, "Then I may read a little. This book is just getting to the good part."

After she was gone, I whispered to Jake, "What was that all about, do you think?"

"It appears you give excellent advice to the lovelorn," he said with a smile.

"I guess, but honestly, I didn't mean to do that good a job," I answered.

"Sorry, I'm afraid you can't take any of it back now. It's not entirely a bad thing, is it, seeing your mother that happy?"

"I'm all for it," I said. "I just hope this date turns out better than the first few did."

Jake kissed me, surprising me so much I nearly dropped the glass in my hand. "We didn't exactly have an ideal beginning ourselves, but look how we're turning out."

I smiled. "I guess there's hope for the world, then."

"At least for the Hart women," he answered.

# CHOCOLATE DONUTS

These donuts are more of a dense and crisp donut than a cake one, and though they're a little on the heavy side, we like them for a change of pace from our regular glazed donuts. It's amazing how just a little icing adds another layer of flavor to these donuts.

## Ingredients
- 1 egg, beaten
- 1/2 cup sugar
- 1 tablespoon butter, melted
- 1/4 cup bittersweet chocolate, melted
- 1 tablespoon cinnamon
- 1/2 cup whole milk
- 2 cups all purpose flour
1 teaspoon baking powder

## Directions
Beat the egg, then add butter, sugar, and cinnamon, and then finally the melted chocolate. In a separate bowl, sift the flour and baking powder together, then slowly add to the egg mixture. Roll out the dough to about a quarter inch, then use a biscuit or donut cutter to cut out the rounds and holes.

Cook in canola oil at 360 to 375 degrees for two and a half minutes on each side or

until dark brown. Drain, dust with powdered sugar or add icing or sprinkles per
your taste.

Makes about 8 donuts.

# CHAPTER 16

Just before we were set to open the next morning, Emma came up front and asked me, "I forgot to ask. When is the funeral? We're not going to miss it, are we?"

"It doesn't start until two," I said. "That should give us plenty of time to get cleaned up and make it even after a full day here. I didn't realize you were going."

"Last night Emily called me and asked me to go with her for moral support," Emma said. "I forgot to ask her the time when she telephoned. She's pretty shook up."

"They were close," I said. "She has a right to be."

Emma wanted to say something else; I could see it in her eyes. "Is there something you're holding back?"

"She's coming by the shop around eight," Emma said. "She wanted to know if she could talk to you for a second."

"She doesn't need to make an appointment to speak with me," I said. What on earth was going on?

Emma shrugged. "It's about the case. She kept asking me if you were making any progress, but I had to keep telling her that I didn't know anything about it. I know she's not satisfied with the answers I've been giving her."

"All I can say is that we're getting closer," I said.

"How close?" Emma asked. How much pressure was Emily putting on her friend?

"I'm not even sure I can answer that. We collect information from as many people who were involved as we can, and we never know when we're going to hit the tipping point when things finally begin to make sense. Something someone says or does might trigger something else we've heard, or we may put two seemingly unrelated facts together. It's hard to quantify, and I probably shouldn't say that we've been making a lot of progress, but I have a feeling in my heart that it's true."

"That's good enough for me. So, who did it?" she asked with a grin.

"I'm not ready to say yet," I answered as I flipped on the lights and opened the front door.

I was surprised to find Stu Mitchell waiting for me outside, and even more surprising, he appeared to be stone-cold sober.

"Good morning," I said as he came in. "Can I help you with something?"

He rubbed the sleep from his eyes. "You actually come to work this early every day? I don't know how you do it. I need coffee before my eyes will even open. Give me the biggest one you serve."

I got him a big cup and filled it to the brim, and as I handed it to him and collected his money, I said, "If you think this is early, we're here by two every morning."

"You must be part vampire," he said as he took his first gulp. "Ah," he said. "Now that's what I'm talking about."

"I'm pretty sure you're not here for a social call, Stu," I said. "What can I do for you?"

"I didn't kill Tim," he said firmly.

"So you said before."

"The last time I said it, we both knew that I was drunk, but I'm sober now, so I wanted you to hear it again."

"Mission accomplished, then," I answered.

He looked long and hard at me before he spoke again. "You don't believe me, do you?"

It was a fair question, and it deserved a

truthful answer. "Honestly? I'm not sure."

Stu took that in. "You know what? I can live with that. I just don't want to see the police rush to judgment. That cop you've been with looks at me like I'm a killer every time he sees me."

I explained, "If it's any consolation, he looks at all his suspects that way."

"I'm not sure if that's better or worse."

"Are you going to Tim's funeral?" I asked.

He took another healthy swallow of his coffee, and then said, "I've been thinking about it, but I'm probably going to pass. I don't need anybody pointing any fingers at me there, you know? Tim and I had our differences, but I didn't want to see him dead, and that's a fact."

Stu took another big swallow, and then pushed the cup back to me. "Anyway, that's why I came by."

After he was gone, Emma came through the kitchen door. "What was that all about? Why would he go out of his way like that just to tell you something he's already said?"

"Were you eavesdropping?" I asked her.

"Wouldn't you have been, if the roles had been reversed?"

I grinned at her as I said, "No doubt about it. Maybe he has a guilty conscience," I said. His sudden appearance was curious, to say the least, and I couldn't wait to tell Jake.

A little before eight, Emily Hargraves came in. She was dressed in black, and was all alone. For one weird second, I wondered if Cow, Spots, and Moose were dressed in black suits back at the shop, but the image of it vanished as quickly as it had come into my mind. This was not a time for fun and frivolity. A man, a dear friend of mine and Emily's honorary uncle, was dead, and he was being buried today.

"I'm so sorry," I said as Emily approached the counter. "This must be brutal for you."

"I'll get through it," she said bravely. "Have you had any luck?"

She didn't have to clarify her question any further. "We're closing in, but I can't say how soon it will be before we're ready to move."

"As long as you're still on it," she said, "then I'll be able to get through this."

"It's sweet of you to ask Emma to go with you."

Emily shook her head. "It's not sweet. I have to have her there to lean on, or I won't be able to get through it. Are you coming?"

"Yes, of course I am. Jake and I will be there, and George and Grace, too."

"Good," she said. "Tim deserved a fine showing of the folks who cared about him."

"Can I send anything to the house?" I asked. "I'd be glad to throw a few dozen donuts in boxes for you."

"Thanks, but the place is loaded with food as it is. We're good, but it's a nice thought."

"If there's anything I can do, just let me know," I said.

"You already are," Emily said, and then left the shop.

Not twenty minutes later, George came in, wearing a jet-black suit. From the way he was walking, it appeared that his therapy was finally showing some noticeable results, though he still had the cane with him.

"You, my friend, are doing great," I said.

"For an old man who had an accident?" he asked with a grin.

"For anybody," I answered. I looked around behind him, but didn't see my boyfriend anywhere. "Where's Jake? I thought he was going to come by with you."

"Do you mean that he's not here?" George asked as he looked around. "We were supposed to meet up ten minutes ago."

I knew it was just ten minutes, but I suddenly panicked, wondering if Jake had gotten himself into something he couldn't get out of. "Don't worry, I'll call him," I said as I reached for my cell phone.

Jake didn't pick up, though, and after four

rings, my call went straight to voice mail. "Jake, this is Suzanne. Call me as soon as you get this."

"It's okay," George said as I stowed my telephone back away. "It's probably nothing."

"Probably," I said. "Can I get you a cup of coffee and a couple of donuts, on the house?"

"I wouldn't say no to either offer," he said as he took a seat at the counter.

I got him what I'd promised, and I was about to try Jake again when the man himself walked in the door.

"Sorry I'm late," he said. "Been waiting long, George?"

"Not even long enough to eat my breakfast," George grinned at him. I wasn't sure who was happier that Jake was working the case, George or me.

He leaned over the counter and kissed me quickly. "Sorry about that. I didn't mean to worry you."

"What, me worried?"

He laughed softly. "Suzanne, I got your voice mail. You were worried."

I smiled at him. "You're right, I was. It's taken me some time to get you close to where I want you. I'd hate to have to start over again with someone else."

"Am I really close?"

I walked around the counter and kissed him again. "You've got a ways to go, but yeah, you're pretty good right now."

"Right back at you," he said, and then turned to George. "I'm ready whenever you are."

"Don't you want something to eat?" I asked.

"Thanks, but I had breakfast hours ago."

I lowered my voice so no one in the shop could hear as I asked, "Who are you going to talk to this morning?"

"We're going after Stu," he said.

"He was here early this morning," I said, suddenly realizing that I'd forgotten to tell either man about the early morning visit.

Jake did not look pleased by the information. "When exactly did he show up, and what did he want?"

I answered, "He was here at five-thirty, if you can believe it, and he was sober as a judge."

"I've known some judges in my day," Jake said, "who might disqualify that statement all by themselves."

"Okay, a teetotaler, then. Stu said that he was coming by to tell me that he was innocent, and it was pretty clear that it was important to him that I believed him."

"Is it just me," Jake asked, "or is that man protesting a little too much?" He slapped George on the shoulder. "Let's go see what he has to say to us."

George took a last bite of donut, and then said, "Thanks, Suzanne. That was great."

After the two men were gone, I tried to imagine Stu Mitchell killing Tim and then hoisting his body up in the Patriot Tree. I wasn't sure if I had a good imagination, or if something on a more subtle level was telling me he was guilty, but the image in my mind was sharp, vivid, and hard to dispute.

By eleven, we were slowing down, as was usually the case in a typical day for the donut shop. Emma and I had discussed closing around then regularly instead of our normal noon. After all, not many folks wanted donuts for lunch, and if they did, they could come by and pick them up a little earlier. I had to admit that the prospect of an earlier closing time was tempting, especially since we were there in the heart of darkness every day. It was something I was going to have to seriously consider in the future.

To my great surprise, Betsy Hanks and Gina Parsons came in together, both dressed in black, and from the look of their makeup, both women had been crying. It was one of the odder pairings I'd ever seen come into my shop, but it wasn't complete, yet. Angelica DeAngelis walked in just a second later, and all three of Tim's paramours were together at the same time.

"Ladies," I said. "How are you all holding up?"

"We'd like a table, some coffee, and a little privacy," Angelica said with a fleeting smile.

"Of course," I said as I pointed to a table by the window. It was probably small of me, but it was also still close enough for me to eavesdrop.

"You two sit, I'll fetch the coffee when it's ready," Angelica said, and they did as she asked.

"What in the world is going on?" I asked her softly as I started filling cups.

"We've decided to bury the hatchet. That's a bad choice of words, isn't it? We each cared for Tim, and we think we owe it to him to forgive him today, of all days."

"Angelica, I'm so proud of you," I said as I patted her hand.

"You give me too much credit," she said. "Betsy came to me at the restaurant last night and convinced me that it was the proper thing to do. She'd already talked Gina into coming along, so how could I refuse?"

Betsy Hanks just came up a few notches in my book. It had to have taken a great deal of nerve to do what she'd done. "Can I get you all a donut as well?"

"They may or may not eat anything," Angelica said.

"After all of the times you've fed me, including very recently, I'm at least going to try." I put together a sampler platter, and then said, "If you give me a second, I'll come back and grab the coffees."

"You take the donuts, and I can get these," she said. "I'm not above serving, you know that."

"Thanks," I said.

As she distributed the coffees, I put the platter down and said, "Ladies, I am sincerely sorry for your loss today. Please accept these as a token of my respect."

"That's sweet," Gina said, but she had trouble making eye contact with me.

"I agree," Betsy answered. She looked so sad and troubled by the loss of Tim, and yet she'd made a supremely self-sacrificing gesture out of respect for him. I knew that one of the women sitting there might be a killer, but I had a hard time believing it at the moment.

Thirty minutes later, they stood as one, nodded and thanked me in turn, and then walked out of the shop.

It had certainly been an eventful day at Donut Hearts.

And I still had a funeral to attend.

As Jake and I stood at the hilly gravesite, I couldn't believe how many of Tim's friends, loved ones, and admirers had come to say a final good-bye. It was amazing how many folks he'd touched during his life, and the town of April Springs would never be the same without him. The day had started off sunny, but as though in deference to the occasion, clouds had rolled in, giving the afternoon an ominous feel to it.

As I looked around at the crowd, I saw the three girlfriends sitting together; Angelica, Betsy, and Gina. They were holding hands and fighting back their tears, and some were handling things better than the others. Orson Blaine was in attendance, the toothpick firmly in his mouth as he watched the proceedings. I squeezed Jake's hand, and when he looked at me, I motioned to Orson. He nodded, and then his gaze went to a mausoleum nearby. I wasn't sure what he was pointing to at first, but then I smelled the cigar. A minute later Stu shifted, and I could see that he was watching the funeral from afar. How odd. He'd told me he wasn't coming, and yet there he was. I looked forward to discussing what that meant with Jake once we had a chance to speak again.

Jake dropped my hand and took off in his direction, but a few minutes later he came back and rejoined me. "Did you find him?" I whispered.

"No, he got away," Jake replied. It was pretty clear he was unhappy about it, too.

I continued to look around and saw that Emily was quietly weeping by the grave, with Emma by her side. I was so proud of my assistant. She appeared to offer some comforting words and held Emily's hand tightly, being the best kind of friend there was.

After the service, everybody went their separate ways. I was sure there would be something for Tim's closest friends at the Hargraves household, but we hadn't been invited, and that was one get-together I wasn't about to crash.

Jake and I walked back to his car, and as he looked around at the crowd one last time, he asked, "Where's Grace?"

"Her boss decided to make it a three-day meeting, so she's staying overnight in Charlotte."

Jake stared at me for a second before he

spoke. "Hang on a second. She's less than two hours from home and she's staying in a hotel?"

"The best place in Charlotte, as a matter of fact. She explained it to me on the phone. It's got something to do with the company having too much cash and her department being under budget for their fiscal year. If they don't spend it this time, they won't get as much the next."

Jake shook his head. "I don't get it."

"Neither do I, but it makes sense the way she explained it." I took a few steps, and then asked, "What do you make of Stu showing up like that?"

"I expected as much," he said. "I'm just sorry he slipped between my fingers like that."

"Jake, is there something you're not telling me?"

He appeared to think about it, and then said, "Suzanne, there's something in my gut telling me that Stu is the killer. I've been wrong before, but not often enough to matter. I'm not a fan of Orson's alibi, and I think any of the three women are capable of it, but I'm going to go after Stu until I uncover something better."

I stopped in my tracks. "You honestly still think Angelica could have done it? She has an alibi, and what's more, she's our friend."

"Just because we're close to her doesn't mean we can ignore her as a suspect. Who is giving her the alibi, really? Her daughters."

"You're telling me you can see her hoisting a body up that tree by herself," I said.

"She could do it, especially if she were motivated. But that's something else I've been thinking about. I'm beginning to think that whoever did this had to have had help. It takes a great deal of effort to hang a man that way. It's not as easy as it looks."

"Okay, you've got me curious about how you actually know that," I said as we approached his car.

He didn't want to tell me, I could see it in his eyes, but he finally gave in. "While you were selling donuts this morning, George and I tried a little experiment. I didn't want to tell you about it before the funeral, but I can now. We took sacks approximately Tim's weight and hung them from the same branch where you found him."

I couldn't imagine such a morbid test, but I could see the validity of it. "What did you discover?"

"George couldn't do it because of his leg, and to be honest with you, it wasn't all that easy for me. One woman couldn't have done it, but two working together could have."

I watched the three girlfriends break up, and wondered if Betsy and Gina could have done it together. Before the funeral, I wouldn't have bet they could do anything that required cooperation, but I wasn't so sure now. "Could it have been a woman and a man?"

"Sure, I don't see why not, but it's just idle speculation right now." Jake's phone rang, and I'd watched him turn it off when the funeral started, so he must have turned it back on when I hadn't been watching.

"I've got to get this," he said as he stepped away. "Hello? Hello? There's lousy reception here. I'm going to walk down the hill a little."

As soon as he was gone, I was surprised to see Betsy walking quickly toward me. "Suzanne," she said, just a little out of breath. "We need to talk."

"Again, I'm sorry for your loss," I said almost automatically.

"That's fine. There's something I need to tell you. I've been afraid to say anything up until now, but I can't live my life this way."

"What is it?" One look in her eyes told me it was deadly serious.

"It's about what happened to poor, sweet

340

Tim. He didn't deserve the end he got. Something has to be done to correct it."

"Betsy," Gina said as she approached. "There you are."

Betsy said quickly, "Meet me at the Patriot's Tree in an hour. There's something I have to show you."

Gina was with us then, and she put an arm around Betsy's shoulder. Was it protective, or was it intended to secure her silence?

"We were just talking about what a lovely funeral it was," Betsy said, clearly trying to distract Gina.

"So many people came out for it," I said.

"He was loved by many, but no one loved him more than the three of us." Gina turned to Betsy and added, "Come on, the car's waiting for us. We're going with the Hargraves family." Gina turned to me and added, "Thanks for coming, Suzanne."

"This was something I needed to do," I answered.

As Betsy was led away to the car, she looked back at me one last time.

She didn't look sad, though.

She looked scared.

# CHAPTER 17

"I've got to go," Jake said when he came back up the hill. "There's been a double homicide in Greensboro, and they need me right away."

"Jake, Betsy just told me that we need to talk at the Patriot's Tree in an hour. Is there any way you can wait that long and go with me?"

He bit his lip for a second, and then said, "I wish I could, but this is critical. Evidently the victims were friends of the governor, so my vacation has been officially cancelled. Suzanne, promise me that you won't go alone. I'm not crazy enough to ask you to skip it entirely, but you have to be safe."

"Who am I going to take with me? Grace is in Charlotte, remember?"

"I'm not sure what kind of backup she'd be anyway. Call Chief Martin. No, that won't work, he'll scare Betsy off if she sees him with you. Besides, he's out looking for

Stu, so he doesn't have time to go. You could always take George."

What he said made sense, and I knew he had no choice but to leave. "I'll do it, for you."

"Thank you." He kissed me quickly, and then said, "This may be kind of corny, but I got you this."

He took a greeting card from his suit jacket and handed it to me. "Open it later when you're alone."

"Okay. Thank you."

"You're welcome," he said, and then asked, "Can you get a ride back to your place? I need to be there as soon as I can manage it."

I spotted Momma talking to the preacher who'd delivered the eulogy. "Go. I'll be fine."

"I know you will." I was happy he took the time to kiss me again, no matter how fast he did it. "I'll call you when I can, but I can't promise anything."

"Be careful," I said, as he got in the car.

"Right back at you," he said with a smile.

I watched him drive off, and then I found my mother. After she finished speaking with the preacher, I stepped up. "Can I have a ride home?"

"What happened to Jake?" she asked as

she looked around.

"He got called in on a case in Greensboro," I explained. "Duty called."

"Of course you can ride with me."

By the time we got back home and I changed, Momma was off on one of her errands. I never asked where she was going, and she never volunteered the information. I'd been trying to call George since the funeral was over, but I hadn't been able to reach him.

When it was finally time to meet Betsy, I considered just not showing up at all to appease Jake, but I couldn't bring myself to do it. I'd be careful, but there was no way I was going to stand Betsy up. She had something important to tell me, and I didn't want to let her down.

As I neared the tree, my gaze went to the upper branches almost involuntarily. Would I ever be able to look at this tree again without seeing Tim hanging from it? Looking back to the ground, I saw that someone was sitting in the shadows, leaning up against the trunk of a nearby tree that was well away from the main part of the park. Perfect. Someone had chosen the worst time in the world to take a break at my rendezvous site. Should I try to run them off, or just wait there patiently for Betsy? As I approached, I suddenly realized that it just might be the woman I was supposed to meet. "Betsy? Is that you?"

There was no response. Could she have come here early and fallen asleep? I didn't blame her if she had. The past few days must have been horrible for her, and from the look of her at the funeral, no amount of concealer would hide those dark circles under her eyes. I thought about letting her rest, but she'd asked me for the meeting, so I couldn't just leave her there.

"Betsy," I repeated, much louder this time.

When she didn't respond, I felt a tingling on the back of my neck.

As I walked around the tree, I found her there, her eyes shut, but not from napping. There was an empty pill bottle on the ground, and a note pinned to her blouse.

It said, "I'm so sorry. I killed him, and I can't live with the pain."

I backed up, horrified, and tripped over a tree root. A few leaves and twigs caught in my blue jean cuffs, and I scratched one hand on a rock as I tried to catch myself. Stumbling back to my feet, I called 911.

"I found a body at the Patriot's Tree," I said breathlessly.

"Again? Don't touch anything. Someone will be right there."

The chief showed up three minutes later, and I pointed to Betsy's body.

He took the scene in, and then shook his head sadly. "She couldn't live with what she'd done. I guess that takes care of that."

"How could she have done it?" I'd meant the murder, not the suicide, but the chief misunderstood.

"It happens, Suzanne. I'm just sorry you had to find another body."

Officer Grant came up behind us, and Chief Martin said to him, "Walk her home, and then seal off the area. I'll call the coroner."

As the officer, who was becoming a friend of mine, walked me back to the cottage, I said, "I don't think she killed herself."

"Why not?"

"She asked me to meet her here," I explained. "Why would she do that if she was just going to end her life?"

"Maybe she wanted to confess to you what she'd done," Grant said. "It wouldn't surprise me one bit. Can you imagine how low you must be to kill another person?"

"I can't," I said. "I just didn't think Betsy was the type."

"I'm not sure there is a type," Grant said

346

as we got to the porch. "Can you call someone to stay with you? I noticed your mom's car isn't in the driveway. Is Grace anywhere around?"

"She's in Charlotte. Don't worry, I'll be all right."

He looked at me for a moment, and then said, "It's bad enough finding one body, but you've found two in one week. I'm truly sorry you had to see that. If you need to talk to someone, you can always give me a call."

"Thanks," I said. "I just might take you up on it."

When I walked into the house, it all felt surreal. Why had Betsy done it? Had jealousy driven her to murder, and then the guilt of her action forced her into killing herself? It was hard to believe. I tried to call Jake, but his line was busy. No doubt he was already working the case. I left a voice mail, then lay down on the couch, blue jeans, shoes, and dirty T-shirt from my fall, and tried to wrap my head around what had happened.

I never believed I could do it, but I must have nodded off at some point. The next thing I knew, my mother was standing over me with a frown on her face.

"Suzanne, why did I just see three police

cars leave the park?"

I sat up and rubbed my eyes. "Betsy Hanks killed herself at the Patriot's Tree, and I found the body. Again."

Her harsh expression instantly softened as she said, "You poor child. That's horrible."

"I don't believe it's true," I said.

Momma looked confused by the statement. "That you found them both? Are you in some kind of denial?"

"No, I'll never forget seeing the bodies. I just don't think Betsy killed herself. It doesn't make sense."

"Does it ever? Let me get you a glass of lemonade and we can talk about it."

After we spent a little time sitting together on the couch, I started to feel a little better. To her credit, she hadn't said a word about the state of my outfit.

"Thanks, Momma," I said. I glanced at the clock and asked, "Isn't it time you started getting ready for your date?"

She looked surprised by the suggestion. "I'm not going."

I got up from the couch and stretched. "Yes you are."

Momma wasn't going to budge. "Suzanne, your system had another big shock this afternoon, added to attending Tim's funeral. I'm not about to desert you in your time of need."

I patted her shoulder. "I'm not having a time of need. Was I shocked to find Betsy like that? Of course I was. Do I need you here to hold my hand? I'm okay. I promise I am."

"I can't imagine that you really are," she said.

I wasn't getting anywhere. It was time for a different approach. "You haven't called your date off yet, have you?"

She frowned. "No, I was just getting ready to call Phillip, though."

I took her hands in mine. "Do me a favor and go through with it. Momma, I know you're having trouble getting back into dating. I'm afraid if you stop now, you'll never try again. This is important."

"So are you," she said. I could swear I saw tears start to form in her eyes.

"I know you love me, but you've got to trust me on this. Even if the real shock of everything that's happened hasn't hit me yet, I need some time alone to come to grips with everything. You'd be doing me a favor by going out with Chief Martin tonight."

She looked a little flustered, almost as though I'd taken away a perfect excuse for her to delay her date. "I'm sure he's busy with the new case."

"He doesn't think it was murder, remember? I'm sure he thinks it's all wrapped up now."

Momma looked long and hard at me. "But you don't. That much is clear."

"I could be wrong. Stranger things have happened. I can't see Betsy killing Tim or herself, but do we ever know why people do what they do? I'm just not sure, and I don't want to overanalyze it. If you stay, we're going to dissect this up and down, and in the end, I'll be no closer to accepting it than I am right now. I just need some time, and a little space."

"I'll call to see if we're still on, then," she said as she reached for the house telephone. I was surprised when she didn't have to look up the number of the police in the phone book before she called. "Phillip, do you need to cancel tonight? No? Are you certain? I don't want to pull you away from anything important." She lowered her voice, and then said, "No, she says she's fine." After a moment, her volume was back to normal. "Very well, I'll see you soon."

She hung up and then turned to me. "He was just leaving the station to get ready for our date," Momma said. "You can't even call Grace, can you? Is she still in Charlotte?"

"The last I heard."

Momma looked concerned. "With Jake on his way to Greensboro, you really are going to be alone."

"No offense, but that's exactly what I need."

She had one more question to ask. "Are you positive?"

"I am," I said with a smile. "Now, do you need help getting ready for your date?"

She returned the grin. "I've been instructed to wear casual clothing this evening. We're eating at the Boxcar, and then he has something along the same lines for later."

"It sounds like fun to me," I said.

"I think so, too, but don't tell him I said that."

At the appointed time, no sooner and no later, there was a knock on our door. When I opened it, Chief Martin was standing there, without a horse-drawn carriage, roses, or a thirty-piece orchestra. He'd changed out of his uniform, but his slacks weren't new, and his shirt clearly needed ironing. "Hi," he said with an unfamiliar smile, at least to me.

"Come on in. She'll be right out."

Thank goodness Momma was on my heels. I wasn't sure what kind of small talk I could make with him after what had just happened. The last thing I wanted to do was pick a fight with the man right before he took my mother out on a date.

"You look lovely," he said the second he saw my mother.

"You are handsome as well."

As they started to go, Momma said, "Suzanne, we'll be just a shout away at the Boxcar if you need us."

"I'm going to be good," I said. "You two kids have fun."

She shook her head at that remark, but I could swear I saw the chief smile for the briefest moment.

Once they were gone, I settled in on the couch with a bag of popcorn fresh from the microwave and a mystery movie on DVD that I'd been waiting for the right moment to watch.

Ten minutes in, when the heroine was in danger from an unseen stranger, I decided maybe a movie wasn't the best idea after all. I remembered Jake's card, so I pulled it from my back pocket and unfolded it.

Instead of a greeting, there was thirty seconds of his voice recorded on it. *"Suzanne,"* he said. *"You mean more to me than I could ever express. Never doubt how I feel about you, and that we belong together."*

It was the sweetest thing I'd ever heard.

I moved out onto the porch as dusk started to creep up into the day, swinging on the swing as I replayed the message again and again. On the back of the card was a button you had to press to record a message, but I knew I'd never tape over what he'd said to me. Finally I tucked it into my T-shirt so I could have it next to my heart, where it belonged.

As I sat there, I thought about all that had happened. The more I considered it, the more certain I was that Betsy hadn't killed herself. She'd been frightened when I'd last seen her, not despondent. When she'd told me we'd needed to talk, it wasn't to clear her conscience; I just knew it.

She was planning to share something about the case with me.

And someone had stopped her before she could tell me what she so urgently had wanted to say.

Against my better judgment, I decided to walk back over to the Patriot's Tree to see if something there could give me some idea about what had really happened to her. There was police tape covering the area, but I ducked under it without a second thought. Breaking that particular warning didn't bother me a bit, but as I'd knelt down to go under the tape, something jabbed me in the ankle. It wasn't a snake, or even a mosquito. Apparently I'd picked something up in the cuff of my blue jeans when I'd stumbled right after discovering Betsy's body. I brushed at the cuff, but couldn't find what was sticking into me.

I thought it was fine, until it happened again.

Reaching down, I unrolled the cuff, and felt a small stick that had poked me.

At least I'd thought it was a small stick.

Upon closer examination, it turned out to be a half-chewed toothpick.

The second it hit my hand, I knew who must have killed Tim Leander, and followed up with getting rid of Betsy Hanks.

It had to mean one thing.

Orson Blaine was a murderer.

# CHAPTER 18

"I see you found it for me," a voice said behind me.

I clenched the toothpick in my hand as I turned around. "Found what?"

Orson was standing ten feet away with a knife in his hand, and he appeared to have no trouble pointing it straight at my heart.

"Give it up, Suzanne. I caught a glimpse of it just now when you were looking at it. I knew I dropped it earlier when I was here, but it's been driving me crazy thinking that the police had that toothpick, along with my DNA. I was about to leave town for good, but I decided to hang back in the shadows when I saw you come out here. It's my lucky day, isn't it?"

"Luckier for you than for me," I said, looking around for some kind of weapon I could use on him. Maybe if I could distract him long enough, someone would come along and find us. "You're the one who stole my recipe book. I didn't even notice you in the shop the day it disappeared."

"The place was so full of customers on your Take-a-Chance Tuesday, I had a feeling you hadn't seen me. I wanted to check you out, and I saw the book on the counter by the register as I waited in line, so when you looked away, I grabbed it and left."

"Why bother stealing it in the first place?"

"Suzanne, the second Betsy told me about what you said the night before your big sale, I knew you wouldn't be able to keep from digging into what happened. Do you think folks all around the county don't know what a snoop you are?"

"But I hadn't even spoken to her when you stole my recipes," I said.

"You didn't have to. Betsy was sitting behind you at the Boxcar Grill with a friend, and she heard you talking about investigating Tim's murder. It didn't take much to figure out what you were up to. I decided to check you out myself the next day, and I was hoping it would stop your meddling when I took your recipes," he said in clear disgust.

Something suddenly made sense that had puzzled me. "You stole my trash that same day, didn't you?"

He nodded. "I thought there might be

something in there that would tell me how much you knew about what I'd been doing." Orson looked at me in distaste. "It was just rubbish, though." He took a deep breath, and then added, "When you didn't quit digging into Tim's murder, I decided to burn the recipe book on your porch as a second warning. It's a shame the whole house didn't go up in flames. That might have stopped you."

I shuddered to think what might have happened. I wasn't sure I could bear losing the cottage where my mother and I lived. It was our haven, our safe harbor from a world gone mad.

And now if I didn't do something, and do it fast, this was not going to end well for me. I had to find a way to fight back, but there wasn't a thing I could use as a weapon in sight.

"I know you had a problem with Tim, but how could you hate him enough to kill him?"

Orson shook his head. "Are you kidding me? He didn't leave me any choice. I know how fake he was, how folks just seemed to love him for no good reason that I could see, but he pushed me the wrong way one too many times. A man can only take so much. Every time I wanted something, it seemed like Tim got it. I got so sick of coming in second place to him that it reached the point where the sound of his voice was enough to set me off. Every time he walked into Go Eats, I wanted to kill him. It became some kind of obsession for me."

"You could have gone someplace else to eat," I said, wondering how a petty rivalry could develop such deep-seated feelings of hate.

Orson looked at me as though I was insane. "And let him run me off? There was no way that was going to happen. I knew deep in my heart that if I could just get rid of him, my life would turn around. When he took Betsy from me" — he paused and ran a hand across his forehead — "that was the last push I was ever going to take. The second I found out about it, I knew I had to set things right. He had to pay, and I don't regret doing it."

It was clear Orson wasn't going to tell me anything more substantial than that. I had to wonder if he even knew just how sick he was. The man was trying to justify murdering a man based on reasons that would seem less than rational for most folks.

"But why kill Betsy?" I asked as I kept looking for something to use against him.

"I didn't know it before, but I found out

that she was weak," he said as he slowly started walking toward me. I backed up instinctively, but he followed at the same pace, the knife point never wavering from my chest. "I knew that Tim would never meet *me* here at the Traitor's Tree, so I used her."

It was no time to correct him, but I hated hearing the Patriot Tree's name changed.

"So you got her to lure him here so you could kill him. How did you do that?"

Orson grinned at me. "I told Betsy that Tim had proposed to Angelica, and that she'd said yes."

"But they weren't going to get married," I protested, backing up another step.

"We both know that, but Betsy didn't. I told her if she could get Tim here, I'd humiliate him so he'd pay for making her look like a fool, but I didn't tell her I was planning to kill him. She would have never gone for that. She wanted revenge, but she was too soft for what I knew had to be done."

"So she lured him here for you and you killed him," I said, backing up yet another step. Maybe if I could get closer to the woods, I'd be able to elude him. I pretended to stumble a little into a smaller tree at that moment, but I did it to hide another action entirely.

"You should have seen her face when I choked Tim with that rope. Betsy fought me, can you believe it? What did he ever do to earn her loyalty? She should have helped me instead of try to stop me."

"Did she help you string him up after he was dead?"

Orson shook his head with disgust. "She lay there on the grass whimpering like a lost child the entire time. I told her if she breathed a word of what we'd done, I'd see her dead before I'd let her testify against me. She was an accessory, whether she liked it or not."

"Maybe the law wouldn't have seen it that way," I said. I backed up one more step, and felt my back hit the bark of the tree. I'd suddenly run out of room, and Orson was still closing in.

"Trust me, I can be very convincing."

"That was smart, offering free drinks to your friends so they could cause a diversion and you could slip out of the bar. It almost worked, too."

Orson shook his head. "It *did* work. From what I've heard, that woman bartender confirmed my story, so I just have one last loose end to take care of. Now, are you going to hand that toothpick to me, or am I going to have to pry it out of your dead fingers?" It was amazing how calm his voice sounded, especially since he had to be barking mad to do what he'd done up until now.

"You can have it," I said as I threw it at him.

I planned to run away as he searched for it in the tall grass, but his gaze barely left mine as it flew through the air.

"Now you're just trying to tick me off," he said.

"You'll never find that toothpick now. Jake knows you did it, and so does the police chief." That was a lie, but he didn't know that. At least I hoped he didn't.

"Your boyfriend is in Greensboro by now, and the police chief is so smitten by your mother, he doesn't know much of anything. I like my chances."

"Think about this before you do something stupid. No one is going to believe that three murders aren't related. Or do you think you can make my death look like a suicide, too?"

"No, you'll be the victim of a random mugging in the park. I'm afraid it's not going to be very pleasant for you."

"Then don't do it," I said, trying to figure out the best direction to run in.

"Sorry, I can't do that. Tim ruined my life by stealing my wife, and Betsy threatened my freedom with her promise to go to the police. I can't leave you free. You're the last thing on my list, and then I'm in the clear. Good-bye, Suzanne."

He was close enough now so that I could smell the onions on his breath. If I timed it right, I had one last chance.

I saw the knife come back, and then he thrust it forward with lightning speed. I barely managed to get out of its way as I tried to knock his arm aside. I missed completely, but by sheer dumb luck, the blade of the knife sunk into the tree bark and not my chest.

As Orson fought to pull it free, I took the one chance I had left and planned to make the most of it.

I raced off into the woods, not caring about where I was going. I needed to get away from him. That was the only thing that mattered. I could try to run to the Boxcar Grill, but I wasn't sure I'd be able to make it across open land.

That left the woods of the park.

I had an advantage, since I'd grown up here, and as far as I knew, Orson hadn't spent much time in the park at all.

I cut right, moved past a pair of red oaks,

and then started for an old maple I'd played near as a kid. If I could get there, I could use one of the lower limbs and climb up onto it. After I did that, there was a place where it touched a hickory tree that I could transfer over to. It was impossible to see from the ground, and it wasn't all that easy to spot from the air. I figured I had a fifty-fifty chance of escaping him, not great odds on my best day, but it was a chance I had to take.

Too soon, I heard the brush crashing behind me. Somehow, Orson had managed to extricate the knife quicker than I'd expected.

"Come on, Suzanne, the longer you run, the worse it's going to be."

I thought about yelling something back at him, but I wanted to save my breath.

The tree I was targeting was just ahead, and if I timed it right, I might be able to jump onto it before he could reach me.

I launched myself in the air, and just as my hands reached the branch, I thought I was home free.

That's when I felt him grab my leg.

He'd jumped as well, but not for the branch.

As he hit me, I heard the branch in my hands crack under our combined weights, and it snapped as suddenly as a broken shoelace, putting us both on the ground.

I waited a split second to die, but then I realized that in the fall, Orson must have dropped the knife. Scanning the ground around us, I stood and searched frantically in the fading light for the blade.

In retrospect, that might have been a mistake.

Orson's hands went around my throat, and I saw that he'd decided to change murder weapons. Abandoning the knife hunt, he was now trying to crush the breath right out of me.

I fell to my knees under his weight and pressure, and the world started to go dark.

As I braced myself on the ground for my last breath, I felt something touch my hand.

It was the knife.

Groping for it as I started to lose consciousness, I finally managed to pick it up and drive it blindly backward.

I'd been hoping to hit his heart, but it buried itself into his leg instead.

The howl of pain from him was the sweetest sound I'd ever heard in my life.

The pressure suddenly eased, but I wasn't sure how long it would last. Forcing myself to my feet, I decided it was time to run again.

Maybe this time he wouldn't be able to follow.

How I wished I was right.

I'd given up all pretense of ambush or confrontation now. All I could do was run, and hope that he couldn't follow with a wounded leg.

When I glanced back over my shoulder, I saw that Orson was on his feet as well, tugging at the knife still stuck in his leg as he ran after me. Where was this lunatic getting his strength?

I was nearly back where we'd first started when I felt a hand grab my shoulder, dragging me back down to the ground. He was on top of me, and I did the only thing I could think to do. I hit him as hard as I could squarely on the nose.

That brought another scream, but he didn't move as blood dripped down his nose onto my T-shirt.

It appeared that I'd fought hard, but not hard enough.

"You're going to pay for that," he snarled at me, his words hitting me like hardened fists. I groped on the ground for something else that I could use as a weapon, but all I could scrape up was some loose dirt. I took a handful and threw it into his face, and as he screamed and put his hands to his eyes, the knife dropped harmlessly to the ground. He rolled off me, writhing in pain, and I grabbed the knife before he could retrieve it. I wasn't sure if I'd blinded him for life, and at the moment, I couldn't say one way or the other if I cared.

"Get up," I said, not recognizing my own voice as I said it.

"You ruined my eyes."

"You don't need to see to stand up. If you don't move in ten seconds, I'll give you a reason to. I've got the knife, now, remember?"

He stood a little unsteadily, and I got behind him and shoved him in the direction of the house. Orson stumbled a little as we moved, but I had no mercy on him.

We were almost to the house when I saw the first police car approach.

It was Officer Grant, and from the odd look on his face, I wasn't sure he even recognized me.

"What happened here?" he asked as he pulled out his weapon. "Someone saw you two fighting and called it in."

I screamed, "He killed Tim, and then he got rid of Betsy when she threatened to expose him. He confessed everything to me."

"She's lying," Orson said, his voice suddenly calm. "This lunatic lured me out here, and then she attacked me with that knife. Look at my leg. I'm bleeding."

The police officer looked at me again, and I said, "It all started when I found one of his toothpicks near the crime scene." It was true. That was where it had been when it had managed to get lodged in my pant cuff, at any rate.

"I dropped it when she cut me," he protested.

"What happened to your eyes?" Officer Grant asked Orson.

"When I broke away from her, she tried to blind me."

"After he attacked me first," I said.

Orson wasn't going to let it go at that. "She's lying."

"I have proof," I said calmly.

Orson looked worried for a split second, but he knew that he'd seen me throw that toothpick away. "Let's see it. You're bluffing."

I pulled the card from under my T-shirt and opened it. I'd waited to hit the button at the precise moment he confessed so they would find some kind of proof that he'd done it if he managed to kill me.

Instead, it was going to help put him away

for two murders.

I didn't get Jake's lovely message when I opened the card this time. Instead, I got Orson's voice, muffled but still recognizable, saying, *"You should have seen her face when I choked Tim with the rope. Betsy fought me, can you believe it? What did he do to earn her loyalty? She should have helped me —"*

It cut off abruptly, but I knew that I'd gotten enough.

"Let's go," Officer Grant said as he slapped his cuffs on Orson, and I finally let the knife slip out of my hand and into the grass.

Chief Martin and Momma pulled up as Officer Grant was putting Orson in the back of his squad car. "What happened? Didn't the date go well?" I asked as I rubbed a little dirt off my chin from where I'd fallen.

"It was wonderful," Momma said, "but we heard the sirens and came running. Suzanne, are you okay?"

"Not yet, but I will be," I said, though I was sore in a few places where I'd hit the ground, and I could barely speak from the pressure Orson had used trying to choke the life out of me. I knew a long soak would take care of most of that, and I'd be good as new soon enough.

At least on the outside.

I brought them both up to date, then replayed the confession from the card for them.

The chief took it from me, and then said, "That was smart thinking, Suzanne. I'm glad you weren't hurt worse than you were."

"So am I," I said with a grin. "Jake's going to kill me, though. He left a really special message in that card, and I erased it."

"I think he'll find it in his heart to forgive you," the chief said.

As he started to go, he turned to my mother and said, "Dorothy, this evening was delightful, even if it was cut short."

To my surprise, Momma laughed and gave him a quick kiss. After that, she said, "Don't worry, we'll get better at it. Just give us a little time."

I don't know who was more surprised to hear that, the chief or me.

I finally managed to get Jake on the phone after a long soak and a quick change into some clean clothes. It still hurt my voice to talk, but it was something I was just going to have to deal with. Jake deserved to hear everything that had happened. As I brought him up to speed, my voice choked up a little when I explained how I had recorded over his message to me.

"It was the sweetest thing I've ever heard," I said, for some reason starting to cry. "And now it's gone."

"It's okay, Suzanne," he said soothingly. "I'll make you another one tomorrow. I'm sorry I'm not there to hold your hand. You were really brave tonight."

"Just hearing your voice is all I need," I said.

"Are you going to close the donut shop tomorrow?" he asked.

"No, we're going to be open as usual."

I loved the sound of Jake's chuckle on the other end. "Why am I not surprised? I'd better let you go, then. I'm glad you're okay, Suzanne. Good night."

"Good night," I replied as I hung up.

I knew I needed sleep, but too much had happened to allow it. I went downstairs, and to my surprise, Emma and her mother were sitting on the couch with Momma.

"Hey, I didn't know we had visitors," I said.

"You were on the telephone, and we didn't want to disturb you," my mother said with a smile.

Emma's mom stood, and I noticed there was a plain white box in her hands. "Suzanne, I hope you can forgive me, but I did

370

something without your permission."

"I can't imagine it being that bad," I said. "Besides, I'm in a very forgiving mood tonight."

"Give her the box," Emma said, grinning at us both.

"By all means," I said. "I'd love to have whatever it is you're offering, though I can't imagine what it could be."

Her mother smiled and handed me the box in her hands, and as I opened it, my heart started to flutter.

There, in my own handwriting, was a photocopy of the front of my recipe book. As I quickly flipped through the pages, I saw that she'd managed to get everything but my very last musings.

As I raced through it, she explained, "I've had a hard time with the recipes when I've helped out in the past, so I made a copy of it without telling you about it. My notes are in the margins, but everything you wrote down is still there. I hope you can forgive me."

"I thought I'd lost this forever," I said as I dropped the box to the floor and hugged her. I was openly crying now, maybe from the stress of the last few days, or it could have simply been because something I cherished had been returned to me.

Emma rubbed my shoulder and said, "Suzanne, you don't ever have to worry about losing it again. I scanned it all into my computer and I've backed it up in a dozen different places. Cool, isn't it?"

"About the coolest thing I've ever seen," I said as I wiped away my tears. I turned back to Emma's mother and said, "I don't know how to thank you."

"Not being angry with me is all the thanks I need," she said.

"Trust me; I couldn't be happier." I turned to Momma and asked, "Do we have any pie left? I feel like a snack. Come on, let's have a party."

Emma looked at her watch. "You're kidding, right? We have to be up in seven hours if we're going to open on time." She turned to my mother and added, "Not that we don't love your pie."

Momma said, "Why don't you children run off to bed and let the grown-ups have a little time together? Good night, ladies."

"Good night," we said in unison, and Emma headed back home while I went upstairs to my room. I knew I should go straight to sleep, but I couldn't help leafing through the pages of my life in that copy of my recipe book.

The last, and most important part of it,

was all there in black-and-white.

It was a special donut I'd been planning to make for Jake, but hadn't had a chance to do yet.

There was just one more thing I had to do.

As I punched in Jake's telephone number, I thought about how delicious it would be to share my news with him.

And that was why it was really so special having someone in my life again.

The employees of Thorndike Press hope you have enjoyed this Large Print book. All our Thorndike, Wheeler, and Kennebec Large Print titles are designed for easy reading, and all our books are made to last. Other Thorndike Press Large Print books are available at your library, through selected bookstores, or directly from us.

For information about titles, please call:
(800) 223-1244

or visit our Web site at:
http://gale.cengage.com/thorndike

To share your comments, please write:
Publisher
Thorndike Press
10 Water St., Suite 310
Waterville, ME 04901